Hannah Goodheart and the Guardian of Time

C. Michael Morrison

FAWKES PRESS

Cover design by Michelle Fairbanks/Fresh Design
Edited by Twyla Beth Lambert

Print ISBN 978-1-945419-36-2
ePub ISBN 978-1-945419-37-9
Library of Congress Control Number 2019933255

TABLE OF CONTENTS

DEDICATION

To my beautiful bride, Dorinda—Thank you for 25 years of humoring my dreams. I'm a better man because of your love and unfeigned devotion.

For Hannah—When I grow up, I want to be just like you.

Above all, my Father—The infinite dreamer who gave all, so I could share in the dream. I'm nothing apart from you.

CHAPTER 1: STARGAZERS

I WATCHED THE bursts of light streaking across the starlit sky, wishing I could control time and freeze the moment, unaware that both time and space were about to take on entirely new meaning for me.

The vast North Texas sky had seemingly exploded with color as the sun was setting for the day. Within an hour, only a faint band of orange would remain, but it wasn't the sunset I had come here to see. A blanket of stars shimmered against the darkness as the hours passed. A meteor shower that had been promised for the next two nights would not disappoint, as occasional streaks of light began to race across the horizon while I watched in awe. My eyes lit up with the majesty of the starry night as I brushed my hair away from my cheeks. Above all else—even turning thirteen, I wanted to just get lost in that galactic sea.

"Special delivery for Hannah Goodheart. Mom thought you might like some hot tea to sip."

"Thank you, Daddy!"

It's in these *quiet* moments that I feel the most—well, like me. Don't get me wrong. I can hold my own in any conversation, if that's what the situation calls for. The Templetons, who used to live next door at my old house, always said I was bright, articulate, and genuine in most every way. Most adults comment to my parents that they're awe struck at how confident and well-spoken I can be, and it's not unusual for me to be mistaken for a much older girl—to my daddy's horror.

I like modest clothes, my style isn't flashy and, honestly, I prefer solitude to being the center of attention. I've even heard people call me "unassuming." Although, I do have a carefully selected group of friends to whom I'm fiercely loyal. I'm all smiles whenever they're around. Which is going to be the case on this night.

The corduroy quilt my great-grandmother had made was spread on the ground and provided the perfect spot to watch the show. A couple of my friends were coming over to watch with me and sleep over, but this was *my* time before they arrived. The contentment I felt at this moment was capped by another flash of light, crossing the night sky above me. "Paradise," I said, as I lay flat on my back with my head resting on my forearm.

I love it here. This was my great-grandparents' homestead. The old Texas ranch has always held a very special place in my heart. My favorite memories always take me back to my great-grandma's kitchen. Nan, as I called her, was always baking or cooking; church dinners, a pie for the fair, or something for a neighbor just to let them know they were appreciated. Nan's kitchen was always the center of everything going on in the home and, from the time I was born, I was not far from the action any time I was here.

I was the apple of my great-grandfather's eye, as well. Paw-Paw made sure my visits to their home were always filled with adventure. Paw-Paw, Paul Learner, was a veteran of World War II. Originally from a small town in northern Virginia, he served in the U.S. Navy in the South Pacific. He met my Nan, Elizabeth, in Mobile, Alabama, right after the war. Elizabeth was a Texas girl through and through, and Paw-Paw would have followed her to the ends of the earth. In fact, at the time, he thought he had. He had never considered settling in a ranching community just north of Dallas, but that's just what he did in 1946.

Together, my great-grandparents raised a son, Tommy. He married a few months before going off to Vietnam, but sadly, never returned. He was captured and later killed as a POW in the now infamous Hanoi Hilton. My mom, Sarah, was born while Tommy was in Vietnam, so sadly, she never knew her father. My grandma, Grace, was devastated by the loss of Tommy for a long time, and so Paw-Paw and Nan stepped in to help raise my mom. They were more like a father and mother to her than grandparents, and she loved them so.

After my mom and dad brought me home, Paw-Paw and Nan became the finest great-grandparents any little girl could have. Paw-Paw died earlier this year, having mourned Nan's passing for the past two and a half years. He willed this old homestead to my parents, and insisted they keep it, saying, "so Hannah could always return for an adventure." And that's why Mom and Dad decided to sell our suburban North Dallas home and move here to the Learner ranch a few months ago.

And so, the adventure of the day had brought me to this open field with the luminescence of this starry night to fire my imagination. But the stillness of the evening was about to be interrupted as I heard footsteps moving toward me. I thought to sit up to see who was approaching, but before I could say or do anything, I heard a familiar voice.

"Hannah. Hannah, are you here?"

I didn't even try to move, but only spoke up and said, "Right over here."

I knew that the quiet serenity of the moment was over, but I was glad, nonetheless, to see Lily Little, my best friend, walking toward me.

Lily Little. What can I say? She is the sort of girl any parent would be delighted for their daughter to have as a friend. My dad has always suspected that she has a mischievous side and, whether he knows for sure or not, he's right. She's pretty quiet, except when things get giggly among the gang; it's always then she can be heard loud and clear. Still, she's well-mannered and smart. Though not particularly athletic, Lily is pretty light and fleet, which tends to lend itself to her ability to remain ambiguous whenever she decides to be… artfully rotten.

Her older sister Annie, on the other hand, is not as stealth about her craftiness. Truly, there is little the two have in common except for their last name and my friendship. Unless, of course, you count the fact that they both wear similar black framed glasses. But while Lily is a blonde, Annie is one hundred percent red-head. She's vocal and expressive with an innate ability to own her space. I envy that about her. The differences in the two sisters are often the source of conflict between them, and yet it's what makes the two a fearsome pair when they are united.

"Your Mom told me to let you know Morgan is on her way," Lily said, as she sat down cross-legged beside where I lay.

I just nodded, saying nothing as Lily laid back to look up into the enormous sky. Lily let out a deep breath, as though the weight of the world had just lifted from her shoulders. A suspicious pause hung in the air before Lily finally said, "Annie had a birthday party to go to, and I kinda forgot to invite her to sleep over."

I sat up and turned to look at Lily, who had a satisfied grin on her face as she gazed upward. "Well, it's a good thing I called and invited her, too," I said.

"I'm busted," Lily exclaimed, with a devilish chuckle.

I just laughed and pulled my long hair back into a sloppy brown bun. Zipping up my hoodie, I said, "Someone is going to drop Annie off after the party. I'm surprised your mom didn't tell you."

"Not a word," Lily replied. "As far as sisters go, she's the best," she continued. "I'm just still trying to get her back for..."

"Being born first?" I asked with a smile.

We both laughed together for a moment as Lily uttered, "True story." Then, quiet settled in as the two of us looked up into the glittering sky.

It wasn't long, though, before Morgan McVey joined us. My relationship with Morgan is very different than with Lily. Morgan's family lived next door to us in the North Dallas suburb I had called home from almost the time I was born. Morgan was more than a year older than me, and while the two of us are very different, we've always enjoyed a friendship that was as deep as two young ladies could have. I've often referred to Morgan as my sister by heart, but Daddy prefers to call her his red-headed step child because of her long, curly, strawberry blonde locks.

While we were living next door to one another, Morgan would spend nearly all her free time at our house, and we loved having her around. Dear old Mr. Templeton, who lived across the street, referred to us as Laverne and Shirley, although we could never quite figure out why. That is, until Daddy schooled us, as he often did, on 1970s television shows he used to watch as a kid. And so, in the evenings after Morgan got home from school, and most weekends, she would leap across our front yard, knowing she was always welcome at our home.

After we moved, Morgan and I have seen less of one another, but it didn't change the bond we had—something I've admittedly struggled with. We'd shed many tears, but we made a point to stay in touch. FaceTime calls and sleepovers have been pretty regular these past few months. I'm probably being paranoid. I'm just afraid she'll slip away; that the distance will cause us to grow apart.

As for the Templetons across the street, they too have tried to keep in touch. Mrs. Templeton was so very fond of us, and we loved them right back. The move has been difficult for everyone.

In contrast, my friendship with Lily had been cultivated through the friendship our mothers have had from the time *they* were young. Since moving to the country, I've enrolled in the same homeschool co-op the Little sisters are in, so the move only brought us closer together. Lily's sister, Annie, is the same age as Morgan, and when the four of us get together, it's usually fun and total mayhem.

And so, all four of us now sat in the field sipping hot chocolate, watching the flashes of light streak across the North Texas sky. I'm pretty sure my parents could hear our bursts of laughter in the kitchen of the old ranch house, where my parents were making some snacks for us. My mother, Sarah Goodheart, stepped outside to check on me and my friends. I saw her silhouette on the back porch and shouted over, "Everything okay, Momma? We're not making too much noise, are we?"

"No, Sweetie," she replied. "It looks like quite an active meteor shower."

"Oh, it is. Can we stay out here for a while longer?"

"Sure, but you might want to grab a jacket or another blanket. It's starting to get cool."

I turned to tell them I was going to go grab my jacket and an extra blanket when something caught my eye. At first, I thought my eyes were playing tricks on me. The streaks of light across the sky had sometimes seemed to linger and even crash to Earth, but this was different. I rubbed my eyes and squinted with uncertainty.

About thirty yards from where we were laying on the corduroy quilt, a faint glow glimmered on the ground. Taking a couple of steps in that direction, I tossed over my shoulder, "Can y'all see that?"

No one else could make out what I was talking about, but I was sure I could see something. I just knew it, and everything within me was driving me to investigate.

"The meteor shower is playing tricks on your eyes," Lily said.

Morgan chimed in, "Lily's probably right."

"No," I said, taking a few more steps closer. "I can definitely see something."

"Where are you going, Hannah?" Annie asked. But before she could even finish the question, I had spanned nearly half of the distance to the glowing object, which I was now certain I was seeing. The other three jumped to their feet and ran to me. Morgan was the first to see it.

"Oh, this is weird. Should we be doing this, guys?" Morgan said with trepidation.

"You don't think it's a meteor or something, do you? Maybe Morgan's right," Lily said.

I kept walking—cautiously, but undeterred by the warnings of my friends. "It might just be a firefly or something, but I want to check it out."

Sure enough, a small object sat just barely exposed on the surface of the ground. It glowed the faintest blue but seemed to fade as we drew closer to it. I knelt and reached out my hand, almost without thinking.

"Hannah," Annie said, "I don't think that's a firefly. You sure you shouldn't get your parents?"

I ignored her completely and brushed the earth away, dislodging the object from the hard, dry soil. It seemed to be a small metallic cube, and almost the moment my hand touched it, it completely quit glowing.

"What is it?" Lily asked.

"I don't know," I mumbled. "It looks like a charm or pendant."

Morgan reached over for it. "Can I see?"

I placed the small cube, which measured about two centimeters, in Morgan's hand. Morgan turned to try to capture as much light on her hand as possible, in hopes that she could make out what this mysterious metallic cube could be. The meteor shower, near its peak, carried on overhead without any notice from the four of us. Our full attention was now on the treasure that was being passed around the group.

"I wonder if Mom or Dad would know what it might be?" I asked, suggesting that we might take the object inside to study closer.

Annie grabbed the old corduroy quilt as Lily, Morgan, and I darted toward the back door of the house, where Momma still stood watching. A flurry of conversation buzzed as we approached, but it was obvious by her expression that Momma could not make out even in part what had us so wound up.

Annie stepped forward and put herself between my mom and the rest of us. She had not stopped to breathe, let alone allow Momma to ask what the fuss was all about.

"Here's Hannah's quilt, Mrs. Goodheart," she said calmly. "They've found something out in the field. Could be something off one of those government spy drones. I think it's harmless, but you never know about these things."

Momma gave Annie a curious look as she entered the house, passing my father, Charles Goodheart, who made his way to the back door to investigate the commotion.

"Alright… alright," he said, as he opened the screen door.

The chatter didn't let up even a little bit. Daddy made a couple of additional attempts to quiet us down, before finally resorting to a whistle so loud it could have been heard a half mile away. We were quiet at last. Momma turned and looked back at Daddy, who had a satisfied grin on his face. In fact, all eyes were on him, including Annie's, who had returned with a big bowl of M&M'S in hand.

"OK, ladies… that's better. What's all the excitement about?" he asked.

That was all it took to whip up another squall of voices, to which Daddy immediately let out another whistle. Silence fell upon the room again, except for the sound of M&M'S being stirred around the glass bowl. Daddy turned to Annie, who, with one hand moving toward her mouth, reached the other one, which held the glass bowl of candy, toward him.

"The green ones are best," she said, as she dropped several pieces into her mouth.

"I prefer the brown ones," Daddy replied with a grin, before snatching the bowl from her hand. Handing it off to Momma, he turned his attention squarely on me. "What's all this about, Hannah-banana?"

Hannah-banana was just one in a long line of nicknames Daddy had ascribed to me, his only child. I smiled for just a second—I loved all of his names for me. But then, I quickly opened my hand, revealing the small metal cube I had found in the field.

"I don't know," I said as I took a deep breath. "I saw it in the field. It looks like a charm, or some kind of locket. Do you know what it is?"

Daddy studied the dark object as closely as he could. "Wait a second," he said. "It's nearly pitch dark out here. How in the world did you even see this?"

Morgan piped up, "Hannah said it was glowing, but then I said her eyes were playing tricks on her..."

"No," said Lily. "*I* said the meteor shower was playing tricks on her eyes, you just agreed with me."

"Whatever," Morgan said with slight irritation. "In any case, I don't see how it could have been glowing. It probably just caught the light of a star or something."

Rubbing her bare arms against the chill, Momma hustled us inside. "I can put on some more hot cocoa, while we can get a better look at your little find."

We quickly filed past my parents, and all six of us made our way to the kitchen island, where a host of snacks were waiting for our weary group of stargazers. Without a second thought for all the excitement we had just shared, the group of us began to pick our way through the goodies that ranged from chips to fresh-out-of-the-oven cookies. Momma set down the glass bowl of M&M'S, which attracted Annie, who immediately began hunting for the green ones after giving her glasses a quick polish.

Daddy, with my find in hand, excused himself and made his way to his small, make-shift study, where he could get a better look at my discovery. He rummaged around a couple of boxes that had not yet been unpacked until he came across a magnifying glass. Extending the swing arm lamp that sat on his antique wooden desk, he directed the light and began to examine the cube carefully. It was somewhat crusted with soil in places, which made for quite a challenge studying the surface.

He set it down and scanned the room as he thought for a moment. "A semi-stiff brush… I know I have one around here somewhere," he muttered to himself as he rifled through several other boxes until he came across a small paint brush. "This will do."

He carefully picked up the small object and gently began to brush away some of the crusty layers of soil. Every few strokes, he would purse his lips and blow away tiny particles of debris broken up by the brush. Daddy was in his own little world, almost oblivious to the occasional bursts of laughter coming from the kitchen.

After a few minutes, he set the brush down and picked up the magnifying glass once again. He had swept away quite a bit of the soil, revealing much greater detail. It was intricately etched, that much was certain, even from where I stood. "Given its relative size, it's masterfully crafted," he mumbled. "It looks like there's a tiny gap at one of the joints, though. Can't tell if it's by design…"

Brushing away a little more filth, Daddy rambled on about what he called "a fixed loop" where he said it might have been designed to connect to a chain, suggesting my find might be part of a piece of jewelry. Putting it gently down on his desk, he sat back and starred at it as though he were entranced. That is until I cleared my throat, snapping him back into the moment.

"So, what do you think it is?"

"I'm not sure, sweet pea. It might be an earring or a pendant," he said. "Maybe even a charm for a bracelet."

"So, you think it's an old piece of jewelry?"

"It's hard to tell," he replied. "It looks like it has something etched on it; very tiny—intricate. I can't make it out because it's crusted with soil and tarnished from exposure. It also looks like there are a few tiny little gears on one side. It's really remarkable. I would clean it up, but I don't want to damage it. It might be worth something."

I brightened up, for sure, at the thought that I may have happened upon a real treasure—maybe dropped by a conquistador, centuries ago. It was a fleeting thought, but exciting, nonetheless. My delusions of wealth and fame were interrupted, however, as Dad spoke again.

"It might have belonged to Nan or Paw-Paw. I'm just not sure. A contact from work has an antique business in Dallas. He might be able to clean it up and give us an idea of what it might be. Maybe we can take it to him tomorrow after we take Morgan home."

"We?" I asked with excitement.

Daddy smiled and said, "Well, it is *your* discovery."

The grin on my face was as bright as the lamp on Daddy's desk. I stepped toward him and collected myself, taking a serious tone as I worked extra hard to contain the excitement I was feeling. "What about the light I saw coming from it?"

"Light? Ah, yes. You did say you saw it light up," he said. "I don't think the light was coming from the cube. It's too small to have any kind of light source or battery to power it. It's sealed all the way around except for a tiny crack at one of the joints. It must have been catching the light from a star or something else."

Daddy's explanation fell short in satisfying my curiosity, but he truly didn't see anything to indicate this tiny object could have been illuminated in any way. Not wanting to dismiss me, he continued. "Yeah, I'm certain it was probably just reflecting light from another source."

Leaving the cube on his desk and turning off the lamp, he walked toward me and put his arm around me. He gave me a gentle squeeze, pulling me close as he embraced me. "We'll get some answers tomorrow," he said. "In the meantime, we better go find out if Lily, Morgan, and Annie left anything for us to snack on."

I smiled and looked up at him as we walked together toward the door. "I'm pretty sure the green M&M'S are all gone," I said with a giggle, brushing my bangs away from my eyes.

Daddy looked back lovingly and grinned warmly. "That's okay," he said. "As long as she didn't eat all the brown ones."

We laughed together and walked toward the kitchen. The rest of the night would be reasonably quiet as my crazy friends and I, along with my parents, would settle in and eventually close our eyes, bringing an end to the day. None of us could have known that the events of this evening would be a beginning and forever change everything for me, my family, and my friends.

CHAPTER 2: NOTHING OF CONSEQUENCE

TRAFFIC WAS MOVING slower than normal for a Saturday on the Dallas North Tollway, and as I sat in the passenger seat of my dad's car, I tried to distract myself from the sadness I felt after dropping off Morgan at her home. It seemed the thirty-minute drive to my old neighborhood had gone by all too fast. It was clear Daddy could sense my emotion as I swiped through pictures and video on my phone, while intermittently looking out the window. It was difficult for him to see his usually happy, warm, and spirited daughter sit silently staring out the window.

"Penny?"

I turned to him with a puzzled look on my face. "What, Daddy?"

"For your thoughts," he replied. "A penny for your thoughts."

I smiled and returned to looking out the window. "It's just hard taking Morgan home. I miss her," I said.

Dad remained silent as he navigated the traffic.

I continued. "I'm glad we moved to Paw-Paw's ranch. I love it there, but I just wish Morgan lived closer to us. We used to see each other nearly every day, and now it seems we're lucky if we talk once or twice a week. I'm just afraid we're going to..." I paused, my voice beginning to crack. Not wanting to think about the distance I perceived growing between me and Morgan, let alone talk about it, I just concluded, "I don't know."

My dad checked his mirrors and glanced over at me as I swiped at a tear. "I understand how you feel, sweet pea. If it were any other friends, I wouldn't say what I'm about to say, but I know you, and I know Morgan, and there aren't two more loyal friends. Your friendship means a lot to both of you. You have a special lifetime bond. Trust me—it wouldn't surprise me if the two of you aren't chasing each other around in wheelchairs when you're ninety-five."

The thought made me giggle and I turned to look at Daddy. "You think so?" I asked.

"I know so," he replied.

Daddy reached into his shirt pocket and pulled out a small manila envelope. He handed it to me, and I turned it upside down, shaking the mysterious cube into the palm of my hand. I put the envelope in the center console's cup holder and fixed my eyes squarely on the object now secured between my thumb and forefinger.

"I haven't really gotten to see it in the light like this yet," I said, as I carefully inspected each side.

Daddy pointed at it and noted the cracked joint he saw the previous night. "That crack is on the joint where the loop is," he said.

I looked carefully. "I'm looking at all four edges of that panel... I don't see a crack or opening of any sort."

"That's odd," Dad replied. "I'm sure there was a tiny opening."

"Nope," I said. "Nothing. Although I have to say, the little embellishments on the two sides look like little gears. So cool—sort of steampunk. Yes, yes, it is. Super cool."

Daddy chuckled as he exited the tollway, alerting me that we were almost to our destination.

I returned the cube to the envelope and began to scan my surroundings through the windshield. I remembered coming to this same place over a year ago, when my dad was doing some research for an article he was writing.

Daddy has been a freelance writer for several blogs and magazines for years, while publishing his own suburban living magazine. One of the periodicals he was a frequent contributor to happened to be an antiquing magazine. Although he got a lot of satisfaction from writing for that publication, I enjoyed it much more when, once or twice a year, he did articles for the travel magazine. That almost always resulted in a trip to someplace really interesting—and really fun!

Writing about antiques, on the other hand, usually meant a visit to Mr. Hoise, of *D. Hoise Antique Emporium of Dallas*. Daddy has said many times that Mr. Hoise was the most knowledgeable antique expert in Texas. Mr. Hoise's shop was nestled conveniently near some of the best shopping in the entire Dallas-Fort Worth area, and it attracted customers from all over the country, and even the world. The store itself was a menagerie of items, from art prints to furniture, jewelry, and coins—everything rare and expensive, to be sure.

My excitement began to build as I exited the car. The fog started to lift from my memory of my last visit here, and I was starting to remember clearly the treasure trove of pieces Mr. Hoise had, all waiting to be discovered. Rare books, music boxes, antique trinkets, tea cups, trunks, jewelry, and oddities of all sizes and shapes and sorts—the possibilities were endless.

Approaching the door, I fed on my father's confidence. I, too, was feeling sure that if anyone could, Mr. Hoise would be able to shed some light on, and estimate the value of, my little treasure. Yes, I'd begun to think of it as mine. The anticipation was swelling to the point I felt like I would burst. "Stay cool," I said to myself, as Daddy opened the door.

Walking inside, I was immediately caught up in the eclectic atmosphere and started scanning the myriad of items in the store, as me and my dad made our way to the counter. A beautiful wood and glass display case held a treasury of jewelry and coins, next to an ornate walnut counter where Mr. Hoise stood waiting at the center of the premises. Daddy extended his right hand to shake, but the middle-aged man stepped from behind the counter and embraced my father, much to my surprise.

"Charles, my dear friend," he exclaimed, in a thick accent.

Not quite as tall as my dad, Mr. Hoise had thick, black hair, just a little long, but neatly combed back, and a full dark beard. Everything about him was polished and well-manicured, right down to his tailored suit. He had deep-set dark brown eyes that almost seemed to look through you. His smile was broad and bright against his beard and olive skin.

Daddy looked down at me with a proud smile. "You remember my daughter, Hannah."

"Ah, yes," Mr. Hoise said, reaching for my hand. "What a beautiful young lady you're growing to be. I hardly recognized you. Much different than the little girl you were the last time you visited my establishment."

He raised my hand and bowed to kiss it gently. I immediately blushed as I looked down and brushed my bangs aside, feeling slightly odd about what I thought was an unusual gesture.

"And equally modest," he added with a wink, as he must have noticed my slight embarrassment to his compliment.

The shopkeeper turned once again to my dad, placing a hand on his shoulder. "I'm so glad you called me this morning, Charles," he said. "I'm eager to see your item. It sounded *most* intriguing."

Daddy wasted no time. "It was actually Hannah who found it. She was stargazing with friends in a field near our home."

I jumped into the conversation, extending the envelope and placing it into his hand. "I thought I saw a light, but it must have been reflecting starlight or something," I said enthusiastically.

Hoise looked at the envelope. His gaze was intense, and his attention was singular. "What kind of light did you see?" he inquired, with a hint of suspicion.

I looked up at my dad and then at Mr. Hoise, whose eyes were fixed squarely on me. "It was… blue-ish. It may have been the streaking lights from the meteor shower, playing tricks on my eyes. Once I got up to it, the light was gone."

Daddy chimed in. "You'll see, it's too small to have a light source of any kind," he said. "It's showing the stress of exposure, but I'm hoping you might be able to clean it up and give us an idea what exactly it is."

Mr. Hoise drew in a breath as he carefully opened the envelope. He reached into the pouch and gently took hold of the cube, pulling it out ever so carefully. He held it delicately as he stepped back behind the counter, walking as though he were carrying something extremely fragile. Reaching down with his free hand, he pulled out a small cherrywood box and opened it to retrieve a jeweler's loupe, using it to meticulously examine my find. "Remarkable," he said under his breath, as he slowly turned the object in his fingers while studying it intently.

"Any thoughts?" My dad asked.

Mr. Hoise raised his eyes and looked up at the two of us, who were watching with curiosity. "You are correct that it is very distressed from exposure, soiled. How long do you suppose it had been left in the elements?" he asked.

I looked once again at my dad, who was shaking his head, trying to guess what the answer might be.

"I'm not sure. Months… years; it's hard to say," Daddy replied.

"Maybe centuries," I exclaimed, trying to contribute. "Maybe it's some treasure left by conquistadors, centuries ago." I immediately felt that my enthusiasm had spilled out maybe a bit too much. But Mr. Hoise smiled politely, although he didn't seem amused with my conquistador theory.

"Can it be cleaned up?" Daddy asked quickly, noticing Mr. Hoise's reaction to my whimsical idea.

Mr. Hoise placed a polishing cloth on the counter and set the cube on it with great care. "Yes," he said. "I believe it can. If you want to leave it here, I can clean and polish it. Once I'm done restoring its luster, I should be able to give you a better idea what it is, as well as its value."

I turned to my dad, whose eyes remained on the cube. "Daddy," I said. I didn't have to say anything else. He knew that I was opposed to the idea of leaving it there. I gave him a long look. I wasn't altogether certain why, I just didn't feel good about leaving it with the antique dealer.

I could tell the idea didn't sit well with my father, either. Daddy remained focused on the item and didn't acknowledge my cue. Mr. Hoise was beginning to appear a little impatient, as he waited for my dad to say something. His dark eyes glared at my dad, and his finger began to tap the counter gently.

"It wouldn't take much time to clean, would it? You mind if we stay and watch?"

Mr. Hoise stiffened, then smiled as he relaxed and began to pull out some tools. "Not at all, Charles, my friend," he said in his thick accent.

He took the loupe in hand again and quickly looked at the cube, checking each side, rotating the tiny box gingerly between his thumb and forefinger, as though he were hunting for something.

Feeling a little less anxious, my eyes began to wander, scanning the treasure trove of unusual items contained within the walls of the antique store. Sitting next to the wooden counter where Mr. Hoise had begun to work, a somewhat tattered hardcover book, with a uniquely embossed cover, drew my eye. As though pulled toward it by an unknown force, I began gravitating in its direction. Just as I was about to touch it, Mr. Hoise's voice pierced through my near-hypnosis.

"It is the oldest translation I have yet to come across," Mr. Hoise said, not taking his eye, or attention, from his work. "*Works and Days*, the finest literary achievement, by the great Greek poet Hesiodos."

My hand stopped cold. I sensed "old" equaled expensive. I quickly put my hands behind my back and diverted my attention back to the counter. Mr. Hoise continued to remove bits of soil and dirt particles from the cube.

"Oh, don't be shy, my dear. Books were made to be touched with searching hands, read by curious eyes, and digested by the inquiring mind," Mr. Hoise said. "It's not for sale at any price, but I welcome you to look at it," he continued, looking up from his work for only a brief second. "Yes, there's something about the feel of the paper in your hand... the satisfaction one gets from turning a page. You just cannot appreciate such experiences with electronic media."

I smiled politely but didn't turn again to the book. The light had caught an item just right and caused a glare, which now drew me toward the glass case next to the counter. With my hands still behind my back, I leaned down to inspect a unique fountain pen, beautifully displayed. The black barrel was crowned by an almost clear top, etched with the words "The President – The White House."

The barrel also appeared to be engraved. I twisted around, straining to see the engraving, but couldn't make it out.

"That pen belonged to President Kennedy," Mr. Hoise said, as though he could read my thoughts, as though he knew the questions without me even asking. "Very rare. Very expensive. The top is made of Lucite. They were custom made for his hand and writing style by Easterbrook. There are very few left. Yes, very few. That one had his initials engraved on the barrel and was found here in Dallas, in November 1963. Some of them sell for upwards of ten thousand. A small collection of fifteen unused pens once brought over forty thousand. This one, I believe, could be worth much more."

Daddy now leaned over to see the rare Kennedy pen as well. "That's extraordinary," he said. "Do you suppose he was carrying it with him at the time he was assassinated?" he asked the eccentric antique dealer.

Mr. Hoise had looked up at the both of us, both equally invested in the prized pen sitting in the antique dealer's display case. "I am... *reasonably* certain of it," he said, sitting down on a stool. He turned his gaze back to the cube he was meticulously working to restore.

"Anyway," he continued, "the museum downtown has been pleading with me to donate it for years now. I say to them I would be glad to sell it to them for a fair and equitable sum. They say I would get a plaque. I say I just want to get paid." Mr. Hoise's rich baritone voice produced a chuckle. "I did not come by that pen easily. It was, in fact, my very first acquisition. So you see, I'm not trying to be difficult. I'm just a simple business man, and a thank you is not a suitable return on investment."

My dad and I looked awkwardly at each other. Daddy patted me on the back of my shoulder—a non-verbal cue to step away from the coveted pen in Mr. Hoise's display case.

I began to look around again, wandering away from the counter, but not so far that Mr. Hoise and my treasure were out of sight. A beautiful snow globe had now attracted my attention. I collect snow globes. I get them here and there. Daddy almost always brings me one back as a souvenier whenever he goes out of town on business, but this particular one was the most beautiful I think I had ever seen. It had a polished silver base; detailed and ornate, cradling an almost invisible crystal globe. Inside was a wonderfully detailed carousel. Three beautifully decorated horses circled the center pole, poised to make chase as the carousel turned. On the front of the base was imbedded a beautiful clear crystal. It looked like a round diamond, larger than my thumb and set in a golden cradle—the centerpiece of the base. I was mesmerized at the realistic detail of the carousel and the beauty of the base.

Mr. Hoise was working away as my dad watched. They engaged in a bit of small talk, as the gentleman continued to assess the cube like a master painter studying a canvas. I could hear much of what the two were saying, in spite of being nearly entranced by the lovely snow globe that, for the moment, held my gaze.

"It appears to be pewter… should be easy to get clean," Mr. Hoise said, grabbing my attention and beckoning me back to the counter.

As I drew near, he had already immersed the cube in a solution. "I would put it in an ultrasonic cleaner, but I don't want to take the chance it might damage it, so I will clean it by hand," he said, as he continued working.

I watched him gently swirl the cube in the solution with a gloved hand. I began to wonder about this curious antique dealer who was clearly not from any part of Texas that I was familiar with. "So, Mr. Hoise, where are you originally from?" I asked.

Mr. Hoise looked up from his work, glancing at me with a smile and replied, "Very far from here. It's called Boeotia—a small village in Greece, near the Gulf of Corinth." He shifted and turned his attention back to his work.

"How did you end up in Dallas, Texas?" I asked, not picking up immediately on his somewhat disquieted body language.

Mr. Hoise glanced up again and smiled. Dad patted me on the back. "Let's allow Mr. Hoise to focus on his work. I'm sure he'd love to share his story with you some other time, but not right now."

Mr. Hoise looked down again as he began to dry and polish the cube, which was showing the intricate detail of a master artisan. "No… no, it's no bother, Charles, my friend. The girl is naturally curious. I very much appreciate that kind of curiosity. Not so common anymore, I think."

Taking his loupe in hand for another close-up look at the detail, he continued, "As much as I love telling stories, the answer to your question is a very long one and perhaps *is* a tale to be told another time."

He set the cube, with all the splendor of its rich matte silver finish, down on a polishing cloth on the counter. "Your charm is all clean. I was correct. It is pewter."

"So, it's a charm, like for a charm bracelet?"

"Not for a bracelet, I think. For a necklace… perhaps."

Daddy interjected, "It's pewter, you said… what period is it from?"

Mr. Hoise removed the nitrile gloves from his hands and scratched his thick beard. "Mid-20th century, perhaps. It is beautifully crafted and exquisitely detailed but is nothing of consequence; a simple charm and nothing of any significant value. I'm sorry."

The excitement Mr. Hoise had previously shown was now seemingly gone. I know my countenance must have showed the disappointment I was feeling. He reached over and patted my cheek and then tenderly lifted my head. "I am truly sorry this isn't the treasure of your conquistador," Mr. Hoise said sympathetically. "Perhaps you might like to sell it to me. I could add it to my inventory. Of course, for you, I would offer a generous price… better yet, perhaps a trade. Yes?"

Mr. Hoise quickly stepped away and made his way through the maze of merchandise, quickly returning with the snow globe that had gripped my attention earlier. He set it on the counter and addressed my dad.

"Your daughter has a very good eye, Charles."

Daddy beamed, as did I. It was a compliment that made me feel… mature. Mr. Hoise continued. "There is a lovely story that goes with this particular piece. There were only two of them ever made. They were commissioned at the request of a young English countess, who was to give one to a mysterious traveler, as a gift for an act of kindness. I came across this one during a recent trip to London. It was packed away in a box of worthless trinkets. I purchased the entire box at an estate auction—a real bargain. The other water globe, the traveler's gift, is said to be priceless, but sadly has never been found. I've searched many years for it with no success. I fear it must have been lost to the ages."

He reached underneath it and pulled out a key, inserting it into the bottom of the base. He began to turn it. After the third crank, he sat it down. "Listen…"

The snow globe began to play a soft melody. My mouth opened in surprise as Daddy pulled me close, sensing my excitement. "It's beautiful," I said. "I… I don't recognize the music."

"Chopin. A lullaby. It's lovely, yes?"

"Oh, yes," I exclaimed.

"So, my young friend, do we, as they say, have a deal?"

I started to reach toward the globe but snatched my hand back with a glance toward my dad. Something just didn't seem right. With a shrug, Daddy let me know that it was up to me. I looked at the charm, still sitting on a polishing cloth, and I looked at the beautiful snow globe, the soft tune now slowing to a near stop. Finally, I looked up at Mr. Hoise, who was eagerly awaiting an answer.

"I'm… I'm not sure." I paused. My heart raced as the room seemed to close in on me. I took a deep breath, then said as politely as I could, "No, sir. I'm sorry, Mr. Hoise. The snow globe *is* beautiful. It's the most beautiful snow globe I've ever seen, but the charm may have belonged to my great-grandmother. I want to research it more before I decide what to do with it. I hope you understand."

Mr. Hoise turned away. I could feel his disappointment, but only for a second, and then he turned back to me. "Certainly, I understand. Things sentimental can often have a much higher value than can be ascribed to the material or artistry in them."

Daddy reached for his wallet. "Mr. Hoise, I appreciate you taking the time to clean and appraise the charm. What do I owe you?"

"No, no, no, it was truly my pleasure—truly!"

As Daddy thanked Mr. Hoise again, I took the charm from the counter and turned toward the exit.

"Wait!"

Startled, I turned to see that Mr. Hoise had produced a small box with a soft, cotton-like material inside for padding. "Please, don't put it down inside that dirty envelope, my dear," he said in a slightly quieter tone.

I placed the charm in the box, took it from Mr. Hoise's hand and turned again to walk toward the door, reaching for Daddy's hand.

"Aren't you forgetting something?"

I stopped and made sure the box containing the charm was still in hand. I turned once more to see Mr. Hoise step around the counter with the snow globe I had admired, carefully nestled in his hands.

"But I didn't want to make the trade, Mr. Hoise."

"I cannot, in good conscience, let you leave without it, my dear. It was meant to be, I think."

My dad spoke up. "Mr. Hoise, thank you so much but I couldn't possibly…"

"It is a gift," Mr. Hoise insisted.

"It must be worth hundreds… thousands," Daddy continued, shaking his head in disbelief. "I can't allow her to accept such an elaborate gift."

I was speechless as Mr. Hoise placed it in my hands and, turning to my dad, said, "You have known me for quite some time—you know I will not take no for an answer." He paused for a second, then continued. "I offend very easily, Charles, and I insist you allow me to give your lovely daughter this gift. I had a daughter once many years ago. She is gone now. Please, my friend, do not refuse me this."

Daddy looked at me, as I was once again mesmerized by the carousel scene in the snow globe. He turned back to Mr. Hoise, who was also watching me stare into the glass globe with wonder. Daddy reached his hand out to the bearded gentleman. "I don't know what to say, Mr. Hoise."

I looked up at my dad with utter excitement. "I can have it?" I asked, as he nodded his head. Turning to Mr. Hoise, whose bright smile had again graced his face, I asked in amazement, "Really? Oh, Mr. Hoise! Thank you so much. I'll treasure this."

Mr. Hoise took the snow globe and wrapped it carefully, to protect it for our car ride home. At that moment, the *D. Hoise Antique Emporium of Dallas* was the coolest place ever.

As I walked with Daddy toward the exit, I could hear Mr. Hoise rifling through a drawer. Reaching the door, I turned to see him holding something in his hand. I wasn't certain from such a distance, but it appeared to be a tintype photograph. I had seen something similar before in my great-grandparents old photo albums. I didn't know it at the time, but it was from the end of the 19th century. I could tell he was studying it intently until he noticed I was watching him. He lowered the photograph and raised his hand, smiled and waved one last time as we exited the store.

As the heavy glass door closed behind me, his eyes return to the photograph. He put it back into the drawer, then fixed his eyes once more upon me as I slowly followed my dad to the car. I felt a chill come over me. Something felt strange about the way he was looking at me. Why was he was suddenly looking at me like an unwelcomed guest to a birthday party?

Daddy and I shared some basic chit-chat as we drove north toward the ranch. While he still seemed shocked by Mr. Hoise's extravagant gift, I was trying to put out of my mind those weird looks I got as we left the antique store. I get carried away sometimes and didn't want to read too much into it. *It's all in my head.* So, my thoughts went to the charm that was now safely boxed in the small purse I carried. I was determined to find out what exactly it was and how it ended up in a field on my great-grandparent's ranch. The mystery of it all gripped my curiosity, and I knew I had to spend some time digging in the attic later in the week if I was going to find any answers. I wasn't yet willing to come to terms with Mr. Hoise's assessment that the charm was "nothing of consequence." Something deep inside me was stirring, and I was certain there was more to it than Mr. Hoise could possibly determine using a jeweler's loupe.

CHAPTER 3: TREASURE HUNT IN THE ATTIC

WORD HAD BEGUN to spread regarding my little discovery. Lily, whose family attended the same church as my family, had told Sean Evans after church. Sean is also a student at the homeschooling co-op I attend with Lily and Annie. In fact, Sean and I both enjoy drama and we're in the co-op's drama class together.

Sean is super bright and energetic. His wide-eyed and adventurous nature was shadowed only by his tendency to exaggerate. Understand, no one had ever accused Sean of lying, but if you told Sean you saw a three-inch house gecko, which is common around North Texas, it would measure at least six inches when *he* told the story.

So naturally, the size and value of my charm had been significantly exaggerated. So much so that, by Monday, my phone had started buzzing non-stop with text messages from friends at church and co-op asking lots of questions about the treasure I had "dug up" here at the ranch. My mom was also getting calls from friends and neighbors, fishing for information. It had certainly elicited a lot of attention for my somewhat private family.

I dealt with the text messages as they came, but my thoughts were on what I might be able to find later in the attic. I hoped to find some clue that might connect the relic to my great-grandparents. Mom, on the other hand, was trying very hard not to let all the calls and inquiries annoy her. Daddy had left early that morning, to meet with his printers and tie up some loose ends for the next edition of his magazine, so it was Mom fielding the calls and answering the barrage of questions. This, Mom muttered as she poured more coffee, was something she rather wished not to have to deal with on a Monday, "or any other day of the week."

Homeschooling was a challenge for us on any typical Monday. My least favorite subjects, Language and Math, were followed by my two favorite subjects, Science and History. This particular Monday was not, however, a typical Monday, and by the second hour, the two of us had barely gotten through half the Language work, and Mom finally gave up for the day after hanging up from yet another call.

"Recess, kiddo," she said, sounding almost exhausted. "I don't have any idea how all of this got blown so far out of proportion, but Lily Little and Sean Evans have made my list this week."

The List was my mother's imaginary record of people who had, either intentionally or unintentionally, irritated her in some way or another. It was usually wiped clean at the end of the day with a few deep breaths and a quiet moment or two alone in prayer. Daddy often teased my mom that "love doesn't keep a record of wrongs," to which Momma would fire back in jest, "it's not rude either, mister." So, I wasn't too concerned for either Lily or Sean, but still, I could certainly relate to Mom's aggravation.

So, Mom declared a sanity break, making this the perfect time to head up to the attic to begin digging through the many boxes of my great-grandparent's things. As I pushed away from my small desk, Momma reminded me that I needed to muck out the barn and brush Gus-Gus. Named from my favorite fairy tale when I was younger, my horse was a surprise from Paw-Paw on my 5th birthday. Paw-Paw had purchased him at an auction in Fort Worth and gentled him, so I could enjoy riding him whenever I visited them at the ranch.

Sometimes, I notice how much like Paw-Paw Momma is—playful, joyous—but not right now. Now, she was all "Mom."

I said nothing in response to her suggestion. I just hung my head and slowly put my school papers in the drawer.

"Do you have something else you want to do, sissy?"

"I want to go up to the attic and have a look around. There are some boxes with photographs and journals I'd like to see."

I was hopeful that mentioning the photographs would do the trick. Momma loves photography like Nan, and that I caught the photography bug, too. "Your Nan would be proud," she'll say, and it's like Nan's there with us.

Sure enough, Momma conceded to let the barn, and Gus-Gus, wait until later. As she always did, she asked me to be careful and added she might join me after a while—if that was OK.

High-tailing it up the stairs, I put my hand on the dark, iron knob of the door which leads to the narrow attic steps. I paused for a moment as my heart raced. The excitement, and even a little fear of the unknown that awaited me, had thoroughly gripped my imagination. I turned the knob and pulled the white wooden door. A loud creaking sound announced throughout the house that someone was entering the attic as I climbed the steep stairway up into the dark, musty space.

The attic's single window provided a little light, but I had carried a flashlight with me in case the natural light wasn't sufficient. Then, I spotted an old brass floor lamp standing resolutely against the wall. Checking the plug to ensure it was plugged in, I turned the switch. Nothing. Tightening the bulb, I tried again, and the lamp lit up, providing some additional light to allow me to see my surroundings more clearly.

There were boxes on top of boxes, things my great-grandparents had collected during the six decades they lived together—most of which were in this beloved old house. A bassinet sat alone in one corner. I walked over to it, gently touching the lacy fabric with my hand. The dust stirred, causing me to sneeze. An old trunk was on the floor nearby, with stacks of books on top. I took one of the books from a pile and looked at the spine. I was unfamiliar with the title but quickly flipped through it, nonetheless, before setting it aside. I grabbed another, and then another, before coming to one that I recognized.

"*Tom Sawyer*! Now that's a good one," I murmured. "I remember this one."

I opened it, carefully turning the musty, discolored pages and remembering how Paw-Paw had read to me as I sat on his lap. I could hear his rasping voice once more in my mind, the way he used such inflection, bringing to life the story contained in Mark Twain's classic. I closed the cover and set it off by itself, intending to take it with me when I finished my little attic treasure hunt.

As I set the book down, I noticed a curious clay jug that looked like something from an ancient ruin that had somehow managed to escape eons of wear and damage. I picked it up and held it in my hand and wondered what the story was behind it and how my great-grandparents might have come across it. "Perhaps one of the artist's shops at Peach Creek," I thought, as I set it aside with full intention to smuggle it to my room later.

Returning to the old books, I quickly sorted through them. I set aside a couple that looked interesting, along with a booklet on anagrams—a subject that most intrigued me. I moved the remaining volumes off the old trunk and quickly opened it. The dark, discolored lid was heavy and the hinges stiff. Inside the musty, wooden container was, among other things, a weathered newspaper, dated August 14, 1945, with the headline "Japan Surrenders" in bold, faded black. Under the paper was a small Japanese flag, which I figured was a wartime souvenir.

Paw-Paw always told such colorful and exciting stories, but few of them were about his Navy service during World War II. I once asked him what he did in the war. He smiled at me courteously, took a sip of coffee, and with his gravelly voice, said, "I followed orders."

A white Naval uniform also sat inside the trunk. Neatly folded, it was in incredible condition, considering it had sat all these years stored away in the antique trunk. I opened the box underneath to find several medals and a set of dog tags. I studied them for a moment before setting them aside. I also happened across a simple silver chain, which probably went with the dog tags I had just found. I reached into my pocket and pulled out the charm I had discovered in the field. Carefully threading the chain through the loop on the charm, I hung it around my neck and continued to dig around the large box. The trunk had plenty of other things in it, all worth exploring later. However, my hunt was about finding some clue about the curious metallic cube that now hung on my neck.

And so, returning to my exploration, the smell of burning dust permeated the stale air of the attic, as the bulb on the lamp had heated up. I turned to look at it, and a familiar box near where the lamp was standing grabbed my attention. *How did I overlook that one before?* I hastily moved over to it, leaving my great-grandfather's trunk open and partially unpacked.

Sitting on top of the box were two rectangular, brown, leather bags. I recognized one of them quickly as Nan's camera bag. I picked it up with care and gently opened the flap, revealing the familiar black and silver casing of the old 35 mm camera my great-grandmother was so rarely seen without. I picked up the camera, which was much heavier than it looked, and ran my fingers across the textured black trim. I recalled being told that this had been a gift from Paw-Paw to Nan, for Christmas in the early 1960s, after a mishap had damaged another camera. I held it up to my eye and peered through the viewfinder toward the single diamond-shaped attic window.

Setting the camera down inside the case, I picked up the other bag and opened it. A looped black strap, attached to a dark plastic box, was the first thing I saw as I reached inside and pulled out the contents. I looked at the face of the strange camera. Mounted under the dark, round lens was a silver plate, which had a red dot logo and the model name in reversed text against a black background. I smiled as I examined the vintage camera intently. It was unlike any camera I had seen before. On one side was what appeared to have been a gray, plastic knob, now broken. An arrow on what was left of the knob pointed counter-clockwise. "Maybe a winding knob for the film," I thought. I was no stranger to old cameras, but this one was really interesting.

Carefully turning the boxy camera around, looking for the viewfinder, I noticed there wasn't one back there. I continued rotating it until I saw at the top, in front of where the leather strap attached to the top of the camera, a window provided a view through another window, just above the lens. I thought about how strange it would have been to take pictures looking down into that little window while pointing the camera at the subject, but I could also recall how Nan spoke so fondly of her "old" camera and lamented its having been damaged.

With the contents of both camera bags unpacked, I reached for the box that had initially drawn me to this corner of the attic. I sat down and slid the box, about the size of a copy paper box, toward me. I knew this box well and had viewed its contents many times. This box was one of the things I had come here to the attic to find. I was certain there would be some clue that would help me unravel the mystery of the silver charm.

The sound of footsteps ascending the steps down below distracted me for just a moment. Turning, I saw Momma top the stairs and enter the dimly lit room to join the hunt.

"Mind if I join you, sis?"

"Pull up a box, sit down and go through this with me," I replied. "You won't believe some of the things I've found already."

Momma stepped over to the center of the room and reached up, taking hold of a braided piece of string attached to a silver chain. She gave it a pull and the attic lit up brightly, as I looked around in surprise.

"You might be able to see better with a little more light," Momma said, with a smile.

I giggled. "I had no idea that was there. True story," I said, watching her head my way.

"Ah, I see you found Nan's camera. I wondered if that was up here somewhere," she said, speaking of the old black and silver 35 mm. "I may have to take it out and see if it still has the magic."

I reached over and picked up the case that contained the older camera with its strange viewfinder and broken knob. "That's fine," I said. "But I'd like to have this one... if that's okay?"

"Oh my! I've never seen this one," Momma said with surprise. "Don't let your Daddy see it," she said, laughing. "He'll snatch it up and put it on the shelf in his study." Examining it closely, she added, "This is extraordinary. I've only seen one of these in pictures."

As I pointed out the broken plastic knob, she added, "Might be hard to find parts to fix it."

I had returned my attention to the box. Inside were several smaller boxes, most containing photographs, and some containing film negatives. I pulled out one of the boxes that held hundreds of negatives and handed it over. "Negatives, right?" I asked inquisitively.

Momma had, on a couple of occasions, talked with me about how things were before the advent of digital photography, but she seemed surprised at how well I had retained it all. As we continued to sort through the boxes of photographs, she told me that Nan, at one time, had everything necessary for a dark room, and it sparked my curiosity that some of it must be here in the attic somewhere.

I've always had these creative impulses and I'll try anything once. But I was intrigued by the idea of developing my own photographs, the old-fashioned way. In fact, I was almost always interested in "old" things and "old" ways. Sewing, baking, growing herbs... these were the things that really piqued my interests. I enjoy the conveniences of my cell phone, downloading apps and playing games—like most kids my age—but I think sometimes Paw-Paw had been quite right years ago when he remarked that I had an "old soul." It was no surprise, at least to my mother, that I would be fascinated by the idea of figuring out the antique camera and developing my own pictures.

Another small box had now come out of the larger box. This one was about the size of a shoe box and, upon opening it, I found dozens upon dozens of old photographs. I handed Momma a handful of them as I started looking through some photos on my own. I could sense her reacting to some of them as she glanced through. I turned my head to see her dab a tear from her eye.

"Seriously," I said lightheartedly. "Already?"

Momma smiled and turned a photograph, showing me the black and white image of a young man, holding a baby. His face looked familiar, but it bore little resemblance to the mustachioed rancher of whom I had such fond memories, and yet…

"Is that Paw-Paw?" I asked, with surprise.

Momma nodded.

"Is that you?"

"Oh no, this was long before I would have been born. The baby would have been my father."

"Wow," I said. "I think the only picture I've ever seen of him is his graduation picture that Nan had hanging in the entry-way." I paused, noticing she looked flushed as she swallowed hard against her emotions. "Sorry, Momma. I didn't know what you were looking at."

"It's okay. It just caught me by surprise. He died not long after I was born."

"Vietnam?"

Momma nodded, as we both went back to looking through photographs.

Another box had come out, as the two of us sifted through, commenting on the pictures from time to time—laughing, and occasionally choking back tears as well. Nan had captured a lifetime in pictures, to be sure. These would now be treasured heirlooms, a memorial to the extraordinary bygone days of Paul and Elizabeth Learner's lives.

"*YES!*" I shouted suddenly. "I was hoping to find this one!"

Turning around the picture of an old barn on the edge of a vast hayfield for my mom to see, I couldn't contain my joy.

"I've never seen that one before," Momma said.

"Nan used to show it to me all the time," I said. "She was proud of this one, I think. Nan and Paw-Paw used to drive me over to The Shops at Peach Creek for ice cream when I would come visit. Nan would always make a big deal about how important it was that I know the way."

Momma took the picture in hand and carefully studied it. "So, what does ice cream at the shopping center have to do with the picture, kiddo? I'm not sure I follow."

"That barn in the picture used to sit right where the ice cream shop is now, over in the shopping center," I answered.

"Oh, my!" Momma gasped. "I guess I knew that but didn't at all make the connection. I remember when they started development of the shopping center—you couldn't have been more than two or three."

Taking the photograph back, I stroked it gently with my thumb. An inner warmth embraced me as I thought of those rides over to Peach Creek. It was a short drive, not more than five miles. I recalled to my mother how Nan had always made a point of saying I should remember my way back to the ranch from the ice cream shop. Paw-Paw would take the trip slow and point out little landmarks along the way. As I shared my memories with Mom, they became more and more vivid. I could almost hear their voices and smell the scent of Nan's perfume. "It's curious," I said. "I don't know why they always made it such a big deal."

"Did she tell you when it was, she took this picture?" Momma asked.

"I think not long before I was born," I answered. "She always said she was going to put some of these pictures in a scrapbook for me... before she got sick."

The mood became a little more somber as my mom reached over and patted my hand. Not wanting to become emotional, I forced a smile and then a quick giggle. "She would always point this photograph out, like every single time I was here. Nan would say, 'It's important to know the way things were. It may help you find your way to where you're going someday,' and then she'd give it a swipe with her apron before putting it back in the box."

I did an impersonation of my great-grandmother when I quoted her and now had Momma laughing out loud. "Oh, my stars! You even sound like her, sis."

Suddenly, a loud thud downstairs sent a shock through my chest. Momma jolted as a quiet rumble could be heard.

I could hardly breathe. Momma, wide-eyed, whispered to me, "It's too early for your daddy to be back."

I said nothing. I couldn't.

Both of us listened carefully, before Momma slowly got to her feet. She walked with caution toward the door, taking an old golf club out of Paw-Paw's bag sitting nearby. Gripping the handle tightly, she stepped down into the narrow stairway and paused. She turned and gestured that I should stay put as she crept downward, almost completely out of my sight.

"Is there someone down there?" I whispered.

Silence.

Mom continued down to the second floor, the steps creaking slightly as she stepped over the loudest treads. I could hear Momma's voice calling out again, as I rose to my feet and moved toward the door. As I passed the bag of golf clubs, I grabbed the biggest one, much like my mom had, and grasped it like a baseball bat before moving to the open door.

Before stepping into the stairway, I caught a glimpse of two journals sitting atop a box. *Remember to return for those later, Hannah.*

Then, I quietly moved to the second floor. I could still hear Mom creeping slowly around, now from the first floor. I descended to the main floor of the old house, as quietly as I could manage, but the stairway creaked with nearly every step.

As I reached the bottom, a figure leaped around the corner. I screamed and drew back the golf club to strike. Standing in front of me, in a nearly identical stance, was my mother—also screaming, ready to take a swing.

"Hannah! My word! I told you to stay put."

"I wasn't going to stay up there! The villain always goes to the attic in those old creeper movies. Besides, I thought you might need help."

"I don't know what that noise was, but there doesn't appear to be anyone here. The doors are locked, and the windows are closed," Momma said, with some relief.

Both of us lowered our clubs and began to giggle. Neither of us were certain whether we were laughing at the hilarity that we had frightened one another, or relief that there was no need for alarm.

Later that afternoon, when Daddy returned home, we told him with laughter how we had nearly come to blows with golf clubs at the bottom of the steps. As I did my chores that afternoon, Dad carefully checked around the house. Later, I found out that he did notice some slight splintering on the front door and door frame, suggesting that someone might have tried to force open the door, but he didn't want to overreact. So, he kept it to himself.

CHAPTER 4: BAD LUCK CHARM

MY THIRTEENTH BIRTHDAY party was happening this weekend, and I had planned to have several friends over on Friday evening. My guest list consisted of about twenty-five friends from my church youth group and the homeschool co-op. Of course, Lily, Annie, and Morgan were all planning to spend the night. And so, Daddy loaded the family up and we went into town to buy party supplies.

I asked if we could go by The Shops at Peach Creek and get some ice cream after we finished our shopping. So, we stopped for a pizza before going to the party supply store, where I picked out party favors and decorations that went with my "glamping" theme.

Daddy didn't get "glamping"—combining glamour and camping—so it took a little explanation before he was completely on board with it. Momma and I had more than a couple laughs at his expense in the party store, before the three of us found ourselves at the little throwback ice cream shop that, at least for me, elicited such fond memories.

Sitting outside, eating our treats, I shared with Dad more of what all Momma and I had found in the attic. He noticed the chain around my neck. I proudly pulled at it and revealed the charm tucked down in my shirt. I told him about finding it in the old U.S. Navy trunk and continued talking about all the other interesting things in the attic. Daddy was particularly fascinated when we described the cameras and old photos.

I started to reminisce and recalled the drives to this ice cream shop, pulling out the picture Nan had taken years earlier. My dad was riveted by the photo but was quickly able to point out where the barn in the picture used to sit in relation to the quaint shopping center, which now occupied the land. He also pointed out where the old road used to run, and how they moved it after the development began, to improve traffic flow. I listened attentively and smiled fondly, remembering such conversations with my great-grandparents once upon a time. It felt so familiar and made me miss them a little more. Daddy, like my Paw-Paw, was a curator of odd trivia and "useless knowledge." Both of them could recall it all in near endless recitations.

But I still had so much I wanted to tell Daddy about the treasures in the attic, so I waited for the right moment. He paused just long enough, and somehow, I managed to take the conversation right back to talking about *Tom Sawyer* and all the other priceless items.

Daddy looked over at Momma, who was listening intently to my account of the afternoon's exploration of the attic, and my cherished memories of Nan and Paw-Paw. Daddy reached over and took my hand. "They were special people," he said. "Paul always told the most fascinating stories, and Elizabeth saw everything around her with such optimism."

Momma chimed in, "It was always like they had some inside perspective—they knew something no one else in the world knew, and no matter what was going on, life was a glorious adventure ever unfolding."

"... And Paul's famous witticisms," Daddy reminisced.

I listened for a while, as my parents shared stories of their own about the Paul and Elizabeth Learner they knew, wishing I could have known them a little longer.

Later that evening, we were nearly home from our outing. It wasn't quite dark yet, but the automatic lights on our car came on, startling a young man who was walking toward us alongside the road. He was carrying a fishing pole and tackle box. The boy darted off the road as we went past.

I turned to look out the back window at him. "Who is that boy?" I asked. "Have either of y'all seen him before?"

Daddy glanced out the rearview mirror, just as the young man stepped back onto the pavement and walked on. "No, I don't think so," he replied. "He looks like he's been fishing, and the only fishing hole near here is the pond on the lower back side of the ranch. Paul stocked it years ago but was pretty choosy about who he allowed to fish there."

"I'll bet that's the Blake boy," Momma said. "They live down the road, him and his mother—moved in about a year or so ago. He's the one who…"

My dad jumped in and cut Momma off mid-sentence, "Oh, gotcha." He glanced back at me in the rearview mirror. "Sam, I think is his name," he whispered to her after a long pause. "I believe you're right, although I've only seen him the one time."

Naturally, I was listening carefully to their conversation but was sure not to let on I was paying any attention. I can't help it. Lily says I'm nosey that way. I like to think I'm just curious. At this moment, I was *curious* what "the one time" referred to and what it was about this boy that made him a topic of a conversation my parents were uncomfortable discussing in front of me. Nevertheless, I tried to control my *curiosity* as Dad made the turn through the gate and onto the ranch, pulling up to the house.

As I collected my phone and charger, Momma had already made her way out and around to the back of the SUV. But Dad was sitting motionless in the front seat, his eyes fixed on the front door.

"Sissy," he said to me with great gravity, "stay in the car." Stepping out, he turned to me with an unusually sober look on his face. "I mean it. Stay here."

Stepping around to the back, he told Momma to get into the car and lock the doors. He grabbed the heavy flashlight out of the roadside emergency kit. I guess now I know why he insists Momma keeps that kit stocked! Closing the tailgate, he slowly approached the dark front porch.

I watched as he took step after cautious step. "We must have freaked him out with the attic story today," I said, half-jokingly. Momma said nothing, as we continued watching. After the false alarm earlier that day, I wasn't the least bit concerned, but she knew something more than an uneasy feeling had gotten his attention.

Except I was certain I had turned the porch light on before exiting the house.

As I was about to ask Mom about it, Daddy clicked on the flashlight, pointing the beam of light toward the front door. Now, I could clearly see the cause for his concern. The door was hanging wide open, and the glass of a broken light bulb littered the porch. He stepped inside, and one by one, the lights inside came on, as my dad walked through the house before waving for the both of us to join him inside.

Daddy had already called 911, and as we waited for a sheriff's deputy to arrive, Mom and Dad walked through our rooms, assessing the damage. Someone had broken into our home and ransacked it, but it was unclear if anything was missing.

Two deputies arrived and began asking all sorts of questions. I sat quietly on the couch as they took pictures and collected evidence.

I couldn't believe this was happening.

Here. To *my* home.

I've heard about it happening in the city. But out here in the country? When my great-grandparents lived here, I don't think they ever even locked the doors.

"My wife and daughter heard something earlier today," I heard Daddy tell the deputy. "I didn't want to alarm anyone because I couldn't say for sure, but it *did* look like someone might have tried to pry the door open."

As my Dad walked the deputy toward the front door, I walked into the kitchen, where my mother sat, staring at the floor.

"Are you OK?"

Momma looked up at me, trying to contain her sadness. "Yes, sweetheart. I'm sorry. I was just coming to tell you."

"Tell me what?"

Momma stood and gestured up the stairs toward my room. As we began to ascend the steps, Momma put her hand gently on the small of my back. *Something's very wrong.* The last time she walked me into a room like this was at Paw-Paw's funeral.

Walking into my bedroom, I first noticed my nightstand's drawer was sitting open, and my dresser drawers were pulled out onto the floor. But then I saw what my mom had brought me in to see. Tears immediately pooled in my eyes and I could barely swallow for the lump in my throat.

Shattered. They're completely shattered.

Two of the snow globes from my collection were in pieces on the floor, water pooling around them. One was my newest acquisition, the one I had promised the antique dealer, Mr. Hoise, I would cherish most. The glass was smashed, the carousel in pieces and the beautiful jewel that embellished the base crushed to bits.

I turned and laid my head on my mother's shoulder and sobbed. Momma held me tightly, as Daddy walked in with one of the deputies. I tried so hard to collect myself, but tears continued to flow as my emotions went from heartbroken and sad to angry. The deputy took a picture and asked if anything was missing in this room. The deputy's matter-of-factness did little to make me feel any better. *He's so disconnected.* I suddenly became infuriated. *I'll bet he wouldn't be so "oh well" if it were his house and his things.*

Aloud, I answered quietly, keeping my anger in check. "No, sir—I don't think so."

As I knelt down to begin picking up the pieces, Momma tapped me on the shoulder. "No, sweetie. I don't want you to cut yourself."

In my anger, I dismissed her altogether and picked up the polished silver base of the beautiful antique snow globe Mr. Hoise had given me. Atop the ornate base was only one of the regal horses. The other two lay broken in a puddle on the floor.

The deputy knelt next to me. "There's nothing here that can't be replaced, Miss," he said, patting my shoulder.

I handed him the remains of the old snow globe. "This one, sir. It can't be replaced," I said, as my voice began to quiver.

The deputy stood up, setting it on top of my dresser. He hesitated for a moment before following us downstairs into the living room. He explained that there had been a series of burglaries, very similar to this, around the county and he had no doubt the incident earlier was someone casing the house, likely scared off when they realized someone was home.

It didn't take too long to determine that nothing was missing from in or around the house, which gave the deputy some pause. He noted that in most of the other burglaries, things like electronics, tools, and firearms had been stolen. And so, he concluded, this break-in *was* different. "Could be a copycat or isolated robbery, but more than likely, it's connected to the others," he said. "Have y'all noticed anyone suspicious around?"

Daddy shook his head and answered, "No, sir."

After collecting all the information they needed, the deputies encouraged us to contact them if we discovered anything missing, or if we saw anyone suspicious. Daddy walked them out to their car, and as they pulled away, he came back inside.

"What did you say to them?" I asked.

"I told them about the Blake boy we saw as we were coming back home."

Momma, trying to clean up, turned to him and said, "Oh, Honey. I don't think he…"

Dad interjected, "I told the deputy he was just a kid, and I didn't believe it was anything, but I thought I might mention it, just in case."

I don't think any of us slept well that night. I laid in my bed, tossing and turning, wrestling with a roller coaster of emotions. I thought about the beginning of this day and how everyone was calling with questions about the treasure they had heard about from Sean. As I pondered these thoughts, it came to me that all this could be because of the charm that now hung around my neck. *Maybe it's bad luck.* I took it off and put it on top of the nightstand, rolled over and turned my back to it. "It's a bad luck charm—that must be why someone threw it out there in the field," I muttered under my breath. "Which is exactly where it's going back to tomorrow."

CHAPTER 5: A NEW FRIEND

TUESDAY CAME AND went, as we cleaned up from the break-in that occurred the previous evening. I had managed to trek back up into the attic, under the pretense of checking to see if anything had been disturbed up there. I found everything just as I had left it, which was at least a little consolation. The items that had been left out the day before went back into the musty Navy trunk, except, of course, for the chain. It continued to hold the curious cube-shaped charm, still sitting on my nightstand.

So, along with the two camera bags, I took the copy of *Tom Sawyer* and two of my Paw-Paw Learner's journals to my bedroom. Another trip up was needed to get the box of photographs and negatives. I trod down the narrow stairway to the second floor, where my bedroom sat just to the left of the attic door. The box was heavy, and I was still chewing on my angry feelings—but still, I was secretly hoping that it, or perhaps the journals, would hold some clue about the small, box-shaped charm.

I couldn't put my finger on why I was so obsessed. In spite of my feelings about the break-in, I *was* admittedly obsessing over the silver cube. Obsessing over things is nothing new for me. It was one of those quirky traits that I had no doubt inherited from my father, but this was different. The obsession was deeper than the usual fanaticism I enjoyed from time to time about things like K-pop or far away cultures. This was eating at me, deep inside, and churned the very core of my being. I was determined not to let this go. I just couldn't seem to shake the feeling that there was so much more to the charm than Mr. Hoise knew. I was still grappling with the notion that it had somehow brought bad luck or was at least connected to the break-in. But, it was a new day, and I was cautiously optimistic that soon, I might have some answers.

As I made my way back to the second floor, I suddenly caught a glimpse of a curious light. The floor at the base of the steps was aglow. The bright blue glare was so bright, in fact, that it lit up the stairway. The diffused light danced on the walls, as I cautiously continued down toward the doorway. *Weird.*

I took another step and noticed the light pulsated in a slow rhythm. *Very weird.* After the break-in, "weird" equaled "cause for concern" in my book.

I stopped at the last step and leaned forward, wondering where the light was coming from. Had I had turned on a lamp, or was the sunlight reflecting into the hallway? Clearly, it was coming from my room, but as I stepped through the doorway onto the second floor, it was gone. "Must have been the sunlight," I murmured, walking briskly toward my room, relieved and even a little embarrassed for being so jumpy. Setting the box of photographs down on my bed next to the journals, I noticed that one of the journals was sitting opened.

I leaned toward it, caught the thick cover between my fingers and pulled it quickly toward me. Looking down, I recognized my great-grandfather's penmanship. Paw-Paw's strokes were smooth and dark. The page was dated Thursday, November 28, 1963, and spoke about a "somber Thanksgiving." One line read, "Elizabeth's pumpkin pie smelled so good as it sat on the counter, but none of us could bring ourselves to eat much dinner, let alone dessert." It seemed very cryptic, but the most peculiar line was at the bottom of the page. The sentence read, "Aphrodite was to bathe her head with grace."

I found myself utterly fixating on the words. I read the line over and over as though, somehow, it would make sense to me through repetition. It seemed to have nothing to do with the rest of the journal entry, and yet, I had a gut feeling that this was Providence at work, and this bizarre sentence was the key to solving the mystery of the silver trinket. I stood nearly motionless beside my bed for what seemed like forever, but in truth was merely a minute, maybe two. I could feel the pressure building inside me until finally I could not take it anymore. "What's it even *mean*?" I blurted, in frustration.

Just then, my cell phone vibrated, once and then a couple more times. Someone was texting. My concentration broken, I reached into my back pocket to see who was blowing up my phone. It was Lily.

"Hey. Just heard. ☹"

"You OK?"

"Luv ya! ❤"

I sent back a quick response. "☹ I'll be OK. Luv U2! ❤"

As I hit send, I could hear my mom calling up to me. I closed the journal, then headed downstairs. The rest of the day was quiet, as we worked together to put things back to normal. I, however, continued to be infatuated with the silver cube throughout the day. I just couldn't put it out of my mind for very long. The added oddity of my great-grandfather's journal entry also plagued my thoughts, and between these two major mysteries, I wasn't able to find a minute's peace inside the solitude of my thoughts.

The following morning started out mostly routine. I had completed my schoolwork by 2:00 p.m. and had asked my mom to let me take Gus-Gus out. I hadn't ridden him for a week or so and, all things considered, I thought it would be good therapy; a chance to take my mind off things. I also thought this might be a good opportunity to get rid of that "bad luck charm." The more I thought, the more convinced I was that it was somehow responsible for the break-in two days earlier. It just felt too coincidental. I know—that's neither reasonable nor rational, but as Annie says, "Consider my age and be thankful it's not worse." The added preoccupation I was experiencing just made it seem more necessary to rid myself of it and be done with this whole frustrating ordeal. So now, rather than throwing it out into the field, I thought maybe dropping it into the pond on the lower end of the ranch would ensure no one else would come across it.I changed clothes, got my helmet, and put the charm, chain and all, into my hip pocket before heading to the barn. Walking in, I saw my dad securing the saddle before handing me the reins.

"Thanks, Daddy. I didn't know you were here."

He smiled and gave me a boost as I mounted the sturdy horse. "I got home a few minutes ago, and your mom said you were taking Gus-Gus out."

I gave my horse a nudge, and Gus-Gus sauntered toward the open barn door, his head nodding in agreement that he, too, was looking forward to the ride.

"Stick to the trails and don't go beyond the perimeter of our property," Daddy said, walking alongside.

"I thought I'd ride down to the pond, if that's okay?"

I could tell Daddy wasn't immediately on board with that idea, so I gave him my best puppy-dog face. He chuckled and shook his head. "Sure," he said. "How can I say no to those big brown eyes? You look so much like your mom, and I can't hardly say 'no' to either one of you. Nice and easy, though—not too fast, and be back here in about an hour."

I smiled and jokingly rolled my eyes as my dad covered the rules. Truth be told, I've always found comfort in the boundaries my parents set, and even when they're occasionally over-protective… well, I don't always like it, but I know I'm important to them and loved.

Daddy patted my leg and said, "Hey, don't give me grief. I can't help it. You'll find out someday when *you're* a parent."

With that, Daddy gave Gus-Gus a pat and ordered the old boy to take care of his "little girl" as we trotted off across the meadow, toward the pond.

Several trails wound around to the pond and I paused to decide which one I wanted to take. As I sat atop Gus-Gus looking toward the trails, I started to become overwhelmed by the sensation that someone was watching me. I looked around and circled the horse, who also seemed a little skittish.

Gus-Gus pointed his ears forward. They were stiff as he let out a loud snort. I instinctively reached forward with my left hand and stroked his neck until his ears relaxed. "Easy boy," I soothed. I wondered if my four-hooved companion was experiencing the same sensation, or if he was merely reacting to me. Nevertheless, the horse settled and with a couple blows, he let me know everything was alright before I gave a gentle tug at the reins, leading Gus-Gus down one of the paths toward the pond.

Riding along, I still couldn't shake the feeling that someone was watching me. At one point, I considered turning back toward the ranch, but let Gus-Gus trot along instead. Coming to a clearing, I gave him the signal to open up a little into a nice gallop. I was definitely feeling more relaxed by this point, as was my beloved horse.

In moments, we were there. It was a good size pond, covering about two and a half acres. I dismounted near a neglected firepit and a bench made of rough-cut timbers with the initials "PL+EL" carved into it. I secured Gus-Gus's reins on a tree branch that stretched out over the still waters, and as he drank from the pond, I sat on the bench and took in the view.

It was quiet and serene. I came here many days fishing with my Paw-Paw. Nan would make sandwiches and throw them into a picnic basket, along with glass jars of sweet tea. She'd grab a couple peaches from the orchard and slice them up, drop them in a glass canning jar with ice and pour the tea right over them. Sometimes she would fry chicken. I sat there on the bench remembering how amazing it was that Nan could fry chicken in the morning, wrap it up in foil and newspaper, and somehow it was still hot when we pulled it out hours later at the pond. A flood of memories was rushing over me like a spring wind. I thought about all the great times I had around this quiet pool.

I recalled once, after I lost my fishing hook, Paw-Paw teased that he was fresh out. "No more hooks, little girl," he declared. Not knowing he was joking, I threw all our fishing worms into the pond. It still gets me chuckling, remembering how he reacted when he discovered his joke had ended our fishing trip for real. These are all precious memories for me.

I tugged at my brown riding boots before reaching into my back pocket for my phone. I barely had a signal, but the clock indicated that I should probably head back before long. Putting my phone away, I pulled the charm out of my hip pocket. Dangling it in front of me, I recalled my excitement—giddiness, even—when I discovered it in the field.

As I looked at it, I noticed the panel where the chain looped through had an opening on the joint, like a box that was cracked open. I recalled Daddy saying he saw the same thing on it the night I found it, but when we took it to Mr. Hoise at the antique shop, it wasn't there. I managed to slide my thumbnail into the gap and gently pry until the point I felt my nail start to give.

While studying it closer, I heard rustling. Gus-Gus also reacted to the sounds, which seemed to be something, or someone, coming out of the tree line and into the clearing. I put the charm back into my pocket and stood, expecting to have to go calm my horse, but he had already gone back to sipping water from the pond.

I looked over again at the tree line, and out walked a relatively tall, dark-haired young man. He was wearing a plain green t-shirt, blue jeans and work boots, and was carrying a fishing pole and tackle box. As he got closer, I could see it was, in fact, the same boy I saw a couple of nights earlier, on our way home from the ice cream shop.

I watched as he crossed the meadow, walking at a casual pace toward us. His kind face held no surprise as he nodded to me and set his tackle and fishing pole down. He reached out a hand to stroke Gus-Gus, who whinnied at his approach. I quickly moved toward them, unsure how Gus-Gus would take to this stranger.

"Hey-ya, Gus-Gus," said the young man. "Long time no see, ay boy?"

Gus-Gus nodded, as if to say, "Yep, you got that right."

Taken off guard, I spoke up. "I see he knows you."

The young man smiled, as he continued to stroke and pat the horse and turn his gaze to me. "I'm Sam… Sam Blake. Helped your grandfather out from time to time 'round the ranch. Gus-Gus here, and me—well, you can say we're old friends. Ain't that right boy?"

I couldn't help but smile, watching my horse react to Sam's attention. "I'm Hannah. Paul was actually my *great*-grandfather."

Sam continued doting on the horse. "Hannah Goodheart. Yeah, I know. Mr. Learner always referred to you as his granddaughter, so I just assumed. He… he was a cool guy."

I stepped around and sat back down on the bench. "So, Sam Blake, you come fish this pond a lot?"

Sam stepped away from the horse and picked up his fishing gear, then sat down next to me. He propped up his pole next to him and opened his tackle box, digging around to find what he needed to rig his pole before wetting a line. "I have been for well over a year now. Mr. Learner said I could anytime I wanted. I guess I should have asked permission after y'all moved in, but I didn't want to bother your folks. It seemed a little... awkward."

I wondered for a moment what he could mean by "awkward." It occurred to me that it seemed to be the perfect word to describe a lot of things these past few months. Thinking about losing my great-grandfather and then moving to the ranch was enough. But then, as it tends to do, my mind wandered, and began to ponder the distance that seemed to be growing in my relationship with Morgan. I forgot for a minute that Sam was sitting next to me and blurted out, "Awkward doesn't even begin to describe it."

Sam, not knowing I was lost in my own thoughts, must have believed I was directing my outburst at him and quickly became defensive. "Look, I just found him. I wasn't even there when he died."

I quickly turned. My mouth gaped in shock. "What do you mean?" I asked in a loud, shrill voice. "What are you saying?"

Sam's eyes dropped to the dusty ground at his feet. "I came over to see if he needed help in the barn. My mom was working, and I came over every couple of days—you know, to help out. Mr. Learner was just lying there. I tried to wake him up, but he was..."

I could feel my eyes welling up as I listened to Sam tell about finding Paw-Paw laying on the ground between the house and the barn. He had run home and called 911 because he didn't have a cell phone. He said he'd felt guilty for leaving my Paw-Paw and by the time he got back, paramedics were already arriving, but it was too late. I realized Sam had held that guilt inside all these months since Paw-Paw's passing. It was clear to me, he had agonized, wondering if he could have done something different, or done more to save his friends life.

"It's not your fault, Sam," I said, trying to console him. "I… I just didn't know it was you. I only knew they found him—his heart just gave out."

Sam sat silently as I confirmed that what he probably already knew in his heart of hearts was true. I could tell it had been such a difficult few months for him, carrying his hurt inside as he had.

"I should have come by," he said, as he struggled to find words to express both his own sense of loss and sympathy for me. "He meant a lot to me; he really did. It's hard to explain. I just know I wanted to come and tell y'all how much he…"

"It's OK. I understand. It couldn't have been easy for you. I'm sorry if it seemed as though I was jumping to conclusions."

Sam's shoulders sagged and his stiff posture relaxed a bit as he told me more about how he had come to know my great-grandfather. He explained that his own father had left when he was five, leaving him and his mother with nothing, near homelessness. The two moved around a lot over the next couple of years as Sam's mother, Manuela, went from job to job, trying to provide for Sam, before landing a good job and settling down.

While we sat talking, he told me that, about eighteen months ago, his mom got lost. She was looking for a house that was advertised for sale or rent and showed up at here at Learner Ranch to ask for directions. According to Sam, Paw-Paw took an immediate interest in him and his mother. I wasn't surprised. Paw-Paw had a way of making people feel special.

"It was like he knew us, as though he had for years," Sam said.

His mother's dream was to be able to buy a permanent home for them, but she couldn't save much of her salary. In fact, she had told him they were barely going to be able to afford the rent on the home they were there to look at, just down the road from the Paw-Paw's. But then, they got a phone call the next afternoon from the owner, saying they were willing to come down considerably on the rent. They moved in and the first visitor to show up and welcome them was none other than my Paw-Paw.

"Paul—Mr. Learner—asked me to come by and offered me a few dollars here and there to do odd jobs around the ranch," Sam recalled. "Paint a fence, muck the stalls in the barn, stuff like that. I would have done it for free. He treated me like I was his own grandson or something."

Sam continued, "Six months or so after we moved in, my mom got a call from the owner of the house saying that they needed to sell the house and wanted to give us the first chance to buy. Of course, we couldn't. Well, I told Paul we were going to have to move. About a week later, we got a call from the owner saying Paul Learner was buying the house. That night, Paul stopped by and asked my mom to sign papers. I wasn't sure what was going on, but after he left, my mom broke down and cried. She kept calling him 'nuestro ángel,' our angel."

"Paw-Paw bought your house and gave it to you?"

"He did. To this day, I don't know why, but he did."

"You must have been as special to him as he was to you. Paw-Paw did a lot of amazing things for a lot of people, but I have to say, that's incredible."

We continued to talk for a couple of minutes before I pulled my phone out to check the time. I leaped to my feet and clambered atop Gus-Gus, wheeling him around as I hollered over my shoulder, "It was nice meeting you, Sam."

"Likewise."

I reined in a moment. "Gus-Gus was glad to see you, too. You should come by sometime and visit. In fact, I'm having a birthday party on Friday evening. Will you come?"

"What should I bring?"

"Nothing," I replied. "I just want my friends to come and hang out—no gifts."

"Then I'll see you Friday, Hannah Goodheart," Sam grinned. I think I must have blushed because he looked away like he was trying not to notice.

With that, I nudged Gus-Gus, and the hearty horse set off at a trot, leaving Sam standing alone by the pond.

It was a less leisurely ride back, as Gus-Gus carried us quickly along the trail. I thought about the conversation with Sam Blake and the bond he seemed to have had with Paw-Paw. How was I never aware of

Sam or the relationship he had with my great-grandfather? I had never even heard Paw-Paw mention Sam or his mother. It seemed somehow strange.

That thought began to fade, replaced with the uneasy feeling that I was, once again, being watched. I scanned around, looking to see if anyone else could be around, but saw no one. I was really starting to freak out. "You're just being paranoid," I said aloud, as Gus-Gus galloped through the meadow toward home, where my parents were anxiously waiting for me to return.

That unsettling feeling that someone was watching me would not go away. A few other times, as the week continued, I felt certain that someone was watching me. It was super creepy. It occurred mostly at home, but not exclusively. I was certain that I was just feeling paranoid and that I was probably still shaken from the burglary. I considered talking to my parents about it, but after giving it a good deal of thought, I decided to keep it to myself, rather than to worry them with my silly "delusions." All that, however, was about to change.

CHAPTER 6: THE BRIAR CIRCLE INCIDENT

THURSDAY EVENING, MY parents, seemingly on a whim, took me to Briar Circle Mall, which was not far from our old neighborhood. They confessed that they still needed to pick up a birthday gift and had arranged a special treat for me. My curiosity went into overdrive. I filled the whole trip with question after question, most of which were answered with "wait and see," but the excitement was almost too much. I could tell as they traded glances and bright smiles, my parents were elated to see me bursting with joy over something after such a stressful week.

At the mall, we went to the upper level to the food court. I was still a ball of excitement as the escalator carried us to our destination. The delightful smell of warm chicken sandwiches followed by the strong scent of pepperoni pizza were enticing, but not necessarily the kind of thing my parents would refer to as a "special treat." At first, I walked a few steps ahead of my mom and dad but fell back as I realized I wasn't sure where they were going. Then, I glimpsed the figure of a girl coming toward us. At that moment, if I could have leaped the span between us in a single jump, I would have. Morgan McVey—Morgan!—walked briskly at first, and then at nearly a full run, as I moved quickly toward her. The two of us embraced and immediately began to talk as though we were merely continuing a conversation from a moment ago. It felt so good.

Mom and dad waved at Morgan's parents who were standing at a nearby table. Momma mouthed a "thank you" to them as she patted Morgan on the back to say hello. Daddy handed me a twenty-dollar bill and told me to get something to eat and to stay with the McVeys while he and Momma went shopping.

Morgan asked me about the burglary, which actually felt good for me to talk about and get it all out, but the subject quickly changed to the birthday party and the sleepover happening the following night. The two of us talked nearly non-stop for twenty-five or thirty minutes before Mr. and Mrs. McVey suggested we tag along with them and check out some stores in the mall ourselves.

Walking ahead of Morgan's parents, I began to tell Morgan about the boy, Sam, I met. Before I could get out the first sentence, Morgan asked, "Was he cute?"

I should have expected that question from her and I blushed at first. Morgan is at the point where she's becoming interested in guys, but honestly, right now, I'm more interested in astronomy, photography, and stuff like that. Don't get me wrong, I certainly know a cute guy when I see one, but I'm just not altogether interested in them.

"I don't know. Maybe…?" I trailed off, unsure of myself. Then, "Yes."

The two of us broke out with a case of the giggles as we walked along, with Morgan's parents shaking their heads while following not far behind.

"That isn't the point, though," I continued.

"So, when do I get to meet him?" Morgan asked, adjusting the sleeves of her bright neon green shirt.

"I invited him to come tomorrow night. True story!"

Morgan smiled, as we walked toward one of the shops, but stopped a few steps short of the store. "About tomorrow night… I'm afraid I can't make it."

It was like getting punched in the center of my chest, and I tried to contain my shock and disappointment. All the joy I was feeling at having this opportunity to reconnect with Morgan was sinking quickly. I didn't want to overreact, but the emotion was quickly starting to surface. I felt that familiar lump in my throat and swallowed hard. I didn't want to tear up, so I tried to think of something understanding to say. All I could muster was, "But…"

Morgan's grave expression began to change as the corners of her mouth started to pull upward until a full-on laugh exploded out of her. Morgan's laugh was usually loud, always hilarious and sometimes accompanied by snorts, which was the case here.

I stood, confused. Her braying laughter and snorts were turning heads, and I was looking around trying to process what had just happened. Morgan reached out and wrapped her arms around me, hugging me tightly. "What did you think, silly?" Morgan said, as she struggled to stop laughing.

The shock and disappointment that I felt quickly gave way to playful irritation as I finally realized Morgan had gotten one over on me. "I'm telling you," I said punching her arm. "You've spent way too much time with Annie!"

"Of course, I'll be there," Morgan said. "I wouldn't miss your birthday party for anything."

I squinted my eyes and peered at Morgan for a second, and then assured her that I *would* get her back for this cruel joke. Morgan's parents sat down on a bench just outside the entrance to the store as the two of us browsed around the boutique full of bath bombs, scrubs, soaps, masks, and all sorts of interesting things we could smell and sample.

"We need some of these face scrub kits for tomorrow night," I said, as I grabbed a product and showed it to Morgan.

Morgan nodded. "Definitely!"

As we looked about, I became overwhelmed with that same nagging feeling of being watched. My relaxed, casual posture was starting to feel stiff and rigid. Morgan noticed the change in me right away.

"You alright?"

I said nothing, but began to search my surroundings.

Morgan casually looked around as well, unsure what I was trying to spot. "Hannah, say something. Are you OK?"

"Yeah," I said, trying to look relaxed and blow it off. "It's probably nothing. I just keep getting this feeling that someone's following me."

Suddenly, I felt a hand take me by the shoulder from behind. Startled, I jumped and spun around. Morgan was alarmed as well and nearly knocked over a display as she turned quickly to see what had alarmed me.

As I prepared to scream, a store associate said, "Excuse me. Here's a basket."

I let out a big sigh of relief and thanked the young woman.

"I'm Lakeesha," the store associate said politely. "If you see something you want to sample, just ask."

The young woman smiled awkwardly, probably reacting to our nervous behavior, and handed me the shopping basket before walking away to greet another customer. I turned to Morgan, the two of us flashing a grin at one another, sharing in our mutual embarrassment.

Morgan started to say something when, suddenly, a loud commotion near the front of the store caught everyone's attention. A woman, who was coming into the boutique, yelled out, "Hey, watch where you're going! Jerk!" I instinctively darted toward the front of the store with Morgan right behind me. We both stepped out of the store and looked in both directions but didn't see anything or anyone suspicious. Morgan's parents jumped to their feet and asked if everything was alright.

I kept looking around but was still unable to spot anything or anyone familiar until I saw my parents walking in our direction. They could tell something was troubling me, but agreed I was most likely still shaken up from everything this past week. They assured Morgan's parents that everything was fine at the ranch and told them they had a company come and install an alarm for safety.

As our parents continued talking, Morgan motioned to me, and the two of us returned to the store where we continued to smell and sample all the goodies on hand before our parents finally decided to join us. We had put together quite a wish list by this time, and, after Daddy had shelled out quite a few dollars for "glamping party favors," Morgan and I said our goodbyes until tomorrow night.

As we were walking toward the car, Daddy said to me, "I did see someone familiar tonight, sis."

I looked curiously at him, while he continued. "The Blake boy, Sam. He was milling around the mall, I think with his mother."

"Freaky," I thought to myself, but said nothing.

"He saw us coming out of a store and walked over to introduce himself and said he was looking forward to coming over for the party tomorrow evening," Daddy said, fishing for an explanation.

"I met him the other afternoon when I took Gus-Gus out," I said before doing a little fishing of my own. "Why didn't you guys tell me Sam was the one who found Paw-Paw?"

"We didn't think about it at the time, to be honest, honey."

"It didn't seem important… until now," Daddy added.

Daddy looked uncomfortable. I think he was trying to be careful not to seem suspicious of Sam. I have to admit the timing seemed a little coincidental. First, there's a break-in at the ranch, and then we see Sam Blake around the property. Daddy was admittedly concerned. Given that he and Momma had seen Sam in the mall, and this latest incident with me, I had to be honest about this creepy feeling of being watched all the time. Daddy was having serious reservations about the boy coming to my party.

"Are you sure it's a good idea to have him come tomorrow night?"

"He seems really nice, Daddy. Besides, I've already invited him."

Daddy pulled out of the parking lot and into traffic as he and Momma talked quietly in the front seat. I tried to listen, but they spoke with hushed voices and, with the radio playing, I wasn't able to hear what they were saying. I know—it's something I need to work on. Like I said. I'm naturally curious.

Momma turned back to me and smiled, "It's okay, but he needs to leave whenever Sean and the other guys leave."

I smiled and gave Mom a nod of agreement.

To tell the truth, I found it difficult to ignore the suspicious coincidences that seemed to be surrounding Sam Blake. I connected the dots in my mind. Sam seems to pop up at unusual times. I wanted to believe he was a nice boy and certainly couldn't ignore Sam's story about his relationship with my Paw-Paw. I reckoned that my great-grandfather was an excellent judge of character, but I wondered if it could have been Sam watching me during my ride to the pond. He showed up conveniently that day, just as he had this evening while Morgan and I were shopping.

But why would he be stalking me? It occurred to me that perhaps he was after the silver box, or maybe something else. My imagination was taking over, and all kinds of scenarios were bouncing around my thoughts, until I finally accepted my first instinct and let go of all the futile and unfounded ideas that littered my mind.

When we arrived home that evening, I was exhausted and decided to shower and turn in. I changed into my pajamas and brushed my teeth. Picking up my jeans from the bathroom floor, I began to empty the pockets and pulled out the box-shaped charm. I immediately noticed that the tiny opening on the one panel seemed to be sealed once again. I inspected it curiously, puzzled by this as one of many bizarre observations and occurrences of late. *I know this thing was open. I know it was!* I set it on my nightstand, shaking my head in disbelief. Amazed, confused, but too tired to even try to figure it out, I shut off the lights and slipped into bed, with not a clue just how much everything in my life was about to change.

CHAPTER 7: THE ASSEMBLY OF THE SENTINELS

LITTLE DID I know, as this crazy week was happening, an unimaginable series of events were unfolding for a being I would never have dreamed existed. Far removed from my little corner of Texas, his world and mine were on a collision course I could not have anticipated. As I slept, unaware, light years away in my warm bed, his steps echoed off the stark walls of a narrow corridor. His accelerated pace was purposeful but exhibited grace of movement almost unthinkable for a being of his large stature. His lean frame moved quickly, and his face held an intensity that caught the attention of passers-by, who seemed compelled to pay him some expression of honor as he flew through the brightly lit and spartan passageway. No one, however, spoke a word as he darted by them. There were only nods and gestures of an opened hand over the chest. As he passed, some would turn to watch in puzzlement and wonder, while the majestic creature continued fervently toward his destination.

At last, he turned the corner and waved his hand over a small, dimly lit rectangular panel, as two massive doors opened into a large room. The warmly lit chamber, with its polished stone interior, was in stark contrast to the bright white institutional corridors he had just traveled. Two beings stood on either side of the ample chamber doors and bowed their heads as he entered with a momentary pause.

His eyes were like obsidian and he scanned the room, which was lined with sixty-six great pillars. There were six large banners on each side of the chamber, each having its own unique color and each bearing a single symbol—a character from a strange, alien language. Though the vast room had all the appearances of being an ancient chamber, built by a bygone civilization, the technology that was in use was clearly more advanced than anything known to any human being living in our current time.

He approached one of the several monolithic stations and activated a holographic matrix. With a sharp finger, he tapped symbols that appeared to float in thin air. His chiseled face was sober. He smacked his narrow lips as he navigated the device's controls, and with a wave of his hand, he closed the display.

All the beings coming in and out, moving about the chamber shared an appearance much like his own. He was certainly not human as most would define it. His dark skin, overlaid with a translucent membrane, shimmered with all the colors of the rainbow as it caught the light. Atop his over eight-foot frame was an elongated head absent of any hair, with three vertical ridges that met at the center, above his nose. Fearsome as he was, there was a regal, even graceful manner about the rawboned giant.

He reached up and stroked his jaw and scratched his square chin. "Now, where can they be?" he wondered, as he sailed toward the center of the chamber.

At the heart of this incredible hall was a raised platform, where twenty-four marble thrones sat. Arranged in a semi-circle, they overlooked an oval pool, which reflected the light of a star, not unlike our sun, that shone brightly through a skylight.

The formidable being made his way up ten steps, which ran the entire length of the platform. Each step illuminated slightly as his foot touched it. When he reached the top, a small monolith extended up from the platform, between the center two chairs, and burst to life with light emitting from a holographic screen. The impressive entity studied the display and then caught the image in his hand. Turning and throwing it toward the pool, the subtly lit field became enlarged and was suspended vertically before him like a massive screen. He swiped at several characters and images until the pool itself began to project an emerging picture. As if changing the channels on a television, he conjured a host of images, which were clearly visible to him within the boundaries of the reflecting pool.

Unbeknownst to him, another being much like himself had entered the chamber and begun to ascend the steps, pulling nervously at the horizontal point of his tiny ear. His gaze was upon the first, who stood atop the platform, manipulating the holographs around them. "Principal, have you word?" he asked the first.

With a sudden wave of his hand, the Principal returned the menagerie of holographic characters, symbols, and images back to the confines of the small console.

"You summoned the Sentinels to assemble, Principal," he said, as he reached the top of the platform and joined the first.

The Principal turned, as though he was about to sit, but remained standing. "I did," he said. "I had expected the assembly to be convened by the time I returned."

Though the two were conversing, there were no sounds that could be heard. Everything that makes up a conversation was present between the two. They were expressive entities, but rather than communicating with words, they reached out to one another with their minds, and connected to one another through thought.

This unique form of communication was exclusive to their kind and thus, of all the beings in the ever-expanding universe, they held a place of prestige among the known species. Suffice it to say, this non-verbal connection afforded them an advantage whenever they encountered other species. The "inner-link" they create with other beings allows them an apperception of that being. However, knowing the temptations of such an ability, their society had very strict ethical standards that determined when, how, and to what degree, this inner-link was to be used.

And so, the Principal waited for an explanation from his subordinate as to the delay of the other Sentinels, who had been called into the assembly. A striking look of frustration came to the face of the subordinate, who was not happy to have to answer for the other Sentinels.

"Answer, Neanias," said the Principal, calling the subordinate by name.

It was rare that a proper name was used among the Sentinels. It was customary, after all, to observe a certain pageantry and pomp within this chamber. Titles were most often used when addressing one another. In fact, proper names among a species who conversed on such a deep mental and spiritual level were mostly unnecessary. Rarely were there ever any miscommunications, no need for subterfuge, or pretense. It was always clear to whom one was speaking, as well as the intent behind the conversation.

Neanias lowered his head. Why he would feel any shame for the tardiness of his fellow Sentinels was uncertain to him. He didn't feel as though it was his fault they were running late to the assembly, but being the youngest of the council came with a certain liability, which was not always comfortable for him. "It is not for me to know where the Sentinels are keeping themselves or why they have not yet arrived, Principal."

The Principal was clearly not satisfied with his answer, but gently patted Neanias' arm and offered him a seat to his right. Sitting down, the Principal conceded that the others would most likely be along shortly.

"Forgive my impertinence, Principal—but I gather you have spoken with him?"

"Mind your thoughts, Sentinel," said the Principal. "Your intrusiveness is pushing the boundaries of appropriateness." The Sentinel gave a glance over his shoulder at the eager young Sentinel sitting on the edge of his seat, hoping for some crumb of information to fall to him before the others arrived.

Disappointed that the Principal Sentinel was not going to be as forthcoming as he hoped, Neanias sat back in his chair. He looked out over the reflecting pool. This chamber, this world, was the birthright of his kind, and for six millennia his people had been made stewards, messengers, even warriors; they were whatever the universe needed them to be. Neanias considered himself fortunate to be one so young and to sit among the honored Sentinels, who kept a vigilant watch over the universe from this very room.

The Principal, on the other hand, was the eldest of the assembly, although little discernible difference existed physically between him and the younger Neanias that would reveal his age. No one was certain just how old he was, but some stories and legends surrounded him, and even the mention of his name, among the inhabitants of this strange world, invoked a sense of reverence.

A chamber steward delivered a small holographic device, which resembled something in the way of a thumb drive, albeit disk-shaped and slightly smaller in size. The Principal Sentinel graciously took it from the steward's opened hand, and each exchanged a bowed head. As the steward descended the ten steps down from the platform, the Principal held it over the stone-like console. A narrow beam of blue light rose from the smooth surface of the console and connected to the holographic device.

The Principal let go of it, and the disk was suspended above the surface of the console. It turned quickly to the left a half turn, then rolled backward in place two complete turns, before two quick quarter spins clockwise. The Principal then set his long index finger upon it and nudged it ever so gently. Immediately, the device disappeared, and the horizontal screen on the console came to life. A series of characters flowed from right to left; it was an anticipated report. The Principal read intently while Neanias leaned forward to get a view as well.

A wave of his hand expanded and turned the screen upright to make for easier viewing. "You might as well have a look at this, Sentinel."

The two of them digested the information. Another purposeful tap by the Principal's hand brought up a graphic which resembled a planet. Another tap filled in the detail to reveal the planet as our own Earth.

"Beautiful jewel, is it not," asked the Principal of the younger Sentinel.

"I do question the wisdom of this plan, Principal," he replied.

The Principal raised his imposing hand over the console and swatted downward into the image, which caused it to disappear. His hand slapped the smooth surface of the table, which echoed through the chamber. Everyone and everything stopped for a second, as curiosity turned the attention of the vast hall onto the platform and the two Sentinels seated upon it.

"It is not for us to question the plan, Neanias."

The younger Sentinel rotated his entire body in the chair and turned to the elder. "They are not ready," he said with fervor.

"It matters not, young one. What is important is that everything is as it was supposed to be, before the dark time, before the rebellion. It is not for us to decide these things. We have our assigned duty, and I have pledged my life to carry out that duty, as have you."

"Of course, Principal. I *have* pledged myself, and it is for that purpose I *do* question," Neanias said. "A beautiful jewel you say. But a pearl before it's time is nothing but a speck of sand and nothing of what it will become."

The Principal sat back and laughed aloud. His booming voice sounded like a rushing river. The wise elder turned to the younger Sentinel, "You are wise beyond your years, my boy. I was not nearly as perceptive as you when *I* was three hundred."

"Three hundred and one," the Sentinel corrected politely.

The Principal smiled and looked deep into the eyes of Neanias. "You are wise, but you lack experience. I have lived many millennia. I fought during the rebellion, and I remember those days well. I came to this chamber the day Erebos fell. He believed as you. His own pride and arrogance consumed him. Don't let it be so for you, Neanias."

A respectful hush lingered for a moment. Neanias could feel the weight and wisdom of the Principal's warning. He let not only the words, but the sincere intent behind them, rest in his mind. After another moment, he turned to the elder Sentinel and said, "My only concern is that entrusting such power to them is unwise—premature. The Pyxis is too much power for a world still unable to find its way in the universe."

"But as the pearl in your thoughtful metaphor, it begins with something as unassuming as a grain of sand and is *cultivated* to become the pearl," said the Principal. "Exceptional character is not inherent in anything, but rather made, when the conditions are right. Perhaps they possess great potential if only given the opportunity."

Just then, the mammoth doors of the chamber opened. At first, it was only one of the beings who passed over the threshold but then a small band of others entered, all similar in appearance to the two already seated. They appeared to be talking among themselves as they entered, though no sound was heard.

The Principal rose to his feet as the group made their way past either side of the reflecting pool on their approach. He reached out to them with his mind and formed a group inner-link, something like a conference call. Immediately, a chaotic influx of conversation, questions and even opinions, erupted. No one was certain, however, why they had been called into the assembly.

The Principal raised his hand. "Order," he called. "Let there be order, here."

Neanias stood and stepped up just behind the Principal's right shoulder. He addressed the Principal but was silenced, as one of the other Sentinels asked the youth pretentiously, "What do you know of this assemblage?"

The Principal interjected, "He knows nothing. Please, let us come to order."

At last, an expectant silence fell as the others looked to the Principal. He moved down one step and began. "As you are already aware, I have been in communion since morning. Many of you can remember the dark days and the rebellion. All of you at least know the tragic history. I fought alongside some of your fathers, and it was I who appointed the two emissaries to confirm the one spoken of in our prophecy. They left here with the Pyxis to seek out the Guardian who would protect time itself from falling to The Darkness."

The assembly listened intently. Some nodded in agreement and others invited the Principal to continue speaking.

"I have been informed that The Darkness is on the move. Forces are gathering in a dimension which remains hidden from us. They have begun surgical strikes, and we have now been put on alert. As of this moment, the time window is to be watched over forty-seven hours a day, and temporal incursions are to be reported immediately, as they are committed."

The Principal Sentinel paused to gauge the response of the assembly. One of the Sentinels raised his hand and spoke. "What of the emissaries; have we any new word of them?"

"We have new information of Hesiodos," said the Principal. "We have no reason to believe the other still lives."

The announcement sent a shockwave through the assembly. Once again open discussion broke out among them and calls were raised to take action.

The Principal raised his hand again, and all was silent. "The Guardian… we have made contact with the Pyxis, or rather, the Pyxis has made contact with us," the Principal said, to the curiosity of the others.

"But the emissaries… The Guardian cannot ascend, because the emissaries have failed," one of the beings said.

With a gesture of the leader's hand, the entire assembly made haste up the ten steps and took their seats. Operating the panel on the stone console, The Principal Sentinel projected a holographic briefing. "Before we begin, what I'm about to show you has been cleared for you to see, but it is forbidden for you to share it with anyone outside this chamber. Only the Sentinels may know of the information contained in this dossier."

The screen duplicated exponentially, and in a matter of seconds, an extensive cache of information was streaming before the assembly. The blue-green glow of the images reflected off their faces as they sat fixated on the streaming data. The Principal observed them, carefully reading their reactions and weighing how they might respond to the files they were examining.

As he studied the Sentinels, the Principal's eyes met Neanias, who had moved from his immediate right to the far end of the row. Their minds touched for a moment when Neanias asked, "Are we certain of these things, Principal?"

The Principal said nothing, as the stream ended and the images dissipated. Rising suddenly to his feet and turning to face his fellow Sentinels, the Principal declared, "So, as you can see, it is critical that the Guardian finally be revealed, or all that we have sacrificed, all that we have defended, will be erased."

Neanias could not contain his thoughts. "As I have already made known to you, Principal, and now say before this solemn assembly, I don't believe they are ready. The Pyxis is too important and too powerful to be entrusted to them—and it behooves us to examine this Guardian carefully before such an article is relegated. To simply commend the potential contained within this device to one unproven would be irresponsible," he said, feeling confident as he expressed himself openly.

His words received mixed reactions. Some agreed with him, while others vigorously disagreed, and called for him to remain silent. The Principal returned to his seat and held up his bony hand, as the thoughts of the others stilled. He turned to Neanias, who was now less certain that he had spoken so well. "You may well have the opportunity to do just that, my young friend," the Principal allowed.

An uneasy hush moved across the platform. Everyone had an opinion, though none were quick to share. The Sentinels traded glances with one another. Like poker players trying to read their opponents, they studied each other until one of them broke the silence.

"So, the legend is true?"

The Principal weighed the question for a moment and then rose abruptly to his feet, his back now to the assembly. Turning to them, he opened his thoughts. "Before the days of the first quest. Even before the dark time—before the rebellion..." Linking his mind to theirs, he released his own memories for the edification of the others. They saw the ghastly images of a great war that pitted brother against brother just as the Principal remembered it.

He continued. "Time was set into motion, and our kind was committed to the trust, to which each of us have pledged our lives. It has long been established that the Guardian would ascend to rebuff The Darkness. I have already told you today: the Pyxis has reached out to us, confirming what has long been foretold."

He paused thoughtfully as he gauged the response. His face strained against the depth of concentration needed to express his own deep emotion fully. "There are some who question these matters, which have been determinately settled since before the Pyxis was forged." He took a moment to look each of his colleagues in the eye. "But let us remember, that one infinitely wiser and infinitely more knowing, who hung our very star in the universe, and set our world into motion around it, has *also* orchestrated the events which are now unfolding."

His uncharacteristic gestures and the intensity of the Principle's thoughts brought several of the beings to the edge of their seats, their eyes fixed on his. Others nodded. Neanias was swept up in the fervor of it all, and studied everyone carefully, as the sound of his own hearts began to distract him.

The Principle's thoughts sliced through the rhythmic pounding. "I have conferred with him and affirmed everything I have presented to this council. So, I say to you all: weigh your doubts and temper your questions in the knowledge that as it is supposed to be, it *will* be. Now is the moment, fellow Sentinels, for which we all have long waited."

His impassioned appeal left little doubt among the others that their leader, the Principal Sentinel, fully held to his conviction, and each understood his duty. Indeed, they had all pledged to watch over the continuum of time and ensure that everything within the universe unfolded as it should, without any outside meddling or incursion.

But incursions were becoming common, and these were uncertain times over which the Sentinels reigned. Trepidation was wide-spread throughout their world, where, for thousands of years, they and their ancestors had awaited the times of which the Principal was speaking. Some waited eagerly, while hope had begun to wane for others. Still, many had all but abandoned the notion that any truth existed in the legend of the Guardian and the ancient prophecy. For them, it was dismissed as something of a myth or perhaps nothing more than a child's bedtime story where good would one day conquer evil. Sadly, for Neanis and most of his generation, and those younger, the stories were often no longer even told, and the purpose for which the Sentinels served had become obscured by politics and ignorance of their rich history. Many were falling to the opinion that "the old ways" were of little value and perhaps this was the time to establish a new order, that might better serve to meet the challenges being faced.

In fact, among the Sentinels who listened to the Principal's eloquent declaration were a number who were sympathetic to those ideas. Not because they were interested in the ideology, but rather, they wanted to hold fast to the prestige of their esteemed position. Knowing their various stations on these matters, the Principal waited patiently for someone to speak up, but at first, no one said a word. He was aware that his statement had hit its target and sent a ripple through the hearts and minds of all who heard him. The respect he commanded ensured that no one would oppose him outright, but he was certain there would be questions. He could sense a swell of curiosity as he sat back in his chair.

Then, one of the Sentinels spoke up. "So, it *is* true… what we have seen and what you have said?" he asked. "And the Guardian will stand before us having the attributes to assume the imposition of such a formidable task?"

The Principal Sentinel took a deep breath, his eyes widened, and he gripped the armrests of his throne. He opened his mouth, and the sound of waves crashing upon the rocks came forth in force, as he spoke aloud for the hearing of all, saying, "It has already begun."

CHAPTER 8: UNBELIEVABLE DISCOVERIES

THE SUN, BARELY risen, peeked through the windows of my upstairs bedroom. I opened my eyes and rolled over to face my nightstand where my phone was plugged in, charging overnight. My hand snaked out from underneath the comforter, tilting the phone to reveal that the time was 6:58 in the morning. My alarm would not go off for another two minutes. I closed my eyes for a few seconds and opened them again, before tugging at my comforter. I sat up and put both feet firmly on the floor, then rose and walked toward the door, after canceling my alarm. I could hear my mom and dad downstairs, and the smell of bacon wafted through the air.

Dressing quickly, I struggled to emerge from the fog of slumber. The excitement of my birthday had begun to build, and anticipation was setting in for my friends' gathering later in the day. I hastily tidied my bed, which was something I sometimes never got around to doing in the morning. Opening the nightstand drawer, I carefully wound up my phone's charger and placed it inside. Before closing the drawer, my great-grandfather's two journals grabbed my attention. I pulled one out and opened it.

The hardcover book seemed to open naturally to the same page I had turned to a couple of days ago. I read, once again, the journal entry about Thanksgiving 1963, and those cryptic words at the bottom of the page: "Aphrodite was to bathe her head with grace." I sat on my bed wondering, as before, what all this could mean. I had a deep, nagging feeling that it added up to something, but what, I wasn't even remotely sure.

Momma called up to me, announcing that breakfast was ready and waiting for the "birthday girl." I darted from my room and raced down to the kitchen, where my parents were waiting with a breakfast of homemade chocolate chip waffles, scrambled eggs and bacon. Daddy was standing next to a large box, wrapped in brightly colored paper, and after giving me a tight hug, he announced that I could open the gift *after* I had breakfast.

As the three of us ate together, I thought to ask about the journal entry that puzzled me so. "I've been reading from Paw-Paw's journal," I began. "There's an entry from November 28, 1963. He's talking about not feeling like eating and it being a somber day. Do you know what he could have been talking about?"

My parents looked at one another, puzzled at first, before pondering the date of the entry again. Daddy spoke up. "That would have been around Thanksgiving."

"Makes sense," I replied. "He was talking about the pumpkin pie smelling good but not feeling like eating it."

Momma chimed in, "1963 is the year that President Kennedy was assassinated, in downtown Dallas."

"Of course," Daddy said. "That all happened on the Friday before Thanksgiving. President Kennedy was laid to rest the following Monday, so yeah, it probably was a somber, sad Thanksgiving that year. The whole country was in shock and mourning the loss."

I nodded along as I listened.

"My father would have been about your age then," Momma said. "It's strange, though. I don't ever recall either of my grandparents ever talking about it. It was probably traumatic."

Daddy took another bite of his breakfast, followed by a sip of coffee and then added, "Nine-eleven happened not so very long before you were born. It was a horrible tragedy. I remember quite vividly the days that followed, the scope of emotions—sadness, anger… it was probably very much like that for the country in November 1963."

I nodded, and then spoke up. "At the bottom of that journal entry is this really mysterious sentence that says, 'Aphrodite was to bathe her head with grace.' It sounds weird and doesn't seem related to the rest of the entry. Does it mean anything to you guys?"

Again, my parents seemed puzzled as they glanced at each other, and then at me.

"Well…" said Daddy. "Aphrodite, let's see… in mythology, she was a Greek goddess."

Clearly, Daddy wasn't making any connections right away, as he took another sip from his coffee cup.

"Grace..." said Momma. "Grace is often associated with beauty in ancient literature, and Aphrodite was the goddess associated with love and beauty. I'm not sure how it relates to Thanksgiving 1963, though."

I sighed, took the last bite of my waffle and pushed my plate away. "Well, enough of that. It's starting to feel like school work," I grinned. "What's in the box?"

Daddy rose from the table and slid the large box toward me. As I turned and took hold of the wrapping paper, Momma spoke up. "Now, before you open this, we wanted you to have it before the sleepover. We thought it might come in handy. I have another gift for you too... a hand-me-down gift."

I looked curiously at my mother as she continued, "I found all the parts and pieces of Nan's darkroom and got some negatives out of the box in your room. After I try it all out later today, I'm looking forward to teaching you how to develop old film prints."

I clapped my hands in joy and then took hold of the box again. "Now?" I asked with excitement.

Momma nodded, and I ripped at the paper in a flurry of anticipation, until I had revealed the gift inside.

"A telescope!"

I let loose a whoop as I jumped to my feet, hugging and thanking my mom, and then my dad, who said he would help me put it together later in the day.

I began to dig in my pocket for my phone. I wanted to text Lily and Morgan ASAP! When I realized I had left my phone upstairs in my room, I asked to be excused. But before either of my parents could respond, a sudden breeze kicked up throughout the house and we heard a door slam upstairs.

Daddy jumped to his feet. "That sounded like your door, Hannah-banana. Did you leave a window open?"

I shook my head, surprise coloring my expression. I was actually pretty frightened, but I tried not to let on. I started having flashbacks to Monday and the attic incident, as well as the break-in.

Walking quickly, Daddy headed upstairs. "It looks like you left a light on."

"I don't think so, Daddy," I called up, starting to feel a bit more settled.

"I can see a bright blue light shining underneath the door."

I shot Mom a puzzled look, maintaining that the lights were off, and the window closed. I was sure! But after the week I'd had, I supposed anything was possible.

Momma and I looked up from the base of the stairs as Daddy reached for the knob.

"Wow! It's so cold!" He turned the knob and pushed open the door. Whatever the light was, it was gone. Daddy started announcing the play-by-play as he gave things a good once over. Other than a window valance that appeared to be settling back into place where it was blown, perhaps from the door opening, everything sounded to be as I left it.

"Daddy?" I called up, after things fell silent for a moment.

"Honey, is everything OK?"

"Yep." Daddy emerged from the bedroom and started his descent. "That was weird."

He reached out and patted my cheek as he took the last step, before announcing there were preparations to be made for a party and heading outside to set up a tent in the meadow.

Later in the day, Momma had taken negatives and disappeared, as Daddy continued working outside, getting things ready for the festivities that would ensue in a matter of hours. I heard a chime coming from my phone, announcing an incoming text message. Realizing I had not sent Lily and Morgan a text about my new telescope, I headed up to my room to see who had messaged me and to text my exciting news.

I went over to the bed and sat down next to Paw-Paw's journal, which still sat open on my bed. I picked up my phone from the nightstand. Next to it was the pewter cube-shaped charm with its ornate markings and tiny, gear-like embellishments peeking out from the sides. It was still attached to the chain I had found in the old trunk in the attic.

After my missed opportunity to chuck the thing into the pond, I was having second thoughts. I had not fully decided if this relic was a lot of trouble or a great mystery to be solved. *Perhaps a little of both.* Nevertheless, I put it around my neck and checked my phone.

Lily! I tapped the screen and opened the message.

"Happy Birthday! CU in a bit."

That put a smile on my face, for sure. I set the phone down before turning to the journal. Picking it up, I noticed right away the entry's date. It was still opened to the same page as before! I scanned down to the bottom, and the line about Aphrodite was there, but the rest of the page looked noticeably different, somehow. There were characters, strange markings, down the outer margin of the page, arranged from top to bottom. It looked like calligraphy or some kind of foreign script—*maybe Japanese?* I had no idea.

"Those weren't there before," I said aloud. "… or were they?" I wasn't altogether sure.

I began to read from the page that, once again, showed the same smooth, heavy strokes of my great-grandfather's recognizable penmanship.

In disbelief, I silently read the passage, which now said:

> "I don't know how this can be possible. I've been gone for what seemed like days, and yet it was as though I never left. I've seen some unsettling things, but nothing like this. It's going to take time to process, but one thing is sure, nothing will ever be the same. How I'm going to explain all of this to Elizabeth, I don't know. How do you explain to someone that the past is the future and the future is the past? I'm not sure I understand it myself. Sosthenes was explicit that Hesiod can't be allowed to get to the Pyxis and that it must remain with me until the Guardian arrives. I have so many questions, and soon, I'm going to return to that strange place to get some answers."

I was in shock. Nothing about dinner. Nothing about pumpkin pie. Nothing about it being a somber day. I stood up, fanning through the pages until I heard the sound of my dad's voice, calling me from outside. I closed the book and tossed the journal onto the bed, running out to see what he wanted.

Daddy asked me to clean out Gus-Gus's stall. I began to tell him about the bizarre entry in the journal, and how it somehow had been changed, but as I started to describe it, he received a call and had to step away. *Timing!*

He pointed to the barn as he walked away, so slightly irritated, I trudged over and quickly mucked the stall.

As I headed inside to clean up, Momma met me at the door with freshly developed prints from the negatives she had taken.

"Check it out, sis."

I took the prints in hand and began to look through them.

"I'm pretty sure that was the last roll of film to come out of the old brown camera," Momma said. "The negatives look like they were damaged, but I'm pretty sure these are from downtown Dallas. Look, I think they're from the day Kennedy was assassinated." Momma pointed at a print that I was studying. "There's the infamous grassy knoll right there, you see it?"

I continued flipping through as she pointed things out. "That's the president's car, right there."

I came to the next photograph, which seemed chaotic and out of focus. It was an old, silver side view mirror. In the mirror, you could see the reflection of a bearded man. His head was turned, so was hard to make out any distinct features of his face. I was intrigued.

"That was the last one," Momma said.

"These are amazing," I said, looking through them again.

I stopped on another photograph and turned it to show my mom. "Paw-Paw?"

Momma nodded. It was my great-grandfather alright—Paul Learner, young and in the prime of life. He was dressed in slacks, sweater vest, and wearing a fedora style hat. In the photograph, he appeared to be pointing toward something. His mouth was caught obviously mid-sentence. I marveled at how different he looked without his familiar mustache. In the photo, it appeared as though he was talking to someone, but the other party wasn't present in the picture. The next print was of Paw-Paw's back. His tall frame was obscuring another subject. It appeared to be a girl. The black and white print was not very telling, but I could see that someone was standing in front of him. I once again turned the print to Momma.

"Who's the girl he's talking to?"

Momma looked at the print. "Not sure," she replied. "Looks like she's wearing jeans, I see a bit of her hair… I don't really know."

I took another look. "Probably no one in particular."

Daddy came to the door and apologized for the phone call. Stepping inside, he took an immediate interest in the photographs, looking through them enthusiastically as I began to tell him again what I saw in the journal earlier. He didn't seem particularly interested but followed me back up to my room as he continued to inspect the freshly printed photos.

Walking into my room behind me, he handed me the picture of the car mirror and made a peculiar observation. "Don't you think the guy in the reflection looks a little like that antique dealer, Mr. Hoise?"

I looked at the print again. "Oh yeah, I can see it... well, sort of."

Daddy continued. "Of course, it's not. But from what I can make out in this print, it sort of resembles him... maybe... a little... okay, it's hard to tell since it's slightly out of focus."

We both had a laugh as I picked up the journal from my bed.

"Seriously, though, Daddy... Check this out," I said, handing it to him already opened to the page I wanted him to see.

Daddy brushed his hand across the page and began to read. His facial expressions changed as he read. He inhaled and exhaled as his eyes moved from left to right, his head bobbing up and down as it did whenever he was invested in what he was reading or writing. Then he fanned the pages and scanned a few before closing the cover and handing it back to me.

"That was definitely Thanksgiving 1963. It sounds like a difficult time," he said, as I took the book from his hand. I was a little surprised and uncertain about what Daddy was saying, and it must have showed. My dad took a step back and crossed his arms—a sign that he was ready for me to come unglued.

"But, Daddy," I said, as I opened the journal again. Going right to the page in question, I read it again. "It's changed... the words are different," I said in disbelief.

"That sounds like what you were describing at breakfast."

I continued, "No, they're different... they *were* different."

I could tell Daddy was uncertain what it was I was getting at, but he wanted to reassure me. "Sometimes, when you understand the context, a passage can take on new meaning, sweet pea. It's natural."

I looked up at him, confused and bewildered. The thought occurred to me that I might be losing my mind. *Maybe it's the stress.*

Daddy rubbed my shoulder and kissed my forehead. For the moment, whatever uncertainty I was feeling melted away as he embraced me. It was times like these, he didn't need to *say* anything.

A chime interrupted the moment. Another text, this time from Morgan: "C U in a while birthday girl. Luv ya!"

Daddy suggested I take a break and rest up before my guests began to arrive and then slipped out of the room. I pushed the journal aside and lay down on my bed, my hands folded behind my head. Closing my eyes for a minute, I tried to clear my mind of the whirlwind of thoughts, but my efforts were futile.

Atop my dresser sat my laptop, and setting my eyes on it, I thought perhaps I could find some clues to this strange and chaotic puzzle, with the help of a good ol' internet search engine. I retrieved it and sat cross-legged on the floor. Booting up the computer and opening my web browser, I began by entering the words from the journal, "Aphrodite was to bathe her head with grace."

I hit Enter and a host of results came up. I scanned the brief descriptions, looking for something that might connect everything together. Then, coming across a reference which read, "Hesiod, *Works and Days*," I paused. "There is something familiar about this one."

I clicked the link, and as it loaded, I continued to grapple with my memory, trying to recall where I might have heard or seen these words before. As soon as the page finished loading, I saw a photograph of a sculpted marble bust of a bearded man. I began reading about Greek mythology, as written by Hesiod, a Greek poet from sometime between 750 and 650 B.C. "Among his most notable writings were *Works and Days* and *Theogony*," the entry explained. I continued reading about this significant historical figure and the influence he had on science, religion, and economics, leaving an indelible mark on the culture of his time and beyond.

As I read, I suddenly recalled where it was that I had heard of *Works and Days*.

"Mr. Hoise, the antique dealer," I gasped. I remembered the copy in his store that sat on the counter. This was an interesting connection indeed. My mind raced, as I continued searching. I found an extensive passage from *Works and Days*, which I began to read until I came across the very words written in my Paw-Paw's journal.

No! Way!

The words were part of a narrative about Pandora, who, according to mythology, was created by Zeus. I tried to remember the altered words that had appeared in the journal earlier—for a moment, at least. I remembered the word "Pyxis," but could not remember how it had been spelled. I entered it as best I could remember into the search field, which brought up an alternative spelling and definition. It was a Greek word, which referred to the shape of a vessel from the classical world: "a box or jar with a lid."

I set my laptop down and tried to take it in, still trying to make the connections. I picked up the photographs again and pulled the odd picture of the mirror, with the man's image reflected in it. I looked at it for the longest time, until my phone chimed once more. It was another text message from Morgan. "On my way."

I set my phone down on my nightstand, and my eye caught the short stack of musty old books I had retrieved from my attic treasure hunt. Atop the stack was the booklet on anagrams, and it gave me a wild, but *genius* idea. "It may be nothing," I thought. But then again, I knew something just wasn't adding up.

Morgan and I had played with anagrams in the past. To us, they were fun little word games. We would take a word and see how many other words we could make using the exact letters. Picking up the booklet, I fanned the dusty pages, which provided plenty of technical information and ways in which anagrams could be a useful tool. One section discussed covert communication using anagrams. I quickly scanned the section—a mere three pages. An idea began to form in my mind, and I quickly grabbed my phone. I entered a search for "anagram apps" and was immediately presented with some options.

Downloading the most popular and best-reviewed free app, I opened it and familiarized myself with it. I could enter any word, and it would automatically generate all possible anagrams for said word. I typed in "Hoise" and hit the green Generate button. Almost immediately, a host of words, and combinations of words, were listed. However, nothing of interest came up; or at least nothing that made any sense. I scanned the list several times, but unless "i shoe" was some kind of secret code name, I had little to go on.

Just then, Daddy passed in front of my door.

"Daddy, what is Mr. Hoise's first name?"

Daddy leaned into the room. "Umm… you know, I don't know," he answered. "It's always just been Mr. Hoise. It's something that starts with a 'D,' probably, since that's what's on his sign."

I thanked him and returned my attention to my anagram generator. I typed in "D Hoise" as fast as my thumbs could pound out the characters. With another stroke of the green button, I had a new list and began to scan through the results until I came to one that was, even for my sometimes-nonsensical mind, too unbelievable to be true.

"I *must* be crazy," I said aloud, as I looked once more at the image reflected in the mirror in the old photograph. Everything was quickly pushed aside, however, as the sound of a car approaching diverted my attention. My friends had started to arrive for the birthday party.

As I made my way down to greet everyone, I was so conflicted and wrestled quietly with the connections I was making and marveled at how impossible it all seemed. *Some time with friends is just the kind of diversion I need.* The lingering, unsettled feeling deep within me, however, would prove to be a warning that this was only the beginning of things: impossible, unexplainable, and unexpected.

CHAPTER 9: THE UNINVITED GUEST

THE DECORATED MEADOW, with the arbor archway welcoming my friends to "Camp Hannah," was buzzing with activity. Music played, and plates of finger foods circulated. Many of my friends had come to celebrate my birthday. The warm spring evening was full of laughter and, for a moment, I had completely forgotten all about the mysterious charm that still hung around my neck, the break-in, the strange occurrences, and the bizarre clues that seemed to be leading to an unbelievable conclusion. It was a welcome distraction, for sure.

Sam Blake had taken me up on the invitation to the party, and I was sure to introduce him around. My girlfriends, in particular, were glad to meet the tall, dark, handsome young man, but Sam spent most of the evening glued to, of all people, Sean. As Sean held court at the party, telling tall tales and entertaining everyone with his colorful stories, Sam could be found close by, laughing and joking right along with Sean.

"That dude is hilarious," Sam exclaimed to me, Morgan, and Lily as we congregated near the table which held the few remaining slices of my birthday cake.

I was all too used to Sean hamming it up from all the time I spent with him in drama class at co-op. "You'll get tired of the Sean Show… eventually," I told him.

"There you go with the 'Sean Show' bit again," Sean said as he drew near. "Just remember Goodheart; on the Sean show, I always get the best lines."

That was always Sean's comeback anytime I mentioned the Sean Show. Although it was always in good fun, Sean's nerdy banter and his almost constant need to be the center of attention was sometimes annoying to his friends. But still, Sean was good humored and fun to have around, as Sam was quickly discovering.

Dusk began to settle in on the warm, spring evening as things were winding down. Everyone had left at this point except for Lily, Annie, and Morgan, who were staying the night, and Sean and Sam. Sean was waiting for his parents to pick him up, and Sam had decided to stick around until Sean left.

Camp chairs were brought out, and the six of us snacked and talked, as Daddy got a fire started in the fire pit. My mom was starting to clean up a little and could hear Sean wrapping up another one of his gilded tales.

"That guy was buried in mud up to his neck," Sean reported. "I ran over and got him by the arm and pulled…"

"Wait," Daddy said, turning around. "If he was buried up to his neck in mud, how did you get hold of his arm?"

Sean sat in an awkward silence, looking over at my dad, who had a mischievous grin on his face. The silence was broken when Sam burst out with laughter and announced, "Busted, Dude! You've been busted! BAM! Yes, that just happened!"

All of us laughed hysterically at Sean's embarrassment over being called on his extreme exaggeration, while Daddy quietly helped Momma carry a table into the house.

"So, when do I get to see the buried treasure you found last weekend, Goodheart?" Sean asked sarcastically, while pushing up the sleeves of his blue, silver, and white rugby shirt.

I pulled at the chain around my neck and revealed the small silver box that had been tucked inside my shirt. A collective gasp came from the group as I pulled the chain over my head and passed it around.

"It looks completely different now that it's all cleaned up," remarked Annie.

Sean took it into his hand and held it close, examining the markings carefully. "It looks like a Borg ship, from Star Trek," he said.

Sam shot back, "Resistance is futile, Bro."

Sean suddenly stiffened up and then cried out as though he were in searing pain. All of us leaped backward in fright as Sean lowered his head.

"Sean are you alright?" I asked.

Sean slowly raised his eyes until they met my concerned stare. He held eye contact for a few seconds, his face expressionless.

Uncertain of what had happened, and afraid something was wrong, I muttered, "Sean, say something."

"I've been assimilated," Sean said, handing the small metallic cube to Sam.

Those two laughed, but the rest of us didn't completely get the Star Trek reference, nor were we impressed with Sean's attempt at a practical joke. I punched Sean's arm while Morgan and Lily rolled their eyes, annoyed with Sean's folly.

Sam noticed something as he looked at the curious object. "Hey, some of those look like Greek characters… you know, like the alphabet," noting the placement and shapes of some of the etched markings.

"I thought so as well," I said, while Sean rubbed his arm.

Taking the charm back and looking at it as it sat in the palm of my hand, I contemplated whether or not to share with my friends what I had uncovered earlier. I questioned if it was all just too crazy to be believed. Would I sound paranoid or worse? These were my friends, though. "Surely, they'll take me seriously," I thought. "What's the worst they can do—dismiss me?"

I took a deep breath and looked up at my friends, old and new, who seemed to sit on the edges of their seats, waiting for me to reveal the mystery of the cube-shaped charm. "Promise me you won't think I'm crazy, you guys," I said with reservation.

While my friends assured me that they would keep an open mind, a black Mercedes pulled hastily into the driveway. I had a sinking feeling, as I looked up to see a dark-bearded man emerge from the car and begin to walk briskly toward us. It was the antique dealer, Mr. Hoise. I leaped to my feet but couldn't muster a word. Annie was the first to notice my attention had waned. She could sense my unsettled demeanor, and so she turned to see who had arrived. By now, everyone had clued into my tension and were on their feet as the well-dressed man drew near.

His deep-set eyes were squarely fixed on me as I closed my hand which held the charm, making a tight fist. "Miss Goodheart," he said in his thick Greek accent. "You know why I've come. You *must* give it to me."

Sam glanced at me and could clearly see I was upset as he stepped toward the man. "Hey, mi amigo," he said. "Maybe you should leave. I don't think you're supposed to be here."

Morgan turned toward the house and yelled loudly for my dad, who came to the door right away.

Daddy stepped out and asked, with surprise, "Mr. Hoise, what are you doing here?"

Hoise said nothing, as he continued to stare intently at me. "Miss Goodheart, you need to trust me," he stated in a calm, quiet voice. "You have no idea what it is you're dealing with. Give me the Pyxis... now, Miss Goodheart."

As my dad hurried over, we all slowly circled, surrounding Hoise. "Miss Goodheart, please," he said, with a growing intensity.

Daddy could tell something was amiss. He walked closer and asked sternly, "What's this about, Mr. Hoise?"

I turned and looked at my dad, who, in spite of the authority in his voice, seemed quite confused. "His name isn't Hoise, Daddy." I turned back to the bearded man in the dark suit. "It's Hesiod," I said, as the man's dark eyes peered into mine. "Isn't that correct?" I asked him.

"Clever girl," the man said, as a sinister smile came across his face.

"D. Hoise—it's an anagram," I said. "I don't know how, but he was in Nan's photograph from the Kennedy assassination."

Lily looked at Sean. "Hesiod? Who's Hesiod?"

Sean shrugged. Daddy took another step toward the man and reached out to grab him.

"Charles, I don't want anyone to get hurt, and if you feel as I do, you will take five steps back, right now," said the man, as he lunged and grabbed my wrist.

Daddy stepped back with his hands up in plain view. Momma had stepped out to see what was going on and could quickly tell something was very wrong. Her first reaction was to get her cell phone and call for help, but she had left it inside on the kitchen counter. As she turned to dart back inside, the man, who now had a firm grip on my right wrist, called to her. "You must be the lovely Mrs. Goodheart," he said. "You should come stand by your husband. I'd hate to have to break the girl's arm chasing you inside."

"Mr. Hoise, I'm only going to say this once. Let her go and tell me what's going on here," my dad said indignantly, taking a cautious step toward them.

"Your daughter is extraordinarily bright and is quite right, Charles," he said. "My name *is* Hesiodos, and this clever girl knows *exactly* what's going on here—don't you, my dear?"

I was overwhelmingly frightened, but I managed to muster the courage to look at the man who was holding tightly to me. I tried to pull away, but Hesiod tightened his grip.

"I saw your reflection in a photograph my great-grandmother took in 1963," I said.

I then looked over at Daddy, whose hands slowly fell, as he listened in disbelief. "That's not possible," he said.

"There are things going on here that you can't possibly understand, Charles," Hesiod said, before turning his attention back to me. "*You* understand, though, yes? Or at least you *think* you do. If you only knew the evils that cursed box contained. Now, open your hand, girl, and let me take it back to where it belongs."

My hand began to tingle as Hesiod's grip grew tighter. My mind was racing, as I tried desperately to understand how the pieces of this puzzle all fit together. I looked at my friends, who were standing around, horrified by what was happening. I glanced over at my parents. Momma's hand was shaking as she raised it to cover her mouth, and I saw a look in my father's eyes I had never seen before. He was both frightened and enraged. Suspecting that my dad was about to make a move toward Hesiod, and not wanting to see anyone hurt, I suddenly opened my hand and dropped the silver cube to the ground.

"A wise choice, Miss Goodheart," Hesiod said, looking down at his prize now laying in the grass at his feet. He immediately let me go.

I stepped back, straightened my knit pullover, and cradled my throbbing wrist, as Hesiod slowly crouched down to pick up the tiny silver charm.

Daddy remained completely still. "Hannah, honey—are you okay?" he asked, straightening his glasses.

Looking back at him, I nodded. "Paw-Paw's journal… the words somehow were changed, Daddy. But the riddle at the bottom stayed the same," I said.

My friends stayed close by, frozen in place with fear. Mom and Dad were a few feet away as I continued. "'Aphrodite was to bathe her head with grace.' I know what this is," I declared, pointing to the tiny silver box.

Hesiod stood holding the box in his hand. "No, my dear… you only know the legend—the myth. To open its truth, you need a key," he said, with a satisfied smirk. "Now… I will finally be able to return home after these many years in exile."

Just then, Daddy made a sudden move, as though he was about to charge at Hesiod, but Hesiod turned and held the cube firmly grasped between his thumb and middle index finger. Daddy stopped dead in his tracks as Hesiod pointed at him. "No closer, Charles, my friend," Hesiod shouted. "I would hate to have to erase you from time."

Daddy stood motionless. "What exactly is that thing?"

I spoke up. "It's a—it's a time machine of some kind… I think."

Hesiod turned to me. He looked surprised. Maybe even a little frightened. It was as if I had just won an award that he thought he deserved. "You *are* clever—indeed," he said. Then he seemed to compose himself a bit as he continued. "But I'm afraid that doesn't even begin to explain the great power of this box I hold in my hand."

With that, he placed the silver cube in the palm of his hand and lifted it to the full extent of his reach. He drew a breath and shouted, with everything he had in him, "Isadora!"

Everyone recoiled. Morgan covered her face with her hands. Sam threw his arm up, as though he were blocking something from striking him, but other than a flock of birds taking flight in a frenzy at the sound of Hesiod's booming baritone voice, nothing had happened.

Nothing.

Hesiod drew down his hand and looked at the cube. He pulled the chain out, which was still threaded through the loop and cast it aside. "You've changed the key which opens the box."

"Box," Momma asked. "The charm?"

I turned to her. "Paw-Paw's journal… the answer to the riddle—it's 'Pandora'…"

Suddenly, a sound like thunder clapped across the sky. Hesiod dropped the small cube, but before it could fall to the grass, it became suspended in an orb of bright—and yet pale—blue light. The loop, which a moment ago, was threaded with a chain, began to extend upward. The panel lifted as the little gears on the side turned. As the opening grew larger, the pale light pouring through became nearly blinding. The cube itself seemed to increase in proportion, as it now appeared to be ten, perhaps twenty times, its former size. The etchings on each side began to glow, even move from place to place. First it was a slither, but then became rapid and abrupt. It was as though the box was somehow alive. Illuminated symbols manifested around the surface in mid-air. Everything on and immediately around it appeared to be in motion, working almost like the cogs of a clock. It was frightening and amazing all at the same time.

My eyes struggled to adjust as the light engulfed my friends and me. I could see symbols and markings erupting from the opening. I saw images of places, people. Flying around me were what appeared to be planets and stars, lifeforms I couldn't even recognize—all within the intense streams of light. The images and symbols were all illuminated, semi-transparent, but still I could sense they were somehow real and tangible. It all looked to be three-dimensional; as if I were looking through a window into another universe.

Hesiod laughed as he got his bearings. His hair blew wildly as the swirls of light stirred the air around us. I could see Lily, Annie, and Morgan, as well as Sam. Sean had been hurled backward and was laying on the ground at the perimeter of the growing orb. My parents had also been thrown back and were outside the barrier of the glowing blue light.

The wind inside the bubble was tempestuous. I began to feel a chill, and I could see a light frost forming on the ground beneath my feet. A deep humming sound arose and was nearly deafening. Hesiod moved toward the center of the bubble and stood at one of the many bands of light, waving his hand, manipulating it in some way. It appeared to me as though he was swiping an electronic tablet and I could tell he knew exactly what he was doing. He clenched his jaw and pounded his fist as though frustrated. His celebration appeared short lived as I heard him growling over the blaring clamor.

I moved toward Hesiod and noticed that, as I got closer to him, the air felt warmer and the noise was not as overwhelming. Strangely, I could tell that I had somehow left my yard and had entered, or rather was entering, a room. It was as though I was coming inside from a storm on a cold day, but there were no discernable walls or a floor. No ceiling above me. The only light was the whipping swirls of blue-green images streaming around me. I looked at Hesiod, who appeared to be in a bubble at the center of all the chaos, barely affected by the tempest raging around him.

"Thank you, my dear," he shouted, regaining his composure. "It was kind of you to open the portal."

I looked at the band of light upon which he was tapping. It was transparent, and yet seemed solid and responsive to his touch. "Make it stop," I yelled as fear grew inside me.

A core of even brighter light began to emanate from the center of the orb, as Hesiod took the cube back in hand. "You and your friends need to go now, Miss Goodheart," he said, as he rushed toward me, pushing me away.

I stumbled but regained my footing. Hesiod turned toward the bright white light, which appeared to be a doorway of some kind. He then looked back at me and my friends, who had huddled up mere steps away, clinging to one another in fear.

A great smile grew upon Hesiod's face as he closed his eyes and bowed his head. "I bid you farewell, Miss Goodheart." With that, he turned and stepped into the large circular opening of light.

Without a second thought, I looked back at my friends and lunged forward, toward the doorway where Hesiod had just stepped and blinked out of sight.

I can't explain it.

I don't know why I did it.

But everything in me was pulling at me to follow him.

Focused ahead, I faintly heard my friends following behind me, with a collective shout.

The light began to collapse in on itself. A fleeting glance backward showed horror etched on my parents' faces. The man Daddy had known as Mr. D. Hoise, the antique dealer from Dallas, had completely disappeared. Momma, realizing I had moved to the spot where he had vanished, stretched her hand toward me just as all went dark—

We were gone.

CHAPTER 10: STRANGE NEW WORLD

THE AIR WAS pleasantly fragrant, and I could feel solid ground beneath my feet. My eyes had not yet adjusted from the blinding light I had just hurled myself into, but I could hear clearly and knew I was not alone. A deafening echo had subsided, and I could hear and recognize voices near me.

"Morgan," I called out. "Where are you?"

"Hannah, I can hear you," shouted Morgan, loudly. "I can't see anything … where are *you*?"

I turned and reached out my hand, touching a figure that had been standing directly behind me. "I'm right here. No need to yell," I said with a nervous laugh.

Sam approached us, followed by the sisters, Lily and Annie, who were both rubbing their eyes, as though they had just awoken. "Somebody, please tell me that whole thing a minute ago was just a bad dream," Annie said.

"I don't think it was," I replied, as I tried to get my bearings.

"Hey," Sam said. "Has anyone seen Sean?"

Annie quipped, "Dude, I can barely see *you!*"

"Sarcasm… at a time like this," Lily asked, pushing up at her glasses. "Be nice Annie. Please? Just this once?"

The five of us fanned out a few feet apart and called for Sean but heard no reply.

"I smell something sweet… like lilacs," I said, inhaling the fragrant air.

Morgan added, "I think it smells like the hot tea my Dad likes—Earl Grey."

"Yes, bergamot… that's it."

A loud, but amiable, sound of a bird calling through the trees drew our eyes upward, toward the pastel violet sky above us. The canopy of trees, with their varying colored leaves and floral adornments, shimmered as the sweet-smelling breeze wafted through this unusual forest.

We all began to look around us in wonder. Lily took note of the curious foliage that surrounded us. Colors and varieties of wildflowers she had never seen crowned the bright, rust-colored blades of grass beneath our feet. Near us, a tree appeared ancient, its trunk and branches twisted and covered in thick, dark bark. The leaves that crowned the tree were large—twice the size of a hand—and in vibrant shades of turquoise, blue, and lavender. Near the tree was a tall, flowering bush with bright yellow blooms, long and pointed, protruding from bright green, leafy pods.

As Lily reached her hand out to touch one of the blooms, the entire bush seemed to recoil, as though it were somehow afraid of her. Lily quickly pulled away as I watched with awe.

"Maybe it doesn't like the color red," Annie sniped, referring to the color of Lily's baby doll top.

"Be careful you guys," I said. "I don't think this place—wherever we may be, is anything like Texas."

Lily continued to watch the bush as it appeared to relax. "It's okay, pretty bush. I won't hurt you," she said, as she again reached for the yellow bloom, gently touching it with her hand.

Sam turned and saw her stroking the flower, as she would pet a dog or cat. "I don't think it's *really* afraid of you. It's not like it's *aware*."

As Lily turned to respond to him, a deep voice spoke. "That would not be a correct assumption, Samuel Blake, of the planet you call Earth."

Stunned, we slowly turned to see what appeared to be a man standing—towering—over us. My Daddy was over six feet tall, but this guy was way taller—like he would probably hit his head on a basketball rim, tall. With skin dark like copper or bronze, he had a glassy sheen, which, when it caught the light, sparkled like glitter in every color of the rainbow. His chiseled features were strange and alien, but not so unlike that of a human, which, as hard as it was for me to take in, he clearly was not. The rolling vertical ridges of his oval-shaped head and the small triangular shape of his ears were most curious to us, as we carefully studied him. He wore a white robe, which flowed to just above his knees, and over the garment, a gold and silver breastplate caught the light and glimmered with brilliance, like fire.

In his long, bare, muscular arm he cradled a matching helmet, which I immediately noticed was decorated with similar characters and markings as the charm that Hesiod had just taken from me.

I should have been afraid. We all *should* have been afraid, but we weren't. In this strangest of moments, in this strangest of places, I actually felt more safe and secure than I had felt in nearly a week. Somehow, in the face of this peculiar creature, I saw something that made me feel courageous. It was as though his gaze drew out of me something buried deep in my own heart. I couldn't speak for the rest of my friends, but they, too, seemed unexplainably calm given the unusual and strange nature of our surroundings, including our new host.

"The l'ali bush is very much aware; *sentient*, as they say," he told us. "You must forgive it, for it has never before seen a creature such as yourself."

His deep voice sounded like the rumble of thunder across the plains. And yet it bore a quality of tenderness that evoked a sense of trust. All five of us stood silent, mouths gaped open, and motionless at the sight of this imposing figure, who once again addressed us. "And it appears you have never seen a creature such as me… Please, do not be frightened."

I took a quick look at my friends and gathered the nerve to speak. "We're not frightened by you. Just… um… startled. You caught us by surprise. All of this is a little *surprising*."

The daunting being tenderly gestured by closing his eyes and bowing his head but said nothing.

"How did you know Sam's name?"

"I know all your names, Hannah Goodheart," he said. "I know from where you have come, and more importantly, I know what it is that has brought you here."

"Where exactly *is* here, and when does the next bus leave for Texas?" asked Annie, with her usual air of sarcasm.

Lily kept her eyes focused on the formidable individual who loomed over us, and she gave her big sister a quick pop in the ribs with her elbow.

The being watched Lily as she hit her sister and he gave her a curious look, his brow furrowed. "Please, come and let us serve you," the giant said, as he put his helmet on his hairless head. "I will gladly answer your questions and tell you all you wish to know. It is not far from here, where we are going."

Though we were all uncertain about any of this, we agreed and followed our new "tour guide." Lily waved goodbye to the bush, which seemed to stretch its vines, as though reaching for her. The giant led us out of the thickly wooded area and onto a roadway, paved with brilliantly hued sandy bricks. His steps were long but delicate considering his great size. He seemed to glide gracefully along as we took two, three, even four steps to his one.

We were quiet for a while but soon began to whisper among ourselves. We questioned whether Sean had followed us through the *doorway*. We speculated about where we were and how we were going to make it back home. However, I said very little as I walked, wondering about what had happened to Hesiod and how my parents were coping with me being gone.

"Should we ask about Sean?" Sam asked. "Maybe this *hombre* can tell us if he's here."

"He seems trustworthy, but we have no idea where *here* is or what his intent might be. I think it's best not to say anything for the moment," Morgan suggested.

Sam looked dissatisfied with that answer, and Annie blurted out, "Speak up, Sam."

Sam blushed, and although he didn't say so at the time, he was crushing on Morgan, which explains why he might have wanted to avoid disagreeing with her. Annie caught on right away and tried to change the subject. "I, for one, think that forest is probably not the safest place for our boy, Sean, if he's here—*wherever* here might be."

Annie looked over at me as I walked thoughtfully along the road, trying to keep up with our guide. "Hannah," she inquired. "Any thoughts?"

I looked up and came out of myself for a moment. I had heard everything that was going on, but as I often do, especially in a crisis, I had retreated into my own thoughts as I grappled with the unsettling notion that I, as well as my friends, had just been thrust into a universe much larger and much more treacherous than I could have imagined possible. "Let's not say anything right away, until we're totally sure we can trust him," I murmured.

The sky grew darker and began to reveal magnificent starlight. Large twin moons hung in the heavens above us, as we approached a scuttling area—an impressive city, where at its center, sat a massive compound, reminiscent of the Parthenon in Greece.

Everything appeared ancient, but we were surrounded by incredibly advanced technology. While many of the beings, who all looked a lot like our escort— super tall, bald, short robes for clothing—walked, some stood on hovering vehicles, zipping through the streets. Looking toward one of the buildings, Sam noticed what he thought were three-dimensional computer panels, suspended in thin air, which the inhabitants of this strange place seemed to use for any variety of purposes. One person appeared to order transportation while another nearby conjured up something that looked like a taco, which it quickly ate. Lily was watching one walking nearby, tapping a screen projected on its arm, as though it was integrated into its skin.

There were seemingly thousands of these beings, but none seemed to quite share our escort's commanding stature. Heads were turning in our direction, people looking us up and down as we made our way through this remarkable city toward a fortified central building complex.

The compound sat atop a foundation of three thick layers of dense stone, resembling granite, with each layer having a distinct color and pattern. The first layer was golden like the morning sunrise. The second layer was comprised of various hues of tans and browns, with spots of salmon and flakes of gold. It was marbled with veins of dark crimson. The top layer was blue, like the Texas sky in springtime. As we climbed the steps, I noticed that the top layer of the foundation changed color, sometimes blue, sometimes shades of purple and white. This will sound crazy, but honestly, I felt like that stone was alive and, somehow, aware of us. Weird, I know. We all looked at one another in disbelief at what we were experiencing. I was sure I was going to wake up any minute to find this was all a strange dream.

Four large pillars lined the front of the structure, which was opulent in design. A double door, which appeared to be made from massive timbers and trimmed with iron, greeted us as we crossed the veranda. Two guards, I later learned were called Sentries, stood tall on either side and seemed to take no notice of our passing, except to step aside as the doors lumbered open during our approach.

The open doors led us into a foyer of sterile white walls and stark lighting. There were no pictures, no statues, no signs, no symbols, nothing to indicate where we were or what purpose this compound served. Our escort turned and said, "Welcome to the Praetorium. Stay close as we enter the chamber. We observe strict protocols, but rest assured, all will know that you are my guests."

Entering a chamber within the incredible structure, the giant who had walked with us removed his helmet and nodded to two others who appeared to be standing guard. We marveled at what we were seeing. At the center of the room was a large pool of what appeared to be crystal clear water. A skylight overhead allowed a single beam of natural light to shine onto the calm surface of the pool, which sat at the foot of a platform, On the platform, we counted twenty-four huge chairs that looked like they were carved out of marble. Thrones? Was this a throne room for their rulers?

"I will request refreshments for you," said our host, as he nodded his head to one of the many beings walking about the chamber.

Within minutes, a corner of this great hall was prepared with pillowed seats, a stone table, and a cart that was plentifully stocked with fruit and confections, bread and cheese, as well as golden cups of sweet, creamy liquid, unlike anything I had ever tasted— something called *ambro* nectar. It was very smooth, growing colder in the back of my throat as I swallowed.

Sam curiously bit into something that resembled a very large, purple grape, as Morgan picked at a rather odd piece of pink bread. "It tastes like pound cake!"

I noticed that Annie was preoccupied, scanning the room, carefully observing everything. We soon realized that none of the beings seemed to speak, except for our host, who only seemed to talk to the five of us. We watched as they seemed to share nods and other appearances of conversation, but without words. Annie leaned over to Lily and me and suggested that they might communicate with telepathy.

"That's not real! It's science fiction," Lily said, scoffing at the idea.

"That is not correct, Lily Little. It is science fact," our host said, as he crossed the room toward us.

Lily blushed, embarrassed, I'm sure, to have been overheard.

Annie smirked in satisfaction to be right. "Told you," she said. "Look around, this is all straight up *not* of our world, right here."

"Don't say that, Annie," Morgan said. "This is freaking me out enough as it is."

"I apologize," the being interrupted. "I know this must all seem strange to you and I am afraid I am unaccustomed to the social graces of your species. I am called Sosthenes and hold the office of Principal Sentinel in this chamber."

He went on to explain that his kind did communicate naturally in a non-vocal manner, although he said telepathy was a crude word to describe the means in which they communicated. As he shared with us tidbits about his culture, it was becoming more and more apparent to me and my friends that we were indeed, very… *very*, far from home.

"You *are*," said the Sentinel frankly.

"I am… *what*?" I asked.

"Very far from home," he replied. "About twenty-two million light-years away, in fact. You are in a galaxy located in what you would call Ursa Minor, on a planet called Kalos. The city we are in is our capital, Sophia."

We were all somewhat in shock but taking the news of our situation surprisingly well. While the Sentinel continued to talk with us, another *"Kalosian"* approached.

"Communicate in the primitive way, Thekla. Speak. Use words," the Principal said, addressing the other. "Our guests are unable to know your thoughts."

"Certainly," said Thekla, with a somewhat less imposing voice. "We located the other alien; shall I bring him in?"

Sam stood up and squared his shoulders defensively, facing Thekla. "Who are you calling alien, man?"

The Principal Sentinel stood quickly with his hand outstretched to alleviate the tension. "*She* meant no disrespect," he said, before turning to the woman and nodding. "Show the boy in."

Sam backed off with a shrug, his head hanging. "Sorry, ma'am."

"It's Sean, they found Sean," shouted Lily, nudging me.

As the large chamber door opened, Thekla motioned subtly as Sean cautiously entered the hall. Seeing all of us, he took off heading right toward us.

"Am I glad to see you," he exclaimed, as we rushed to greet him. "I thought I lost you all for good!"

Thekla explained that they had found him asleep about a *"disset"* from where we were originally located. I have to admit, we were all glad to be reunited with Sean, and he also seemed happy to see us. Sean told us he "blanked out" while looking for us. "The next thing I knew, I was being hauled in here by these *people*."

"He was near a mizcus patch," Thekla added. "Master Neanias collected the residual dust and it has been put in containment."

Unsure what that meant, I looked to Sosthenes, who was already prepared to answer my question. "*Mizcus* is a feral weed that grows in patches throughout our forests. He probably walked through it and stirred up the release of its pollen, which would have quickly rendered him quite unconscious."

Clearly, Sosthenes could sense my thoughts, and his studious glances indicated he knew I had questions. So, as we settled back down, he turned to me and said, "I think it is time, Hannah Goodheart, that I tell you of Hesiod and the Pyxis."

And so, he began by telling us how, very long ago, all of time and space, as well as diverse dimensions, had been created, and a gateway constructed. As Sosthenes put it, "no one builds a house without a door."

A window was also made, for which to see through the veil of time, into other worlds, other galaxies, even other dimensions beyond material existence. Twenty-four Sentinels were chosen to keep watch.

Annie made the connection right away to the twenty-four marble chairs near the center of the chamber.

"The reflecting pool... the time window?" I asked.

"Very perceptive... very perceptive, indeed." The *Kalosian* Sentinel nodded his affirmation, before he continued. "It was decided that it was too dangerous to have the power of both these objects in one place. It was then a construct of pure gold was made to contain the matrices and power source for the portal... the Pyxis."

"Pandora's box—my charm?" I interjected. "But it's not made of gold, it's pewter—silver in color."

"Purest gold, like that used to make the Pyxis, is as transparent as crystal. It is the impurities in gold that give it color," Sosthenes replied.

I immediately questioned, "So the Pyxis is dark silver because it's full of some kind of impurity... like maybe dark *magic*?"

"Oh child," replied the Sentinel. "There is no *dark* magic or *light* magic. There is only *magic*. Whether it is dark, or light, is determined by the one who wields it."

Morgan spoke up and asked, "So, you're telling us that Hannah's little silver charm is some kind of magic time portal?"

"That is precisely what I am saying."

"But, how do you put something like a time portal into a such a small box?" Sam asked. "I mean, I saw what came out of it. That's just not possible."

"The principals of physics used to construct the device have been theorized on your own world," Sosthenes replied.

"So, it's *not* magic?" Lily asked, with disappointment.

Sosthenes laughed as he leaned toward Lily to respond. "To you, perhaps it would seem like magic. And a powerful kind of magic it possesses, indeed. But what may seem like magic to you is, to my kind, a piece of technology. Such is the case with your Pandora's box."

Annie chided. "Pandora's box is nothing but a myth, a story."

"So, you accept that all of this around you is not of your world because you see it, but you reject a truth because it's surrounded by misconceptions and myths? What is sometimes dismissed as myth is often rooted in truth," said Sosthenes. "You need only look a little deeper. Examine *all* the evidence. Investigate what lies *below* the surface and you'll often discover a reality that is most certainly more incredible than the lore itself."

I said to him, "In Annie's defense, what you're describing doesn't sound *anything* remotely like the Pandora's box *I've* read about."

"Right! According to the story…" Morgan said, "Zeus filled a jar with all the evil of the world, and when he gave it to Pandora as a gift, she opened it and released into the world the evil within it."

The Sentinel leaned back thoughtfully, then said, "That *is* the myth as told by Hesiod, in your world and in your time."

Silence hung in the air as Sosthenes continued. "Two emissaries of this world were chosen, to take the Pyxis, and travel through time and space, to find a Guardian who, according to an ancient prophecy, would be able to fully wield the power it contained. Hesiodos and another, one called Theseus, were selected, but the task was never completed, and the two never returned."

Lily finished her drink, and as her cup was being refilled by one of the *Kalosians*, she said, "The guy that crashed the party didn't look anything like you. Believe me, I would have noticed… no offense."

Sosthenes cracked a reserved smile and said, "No offense is taken, Lily Little." He appeared to relax, just a bit, as he continued. "Would it surprise you to know that we are very nearly identical to you genetically, with only minor differences in our dominant traits?"

Lily's eyes widened, surprise coloring her face as she took a sip of her drink. "*You're* human?" she inquired.

"I am *Kalosian*," replied the man. "A child of my own world, just as you are children of yours. What we *share*, however, runs much deeper. We share a common origin and a common creator. *Human… Kalosian… Attiqan*—these are all mere labels which distinguish us. But what we share in common is far more than what differentiates us. What is flesh? What is race? It is nothing, for we are all created beings whose true self cannot be defined by a name or even our appearance. We are what we are."

"Or what we choose to be," added Sam.

Sosthenes glanced at Sam and tilted his head. "Yes. To a degree, perhaps."

"Mr. Hoise… Hesiod… I'm sorry, but this is all so unbelievable," I said, shaking my head, tying to come to terms with the incredible nature of what I was beginning to discover.

Sosthenes the Sentinel lowered his voice and tried to offer some reassurance. I explained to him how I had begun to suspect the antique dealer was not who he claimed to be.

Then, I was totally blown away as Sosthenes told us more about his people, including one astonishing ability they have. They're metamorphs! He explained how they're able to change and mimic the characteristics of many species from other planets with whom they shared genetic compatibility. Sosthenes continued to challenge our notion of "humanity."

"Just consider that the universe is full of human beings—some who appear very much like you and some who do not," he said to our surprise. "*One* of our unique attributes is in our ability to camouflage our appearance… an ability that is lost, in time, if we do not revert back to our natural state."

The Sentinel went on to say that the *Kalosians* were naturally curious and had once been a race of explorers, until the responsibility was placed upon them to guard the window of time. That is, until the Pyxis was commissioned to be forged and sent forth with the two emissaries.

In the hours that followed, Sosthenes told us a great many things and shared his vast knowledge of the universe. Talking with me at one point, he mentioned that *Kalosians* have extremely long lifespans, by nearly any standard, but Hesiod was protected, even against aging, by the presence of the Pyxis. He said, "Overcome by the temptation of its power, we know most certainly

Hesiod succumbed and never returned. We do not, however, know for certain what has come of Theseus, but we fear the worst."

Sam, overhearing the conversation, asked, "Didn't you think to send someone after them?"

"We did," replied Sosthenes, as he stood. "We... we do not speak of it."

"So, let me get this straight," I said. "You sent two of your own with this Pyxis to find a Guardian. They end up on Earth, 700 B.C. and disguised as 'humans'." I said with air quotes for irony, "one of them becomes a famous poet who influences the history of Greek culture. Oh. My. Goodness. Maybe the entire course of history on my world?"

"That would seem to be an accurate assessment," the Sentinel replied. "It would also seem reasonable to assume that he has used the Pyxis for his own purposes, whatever they may be. Understand, he has hidden in plain sight and we have watched helplessly as he has polluted the development of your world. He has the power to change history and alter time, and he must be stopped."

"He was," I said. I paused and lowered my head, muttering, "At least for a while."

That was the moment, I began to think this situation—Hesiod... the Pyxis... the six of us stranded on a remote planet out in the universe somewhere... my parents at home, probably losing their minds—it might actually be all my fault.

Sosthenes turned to me with a curious smile and said, "Paul Learner. Your great-grandfather."

"You *knew* him?" I asked, surprised to hear his name. Then it hit me. "The journal! It was *here*. He came *here*."

Sosthenes stroked his sculpted jaw and said fondly, "I am fortunate to call him my friend."

"You know," I said sadly, "He passed away a few months ago."

Sosthenes turned and looked at me with an expression that revealed the confidence that could only come from the most deeply hidden knowledge of the universe. It was so assured, I was immediately drawn in. "I know in *your* linear understanding of time, Paul Learner is deceased," he said. "We are the watchmen of time, the Sentinels of forever. Mortality is but a shadow of the eternal realm. What was, what is, and what will be... there is no difference. These things are all the same to me."

I was astonished at his words. The idea that this world, and these people, existed somehow outside of time was mind blowing.

Sosthenes explained that the Pyxis had, by some twist of luck, been found by Paul and that he had indeed been to Kalos many, many times. It was decided that *he* should care for the Pyxis, until the time in which the Guardian would be revealed. Hesiod was trapped, and the responsibility fell to Paul to make sure the Pyxis didn't fall back into his hands. "It has been foreseen that the Guardian will put all things right, and with great wisdom, return our lost brethren to their proper places," Sosthenes said.

"And now, because of me," I said wistfully, "Hesiod has the Pyxis again and is nowhere to be found."

Sosthenes walked toward the center of the hall, asking all six of us to accompany him. As we walked toward the marble chairs, where all but two were occupied by more *Kalosians*, we noticed a transparent panel, holographic perhaps, separating the reflecting pool from the Sentinels, who sat stoically, seemingly paying no attention to our approach.

"I can send you through the window to your home," Sosthenes said, with authority. "It will be as though you never left."

He waved his hand across the holographic panel and I could see my parents in the reflecting pool, by the very spot we had been hours earlier, before we leapt through the portal.

"What about Hesiod?" I asked.

With another wave of his massive hand, the scene was cleared. He turned to me. "He has slipped from our realm and has the ability to hide from our gaze. He will run through time and space, bounce from dimension to dimension and no doubt wreak havoc. Our only hope is to, somehow, find the Guardian and stop him."

"So, you *will* go after him?" asked Sam.

Sosthenes shook his head. "No, Sam Blake... once a *Kalosian* leaves this purview, we cannot always see them in time. We are like moving shadows in dimly lit rooms. And with the Pyxis, it will be much easier for him to elude our watch. Theseus is feared to have slipped the realm of mortality, perhaps lost in some uncharted dimension. Most grievously, Hesiod holds the power of time and space in his hand, so we have no choice but to wait. In time, the Guardian will be revealed, and all will be as it should be."

The six of us listened intently, as Sosthenes explained their plight.

"Sit on your hands much?!" Lily exclaimed.

Annie put her hand on her heart and stepped back, astonished to hear Lily pop off with such sarcasm. "It does seem kind of… pacifistic," Annie added, collecting herself.

Sam agreed hesitantly, as Sosthenes gave the sisters a long look.

I looked up and, without hesitation, I said with conviction, "I'll go!" I don't know what came over me. It was almost unconscious, and yet I felt so compelled to do something. I had to fix all this… somehow.

The Sentinel looked down at me. A spark came into his eyes, which had the appearance of a vast galaxy full of stars.

"There would be significant risks, Hannah Goodheart," he said. "I can send you through the window, but it would be a one-way trip. Without the Pyxis, you would remain in whatever time and place you're sent."

"This is my fault," I said. "You can send us back, but now that I know about all of this, I can't just go back home and forget it. I have to do this."

Sosthenes turned to a sand colored disk, suspended beside him, atop a table size monolith and took a stark white band that had materialized above it. Placing it on my wrist, he said, "I can send you to wherever the Pyxis is. This will help you locate it, but more importantly, it will lock onto the Pyxis. Wherever Hesiod goes, you will be pulled with him."

"Like a tether," said Morgan.

Annie looked down at the band on my wrist. "It looks like a seriously high-tech smart watch."

Lily took hold of my hand and looked up at Sosthenes, asking, "You got two of these, big guy?"

"No," I said immediately. "I can't ask you to go with me." I looked up at the imposing Sentinel. "You can send them home, right?" I asked. "Because, that's the deal."

Sosthenes nodded in affirmation.

Lily turned to look right into my eyes. "I'm going with you," she said bravely.

"*We're* going with you," Morgan said, as she stepped forward.

"All of us," Sean added, as the others rallied around me.

Each of them was given a small diamond-shaped pin to attach to their shirt; a temporal tag, which allowed them to stay temporally locked to my device. Wherever I was taken by Hesiod and the Pyxis, they would be taken as well. I turned once more to look upon the stately Principal Sentinel, Sosthenes, as I stepped into the pool. I noticed that while it appeared that I was standing in water above my ankles, I was not at all wet. I smiled when I felt the warm pool, as it caused my feet to tingle. Sosthenes watched with admiration, as though he somehow wished he could go along.

"Remember," he said, "after you find Hesiod and retrieve the Pyxis, you will know where to find the Guardian. *Everything* depends upon your success. Once you have found the Guardian, you must return here."

I turned away and looked downward into the event horizon. My reflection looked back up at me from the ripples, as I stepped down deeper into the pool. Although it was me that I saw, it didn't feel like I was looking back at *myself*. We all held hands as our reflections faded.

"Find the Guardian," we could hear Sosthenes say, as the pool turned a translucent blue. And so, we slipped out of sight, while the Sentinels continued to keep watch.

CHAPTER 11: THE DEALEY DILEMMA

THE JOURNEY THROUGH the portal left all six of us feeling a little disoriented. My skin still had that strange tickling sensation I first felt as we were being pulled from Kalos to… wherever this place was we now found ourselves. I took in the sights all around as we emerged from between two buildings into a bustling sea of people. The throwback styles people were wearing immediately caught my attention.

"So, do you have any idea where we are?" asked Sam.

"No," I replied. "After where we just came from and what we've seen today, I'm not sure of anything anymore."

"I don't think it's a case of where, Hannah," said Annie nervously. "I think it's more like *when*."

An older model light green car slowly cruised by. The windows were rolled down and we could hear music coming from the radio inside.

"Yeah, you're right," I said pointing to a large brick building just down the street. "I think I know this place, guys."

"I see it," said Morgan.

All of us except for Sean were staring at the seven-story building in wonder. "Does someone want to clue me in?" he asked.

Lily turned to him and punched his arm before saying, "It's the museum... the old book depository. This is downtown Dallas!"

"Dealey Plaza," I added, pointing in the direction of the well-known landmark.

The familiar building stood proudly at the corner of North Houston and Elm Streets. A sign atop the brick structure said the temperature was sixty-one degrees and it looked as though the cloudy sky was clearing.

"The song coming from that old car," I began.

"The Rambler," asked Sam.

I must have looked puzzled as he continued. "It's a 1958 Rambler."

"I know that song. My dad has it on vinyl. *It's All Right*, by The Impressions," I added.

A brisk, gentle breeze blew through the streets, and as we scanned the crowd, we noticed an excited buzz in the air. A few people were holding American flags, and a larger flag was planted behind a simple pole and rope barricade in the grass on the other side of the street.

A man rushed past us wearing a dark suit and hat, followed by a woman in a gray skirt, white blouse, and red sweater. She wore "grandma glasses," as Morgan called them, which referred to the vintage cat eye glasses that were common in the 1950s and 60s. We passed two kids sporting crew cuts, playing with yo-yos and wearing cuffed jeans, with matching mustard colored jackets, as we continued to walk down Houston toward Elm.

It was apparent by the way everyone was dressed, coupled with the previous observation regarding the vehicles, that we were in downtown Dallas, sometime in the early 60s. Sam had suggested we find a newspaper to figure out exactly what the date was, but Sean was quick to offer his own opinion. He suggested that our only priority should be Hesiod—to return him and the Pyxis to the Sentinels.

I reminded him that we needed to find the Guardian as well, suggesting that perhaps this was why Hesiod had come here; to this place and this time. "The Guardian could be here somewhere," I said. "Hesiod may know something we don't."

"You don't think he would come here to eliminate the Guardian, do you?" Lily asked.

"He *did* threaten to erase my Dad from time," I replied. "So, I guess it's possible, if he has that kind of power."

"The bottom line is, Hesiod is dangerous. We know he's here, so eyes open and stay alert," Sam said soberly.

Morgan proposed we split up and search the crowd for Hesiod. Sean agreed, suggesting that we could cover more ground. But as we debated whether it was wise for us to go off in different directions, a man stepped up behind me.

"Miss, can you pick that up for me?" the man asked.

I could barely hear due to the noise of the crowd but turned around and looked up at the man. I recognized something about his handsomely rugged face—especially his eyes. I was trying to put my finger on what it was that struck me as familiar when the man spoke to me again, saying, "I'm sorry, my wife dropped the cover to her camera face. Would you care to pick it up there, at your feet?"

The moment I heard his deep, gravelly voice, I knew what was so familiar about this gentleman. I crouched down and picked up the brown leather cover, and with trembling hands, I handed it back to the man. I was altogether in shock as he took it from my hand and politely thanked me with a smile.

"Got it," a woman exclaimed, as she stepped up beside the tall man standing in front of me.

The dark-haired woman put her hand on the gentleman's arm. Wearing rose and light-blue plaid pants and a rose-colored sweater, she smiled admiringly, as she took her dark sunglasses off and put them on her head.

The man smiled at me and then turning to the woman, asked, "Got what, dear?"

"A picture of your back," she replied with a note of sass, as they both shared a chuckle. "No… I finally got the film in, and I'm ready to take some shots."

The man handed the leather cover to her, giving credit to "the young girl" who was kind enough to pick it up. At that moment, I suddenly realized! I was standing face to face with Paul and Elizabeth Learner, my great-grandparents. They were both in the prime of life, not at all as I remembered them. I took it all in and wanted desperately to remember every detail of this version of my Nan and Paw-Paw, who were standing here with me now.

"Why, thank you, miss," Elizabeth said, crinkling her nose and flashing a smile. Her smooth southern charm brought a flood of memories to my mind. Nan always had a quiet sort of dignity, but I could see why Paw-Paw always said she could sweeten the sourest lemon with a wink and a smile. Seeing her like this, reminded me so much of Mom.

I just nodded, trying very hard to play it cool and contain my emotions, which at this moment were all over the place. I was afraid of saying something that would give me away and didn't want to do anything that would seem weird. However, no way could I have anticipated such a meeting. *I can't let on who they are… who I am.*

Unaware of my most strange encounter, everyone had decided to split up and were all moving away, each in their own direction, hoping to catch a glimpse of Hesiod so they could grab him and return to Sosthenes and the Sentinels of Kalos.

So, I stood… silent, unable to move.

"This is exciting isn't it?" asked Paul.

Still struggling with the reality that this much younger, dark-haired gentleman was actually my Paw-Paw, I couldn't respond, as I wasn't even sure what exactly he was talking about. Not wanting to seem rude or otherwise ill-mannered, I finally reached my hand out and said, "I'm Hannah—Hannah Goodheart, it's a pleasure to meet you."

Paul took my hand and shook it cordially as he replied, "I'm Paul, and this is my wife, Elizabeth." He gestured over at a boy, who looked to be about my age. "That's our son, Tommy, over there."

I looked over at the boy who was wide-eyed with wonder, as he stood on the curb waving the flag he held. He was about the same height as Sam—a little tall for a boy of what would have been twelve. Tommy wore a light tan jacket and jeans that were about an inch too short, which made his white socks stand out. A blue ball cap that said ".45s" rested snugly on his head, covering a fresh barber shop haircut.

He quickly turned around when his father called to him to say hello. The blush on his cheeks made it clear that he wasn't at all comfortable talking to girls, but nevertheless, he smiled and waved. I thought again about my mom, at that moment, and the regret she felt never having had the opportunity to meet her father. And yet, there he was, mere feet from where I stood.

My thoughts were interrupted as Paul spoke again. "It's not every day the president's motorcade comes ridin' through your city. This is a day you'll remember the rest of your life, Hannah." As he and Elizabeth walked toward where Tommy was standing, he thanked me again, but I barely heard his words. While people continued to pour into Dealey Plaza, it suddenly occurred to me exactly where, and more importantly *when*, we were.

Morgan and Sam were the first to arrive back. "Have you seen the others?" Morgan asked.

I just shook my head, but Sam must have caught on that I was freaking out. "Are you OK?"

"I know where we are… I mean, *when* we are," I said. "It's November 22, 1963, and President Kennedy's about to be assassinated, a little over a block away from here."

"How do you know?" Morgan asked.

I pointed over at Paul, Elizabeth, and Tommy Learner, who were swept up in the thrill of the moment, as the sound of the coming motorcade filled the plaza. "Nan and Paw-Paw just told me."

Sam's expression fell from his face as Morgan gasped. Lily and Annie reached us, just in time to watch two police motorcycles turn right on Houston Street in advance of the president's car.

"We have to do something," exclaimed Annie. "We can stop it… change history… save the president."

"We can't," said Sam somberly. "We can't mess with time and change the events of history." He looked around. "Where's Sean, he'll tell you—Temporal Rules…"

Morgan rolled her eyes. "That's what they may say in those old science fiction shows you guys watch. It's TV. It's not like that stuff is real."

"Maybe that's not what was supposed to happen," Annie said emphatically, pointing toward the motorcade. "Maybe we're here for a reason."

"Well, we can't just stand here and *not* do anything," Lily declared, tugging at my arm.

The crowd began to cheer, and as I watched the president's black convertible roll by, I caught a glimpse of the handsome young leader, sitting next to his wife, oblivious that his life was about to be snuffed out by an assassin's bullet. I felt a strange sense of wonder, watching history unfold before my eyes. And yet a feeling of helplessness gripped me, knowing I was in a position to change this dark chapter. Still, I was sure in my heart that it would be irresponsible to interfere, regardless of how tragic a moment it would be. Who could predict how it might change the future?

Time seemed to stand still as he looked right at me and waved. The smile on his face was sincere and the twinkle in his eye left me conflicted. As they passed, Jackie Kennedy, the president's wife, looked over her shoulder and waved in our direction. My heart beat hard against my chest watching the limousine go by.

Suddenly, the thought washed over me like a flood. "Oh, my," I exclaimed. "Maybe that's what *Hesiod* is here to do!"

The others turned to me with various expressions of confusion. "What do you mean?" Lily asked.

Morgan turned to watch as the motorcade passed. "Change history," she said. "My gosh—He's here to change history!"

The president's car made the turn into Dealey Plaza, on Elm.

I held my breath.

Some of the crowd had already begun to dissipate as I heard two shots echoing across the plaza. People started running in all directions. Some took cover behind cars, while others just lay flat on the ground. Several people had quickly moved from Houston Street, across the grass, toward Elm. Mass confusion erupted all around us. I could only describe it as total chaos.

The five of us huddled together. "Where's Sean?" I asked frantically.

Tommy Learner came and took me by the hand. "C'mon... my pop said we need to take cover," the boy said, with a proper southern drawl.

We moved quickly, over to where Paul and Elizabeth were standing. A 1961 white Chevy Impala, parked along the street, served as cover while people continued to scatter.

Just then, I caught sight of a dark bearded figure running toward us. He was clothed in a dirty woolen robe. He looked frightened as his sandaled feet pounded against the pavement. Although he didn't look nearly as well-manicured, I was sure it was Hesiod, but before I could say a word, he slammed into a passer-by. Hesiod bounced off the bystander and stumbled into Elizabeth. The impact threw her against the car. Paul reached out and caught her before she fell, but her brown boxy camera hit the car, breaking the grey knob that advances the film.

I could see that Elizabeth was okay and turned my attention to Hesiod. He fell to his knees but recovered quickly, before tripping into another bystander and finally, falling to the ground. His head hit the pavement hard. But before I could move toward him, Sean came running over.

Nearly out of breath, Sean, pointing toward Elm Street, exclaimed, "I found him. He's over there. Hurry, we have to catch him!"

I gestured toward Hesiod, or should I say Hesiod from the past, who was now laying on the sidewalk.

"That's not *our* man." Seeing Paul standing within earshot, Sean tugged at his ear as he gave him a side-eye. Pointing at the robed man lying unconscious on the ground, Sean said in a hushed voice, "*He* saw our... *companion.*" Not being at all subtle, Sean's eyes got big as his head bobbed back and forth in the direction of Elm. "He shot off in that direction." Paul glanced over and smiled awkwardly at Sean as he continued. "You need to come with me. Our *friend* is this way," Sean said, pointing across the way once more toward Elm Street.

I looked up at Paul. "Go with your friend," he said. "I'll get this gentleman some help."

I gave him a nod and took off running toward Elm Street with Sean and the others. As we cut across into the grass, we scanned the perimeter. "He was just here," Sean said. "I saw him."

"There," Lily cried, pointing over toward a grassy bank, in the direction of the railroad overpass.

All six of us took off running toward the grassy knoll, but as we approached the street, Hesiod vanished into the crowd. We agreed to stay together this time, as we tried to make our way around as best we could. However, the Plaza was too crazy for us to stay, so we made our way back toward Houston Street, where I saw the Learners, their expressions grave, walking away from the Plaza, on Main.

We all made our way toward Paul and his family. Paul turned to me, "The president's been shot," he said in a quiet voice.

"I know," I replied, looking around. "Where's the man—the one who fell back there," I asked.

"Probably on his way to the hospital, I imagine," Paul replied. "I flagged down a couple medics who showed up and they put him on a stretcher and took him away."

I asked Paul if he could drive us to the closest hospital. He reluctantly agreed, and we all climbed into the back of the Learners' pickup truck, as he took us as close to Parkland Hospital as he could get us. There were reporters and police everywhere. Paul was not keen on the idea of leaving the six of us there, but after I had assured him that my guardian was there, he got back into his truck and, with a wave, drove away.

It wasn't nearly as difficult as we thought it would be to make our way inside, but the hallways of Parkland Hospital were crawling with police. There were dozens of men in dark suits, pacing around near the emergency department. I approached an information desk and asked if a man dressed in white robes had been brought in. Before the woman could respond, Morgan caught a glimpse of *our* Hesiod coming through the main emergency room doors and into the corridor. Right away, he saw me as well as the others, and darted toward a door leading to the parking lot.

"How did he get here so fast?" Sean asked, as he took off after him. "We had transportation!"

The rest of us followed, but Hesiod had managed to evade us again.

"Wait," said Annie. "So, there are two of them?"

"You're behind, sister of mine," Lily said in jest.

"One past and one present," said Sean. "I mean… um… the one in robes you mentioned, he must be Hesiod from the past. The Hesiod we're looking for just got away."

"But, why would he come here, to 1963?" I asked.

"Like I said, maybe to prevent the assassination… change history," replied Morgan.

"No," Sam said. "The robed Hesiod was running *away* from the plaza. He looked frightened. Besides, if he was trying to prevent the assassination of JFK, he totally failed."

"I told you," Sean said. "He saw *our* Hesiod… that's what set him off."

"*Our* Hesiod was hiding," Lily said. "Like he had an agenda."

"He's got an agenda, alright," fired Annie. "Fueling conspiracy theories for the next hundred years."

"What are you talking about, Annie," asked Morgan.

"Do you *not* watch documentaries about conspiracies?" Annie responded. "The shadowy figure photographed in the grassy knoll is our time-traveling thief!"

Sean spoke up. "I think you're right, Lily. He came here for a reason, but I doubt that it had anything to do with the assassination of the president."

Suddenly, I remembered the locator and raised my hand to look at the strange device on my wrist. With a tap, a projection originating from the device could be seen on the sleeve of my sweater. I pushed up at the sleeve of both my sweater and the pink plaid shirt underneath to expose my bare arm. The image was much clearer, and now I could study the strange symbols, with Sean looking annoyingly over my shoulder while I tried to decipher them.

"There's still at least one Hesiod who's likely in this hospital. Maybe *he* has a Pyxis," Morgan said.

I turned back toward the hospital and said, "There's only one way to find out."

We made our way back into the hospital and were able to sneak past the guards standing at the emergency room doors. As we entered, Lily's eye caught a fancy pen laying on the floor by the wall. She grabbed it from the floor and inspected the engraving.

"This is the president's pen," she gasped, as she showed it to me.

"Put that down, Lily," said Annie, shaking her head. "We're not here to swipe pens and gather artifacts, there, Indiana Little."

Lily ignored her sister's comment and held onto the unique pen. She shuffled along behind as we walked cautiously through a maze of hallways, until Sean noticed a pair of sandals on the floor behind a curtain.

"Here, everyone," he said, slipping behind the veil as we followed him.

The bearded man lying in the bed was still unconscious. As we all searched around him, Sam picked up the clipboard at the end of the bed and flipped through the papers. "Says here he has a possible mild concussion."

Sean pulled the thin sheet away from Hesiod. His discolored robe was torn near the knees and was bloody. I checked to see if a chain perhaps hung around his neck, and Lily lifted his hand. But, as she pried his fingers open, he suddenly opened his eye and grabbed her hand. This Hesiod was awake. Lily cried out and dropped the prized pen in his lap as she pulled away.

Sam said frantically, "We need to get out of here before we draw unwanted attention."

"I think we already have," Annie said, pointing to a uniformed police officer walking briskly in our direction.

All six of us quickly made a break for it and worked our way out of the emergency department and back into the street, avoiding any direct contact with the authorities.

"This is a waste of time," Sean said with irritation. "*Our* Hesiod's not here."

"I have to agree," I said, near breathless. "He doesn't seem to have a Pyxis either."

Relieved to be back outside and still trying to catch my breath, I gave Sean another nod of agreement as I began to feel a faint vibration. I looked down at the locator on my wrist, which was now lighting up and flashing. Almost instantly, the six of us were pulled into a cold, darkened tunnel, which slowly began to light up with three-dimensional symbols, maps of places, dates… charts, it was the time vortex again, just like when Hesiod first took the Pyxis and ran.

From within a calm bubble, protected from the chaos of the vortex, I yelled, "Morgan, Lily…"

"I think we're all here," shouted Sean.

"Stay close, everyone," exclaimed Annie.

The turbulence had subsided, and slowly our surroundings regained focus as a bright sun beat down on us in what appeared to be, quite literally, the middle of nowhere.

CHAPTER 12: THE MARKET, THE MATRON, AND THE MOUNTAIN

A BEAUTIFUL ROLLING mountain sat majestically off in the distance, looking over the valley below. The saltiness of the arid wind should have been an indication that a sea was nearby, but being novice travelers, none of us picked up on the clue. The terrain was somewhat rocky, but everyone agreed we were on a road or path, of sorts, and that it must lead somewhere. The heat was nearly unbearable as we walked. One thing seemed certain: I was finally beginning to figure out the locator, and it appeared now that we were at least heading in the right direction.

It was fortunate that we came across a spring. Stopping to rest, the six of us enjoyed the cold, refreshing water bubbling up out of the rocks. I removed my sweater while the others also shed extra layers of clothes. It was hard to miss the purple and blue bruising on my right wrist from the tight grip Hesiod had on me. It was tender to the touch, so the cold water felt really good.

The water from the spring flowed into a nearby pool, and Annie threw her denim jacket aside and unlaced her black combat boots, saying she planned to jump in. Sam and Sean were both busy speculating that this was a sign we were getting close to a village or settlement and paused only to overrule Annie's suggestion. Lily, Morgan, and me, on the other hand, were more concerned with where and when we were, for it was evident to everyone that this was nowhere near Dallas, and it was anyone's guess what time period we were in.

I started to wonder if we were even still on Earth. I knew by now that no range limits existed with the Pyxis device. From what Sosthenes had explained while we were in the chamber of the Sentinels on Kalos, the Pyxis could open portals to other times, other planets, even other dimensions. It all seemed so... science fiction to me; like one of Sean's crazy stories—almost beyond reason.

My thoughts were also consumed with what we had just witnessed. Paw-Paw's journal took on new meaning as I contemplated the melancholy tone of what he wrote, now weighed against what *I* saw happen on November 22, 1963. In my heart of hearts, I wanted to do something... anything to prevent the tragedy that befell the world that day. There I was, right there with all the knowledge necessary to prevent John Kennedy's death and I couldn't do a thing. "How unfair," I thought as my mind wandered back to the matter of where in universe we might be, still questioning whether we were on Earth or somewhere else in the cosmos.

As we carried on with our journey, my questions began to dwindle for the moment as the locator brought us to what seemed to be a busy village market teeming with people.

"They're all speaking English... that's a good sign," Annie said, optimistically.

"No," said Sean. "I don't think so. The locator has a translation matrix. You can hear them in your own language, and when we speak, they hear theirs."

"Wait," I said, looking up suspiciously at Sean. "You know this... how?"

"The big one," Sean replied, quickly. "Uh... Sosthenes. He mentioned it. Remember?"

I thought for a moment, trying to recall, before Sam chimed in. "Yeah. I think I *do* remember him saying something like that."

"It works," said Morgan, trying to keep everyone focused. "That's all that matters. We need to keep moving."

We continued to walk cautiously through the crowded area, looking around in hopes of catching a glimpse of Hesiod. I stopped and asked a man where we were. His reply sent a chill down my spine.

"Guys, I have a bad feeling about this," I said to my friends. "We're in Boeotia. I think this is ancient Greece."

"Well, the good news is, we're still on Earth," Lily quickly replied, with an awkward smile.

"How ancient?" asked Morgan.

"I guess somewhere around 700... *B.C.*" I replied.

Sam smiled nervously. "What makes you guess that?"

"I remember Mr. Hoise... Hesiod saying he was from Boeotia... right here. If he's *the* Hesiod of antiquity, then maybe he's decided to come home."

"Home is thousands of light-years from here, if he's *the* Hesiod," Sean chided.

Silence fell over us until Sean sidled up to me and tapped my left wrist.

"What does your device say?" he asked.

I pulled my sleeve up, gave it a tap, and studied it for a moment, trying to be discreet, as the marketplace was bustling with people buying and selling. I told the group that it looked like he was close by.

"Let's spread out again. Maybe we can flush him out," Sean barked.

"No way," I said. "This isn't Dallas, this is… well, it's feasibly ancient Greece. We're staying together. We need to make our way around and try to find him."

I noticed that we were getting some attention from the villagers and realized that everyone there was wearing wool or linen robes and were either walking barefoot or wearing leather sandals. How strange we must have looked to the Greeks. And then, it suddenly occurred to me that Hesiod might look equally as odd.

"I've got an idea!"

I approached a woman and told her that we were foreigners from across the sea and were looking for our friend. "He's tall and dressed similarly to us."

The woman shook her head and told me there had been no other foreigners with our appearance come through the village. Unbeknownst to us at the time, however, Hesiod had stolen a long tunic and was blending in, watching us as we mingled in the square. He was careful not to be seen, dodging us anytime we looked in his direction or drew anywhere near. He was also careful not to be noticed or draw attention from anyone else in the village, by covering his head and partially masking his face with a strip of linen cloth. After a while, however, he was forced out of the village square and lost sight of us.

Finally, I conceded to the rest of the group. "We stay together, but we can fan out a little bit and see if anyone has seen a bearded man dressed like us."

We asked around for nearly half an hour, yielding no result other than to draw more attention to ourselves. The villagers looked at us suspiciously as we made our way through the market. The fruits and vegetables, as well as the cooked meats, were an unwanted reminder that none of us had eaten since leaving Kalos, and I honestly wasn't sure if that had been hours or days ago.

Annie was the first to speak up. "Suffice it to say, it's been twenty-seven hundred years, give or take, since I've had anything to eat."

"Yeah guys, I'm starving," Sam added.

We all agreed. A courtyard nearby beckoned us, and we slowly migrated there, where we sat down. Lily asked, "Does anyone have any money?"

Sean spoke up, "Our money is worthless here. We need something to barter with."

As we dug through our pockets, pulling out everything from used hair bands, cash and coins, to Sam's cherished pocket knife, a woman walked through the courtyard. She was carrying a small child in one arm and a large basket in the other. I watched the beautiful woman walk past and into the market.

"What are you staring at?" Morgan asked me.

I stood to my feet and said, "I think she could use a hand. C'mon you guys. I have an idea."

I walked up to the woman and addressed her. "Hi, I'm Hannah. My friends and I are traveling from a distant place." Reaching into my pocket and pulling out a couple of quarters and a five-dollar bill, I continued. "I'm afraid our currency has no value here. Could I help in some way; carry your basket in exchanged for some bread or fruit?"

Sam interjected, "Or one of those kabob things over there."

I quickly gave him an elbow and continued, "Anything would be appreciated."

The woman smiled, "I like how you handle yourself… Hannah is it?"

Slightly embarrassed, I could feel the blush on my cheeks. I smiled shyly and nodded.

"Hannah… yes," the woman continued. "I'm Isadora. My husband is usually in the *agora*, telling stories or debating philosophy. Normally *he* would be doing the shopping, but I don't see him, so my daughter and I would appreciate your assistance."

We followed Isadora through the market as she collected bread, fruits, vegetables and other items. I watched her carefully as she negotiated with the merchants. The basket I carried was beginning to get heavy, and after a while, Isadora offered to trade the basket for the child.

Dora, the baby, was not yet a year old and was full of joy. Lily, Annie, Morgan, and I passed Dora around, taking turns making faces and noises to elicit giggles from the little bundle.

After nearly two hours in the market, Isadora walked us back to the courtyard and filled our hands with warm pita and fresh nectarines and dried figs. Coming to Sam, the woman gave him a kabob of cooked lamb and smiled. Sam blushed and smiled back at her.

"Thank you," he said. "That was unnecessary, but very kind."

"You should share with your friends and, perhaps, they will share their bread and fruit with you," Isadora responded, mussing his hair.

I carefully handed Dora back over to her mother, who now clearly had her hands full. As the others started to eat, Isadora smiled at me and asked where we were planning to stay while we were in Boeotia.

I looked around and said, "I'm sure we'll find a place."

"It will be dark soon. You'll need a place to sleep, and the streets here in the *agora* are no place for young ones after dark. Why don't you come with me?"

"That's very nice of you," I replied. "We're actually trying to find another person, a man, dressed like us—he's from the same land we're from… well, more or less. Anyway, we should stay here until we find him."

"I insist," said Isadora. "Perhaps my husband will be able to help you find your friend. He's usually around here most days, unless he takes one of his pilgrimages up the mountain. Besides," she said gesturing with her head to her load. "I could use the extra help getting home."

Isadora handed the baby back over to me, and we followed the kind woman home. Passing a small well in a courtyard, Isadora said to Sean and Sam, "I know it's not normally a man's job, but if you would be so kind as to fetch some water from the well, I'll take the ladies inside and begin preparing a meal."

Entering the home constructed of mud brick and stone, Isadora quickly made her way to a large clay bowl with a metal pot sitting on top. Lily, Annie, Morgan, and I watched as she lit a fire and began chopping vegetables she had purchased from the market. "If you want to take Dora to the *gynaeceum* while I prepare the meal, I can join you shortly," she said, while adding the vegetables, garden peas, and lentils to the pot.

As Sam and Sean entered with two clay pots full of water, Isadora smiled and thanked them. She continued to add food to the pan atop the clay stove. "The young men can retire to the *andron*," she said, pointing toward the back of the dwelling. "I will serve your meals first as soon as my husband returns."

I spoke up and said, "If it's no trouble, we'd like to all stay together."

"No trouble," Isadora said with a smile. "I don't usually entertain men in the kitchen, but if you fine men want to help, we can get our meal prepared much faster." Sean seemed unphased by the compliment, but Sam stood a little taller and stuck out his chest. "Fine men…" I heard him mutter under his breath as he pitched in to help. "Fine men."

Isadora had reluctantly decided we should all go ahead and eat, ditching the usual custom of serving the men their meal first. The sun had disappeared behind the nearby mountain, and we sat with full stomachs. Isadora was quiet and looked concerned as Dora slept peacefully in her mother's arms. The air was turning much cooler, and Annie was first to put on her denim jacket. Soon, all of us had put back on the extra layers we had shed earlier in the day by the cold spring.

"Can we clean up?" Morgan asked, politely.

"No, that's not necessary," replied Isadora. "My husband should be home anytime. In fact, he should be here by now."

"You look worried," said Lily.

Isadora nodded. "He usually does the shopping at the *agora*, but he left the basket here, which is why I went instead, but he was nowhere to be found. I do hope he is alright." A worrisome pause was finally interrupted as Isadora added, "Even when he goes to the mountain every few days, he is never out so late."

The baby stirred slightly as the sudden sound of a door opening and closing in the room Isadora called the *andron* could be heard. Isadora immediately rose to her feet, handing Dora to Annie. She moved with grace, as she quickly left the room. I was sitting by the wall and could hear the sound of their voices. I heard Isadora say that they had guests and that food was already prepared. She finally reentered the room and said to us, "May I present my husband..."

A shadowy figure entered the light. "Hesiod," I shouted.

The baby awoke and began to cry.

Sam leaped to his feet, "It's him!"

Hesiod froze for the briefest of moments, his eyes wide. He turned and ran out of the house and into the night.

I quickly pulled up my sleeve to expose my arm and the locator device. I saw the illuminated projection directing me out of the house, to pursue. I turned to a frightened Isadora, who now clung tightly to her baby. The confusion and shock of the moment was written all over her face. No one had even realized that Sean had already taken up the chase until he burst back in, near breathless and said, "We can catch him, but we have to go... NOW."

Annie hurriedly collected a few pieces of bread and a clay jug of water as Lily, Morgan and the others quickly ran outside. I stood, my eyes locked on Isadora and her child. My thoughts were all over the place. I struggled to piece it all together, but now knew that Hesiod, the *Kalosian* emissary, was married to this kind woman and was the father of her child. I had at least a dozen questions for her. I suddenly felt badly for her and wanted to explain myself to the woman, who was still motionless, protectively cradling her baby. Hearing the others outside, however, I turned, and left Isadora and the child, as I set out to pursue Hesiod.

We were all spread out, with Sean and Sam completely out of sight but not out of earshot. They were calling us to hurry. I met Morgan and then caught up to Lily and Annie. It took several minutes and pleas to them to slow down, before we were able to catch up to the guys. We quickly huddled up as I carefully studied the illuminated field being projected onto my arm. "That way," I said pointing the way.

Our eyes quickly adjusted to the night, which was brightly lit by a full moon and a sky ablaze with starlight.

I looked up for a moment and was in awe of what I could see. I allowed my mind to wander for a moment, and I wished for my new telescope as I had never seen a sky so full of stars. Lily flew past me and I snapped out of it, pointing toward a mountain. Confirming the direction once more on my locator, the six of us were off with great haste, to catch the rogue emissary, Hesiod.

It was clear to us that he was headed up the mountain and, as we pursued him, we speculated about what the connection to this mountain might be. Isadora had mentioned that he often made pilgrimages there. Almost without noticing, the six of us had ascended quite far, before coming to a narrow pass. I brought up the rear—which was typical for me, being the least athletic of the group and, by far, the slowest runner. This troubled me greatly as I tried to catch my breath.

"Is there some historical significance to this mountain?" asked Lily, snapping me back to the chase and out of my own head.

I'd barely heard the question, but Morgan spoke up. "Possibly, but I don't know what it could be. It seems to me, he's trying to somehow change the course of our history."

"Not *our* history," I said. "I think he's trying to change *his*!"

Sam, who was trailing Sean by only a few steps, put up a hand and said, "Okay, we need to stop for a second."

I checked my locator again, which as best as I could tell, confirmed we were at least heading in the right direction. I noted that Hesiod couldn't be too far ahead of us.

"It's too dangerous," said Sam.

Sean disagreed. "We continue, or he gets away," he said with certainty.

I looked down once more at the locator and then to the pass. "I'm with Sam. He has to come back down sometime."

Morgan chimed in, "We know where he lives now. We can stake it out. Besides, none of us are equipped for this. I'm wearing riding boots, for Pete's sake... not climbing shoes."

Morgan made a good point, but Sean was growing even more impatient and confronted the rest of us. "We've got him cornered. He doesn't have to come down. What if he decides to open the Pyxis and bounce?"

"Bounce" is a term we picked up from Sosthenes and started to use to describe the trips through the portal, via the Pyxis.

I quickly replied, "Then he takes us with him. Either way, we have him."

Annie spoke up, "There's no guarantee. We have him now... I say we go get him." With that, she cradled the clay water pot close as she joined Sean at the front of the group and started walking toward the pass.

Lily muttered under her breath, "I've got a bad feeling about this." But she reluctantly followed behind as Sam, Morgan, and I entered the pass.

The narrow ledge felt solid, but we had no margin for error as one misstep would result in sure death. The drop was straight down, and as best we could tell, the bottom of the ravine was several hundred feet. At its widest, the pass was less than twenty-four inches and stretched for some twenty feet or more.

Sean and Annie, followed closely by Lily, were more than half way across as Sam firmly rested his back against the rock face and carefully made his way. Morgan was next, with me last to begin the tedious trek. At about the halfway point, though, Morgan stopped. The pathway had narrowed some, and the moonlight reflected off something in the gorge that drew her eyes downward.

Sean and Annie had just reached the other side, and Annie turned to take hold of Lily's hand as the sound of falling debris drew everyone's attention to Morgan, struggling to maintain her footing. Sam turned his face toward her as he carefully clung to the rock face still at his back.

Morgan's balance waned.

Sam shouted, "Morgan, take my hand!"

I quickly reached for her, but to my horror, Morgan slipped. Wobbling forward to try and regain her footing, the rocky base began to crumble. She screamed as her foot left what little remained of the ledge. Her body rotated instinctively around to grab for something to hold. Sam and I both tried to catch her as I shouted, "Morgan!!!"

But it was too late. Morgan was out of reach. Her screams echoed through the chasm as she fell.

I stood motionless, unable to breathe—watching helplessly. I couldn't catch her.

I couldn't *do* anything.

I prayed in my heart that this was all a bad dream. *This can't be happening!* Reaching out, I cried, "No!" The shock left me unaware, however, that I was being pulled through the time portal once again, as Morgan plunged out of sight into the abyss of that ancient ravine.

CHAPTER 13: NOT SO UNEXPECTED

THE SILENCE WAS deafening. None of us could utter a word or comprehend that we were now standing in the loft of an old barn looking out, the light of the sun dancing through the trees surrounding the clearing. On the other side of the trees was a vast hayfield, far from the narrow pass overlooking the deep ravine that had just claimed Morgan. It was all so unimaginably horrific and yet so overwhelmingly serene.

I stood expressionless. All I could do was just stare at the ground from the edge of the loft. The brilliant green grass, still shimmering with the morning dew, was such a stark contrast to the dark cavern I was staring into just a moment ago. Being pulled into the portal and deposited elsewhere was disorienting to say the least. There's the tingling feeling followed by the brisk chill, which is capped by a feeling of weightlessness and nausea. It's a shock to the senses, but the dizzying bounce this time was coupled with the staggering reality that Morgan was...

Gone.

Sosthenes said there would be risks. I never dreamed, however, anything like this could have happened. A sick feeling came over me.

My hands were in tight fists at my side as tears began to pool in my eyes, creating a watery veil that obstructed my sight. Lily drew near to comfort me, but I pulled away. I could no longer hold back the flood of emotion, and I began to weep bitterly. Through my sobs, I could only utter words of regret. I've felt that my relationship with Morgan had suffered since my family moved out of the old neighborhood where I once lived next door to the McVeys. We were so close. As close as two friends could be. I turned to Lily and said through my tears, "Tell me! Tell me this didn't just happen... say this is all just a bad dream. Say it!"

My friends gathered around, trying to calm me but, inconsolable, I continued to weep. Sam reached into his pocket and produced a scrap of linen cloth that still contained crumbs from the bread it was wrapped around in the Greek marketplace earlier. He shook it and offered it to me, as I tried very hard to collect myself.

I wiped my nose as I sniffed and dabbed my eyes. "I've felt like I've been losing her and now... she's gone," I said, as I fought back another round of tears. "She's gone," I said, once more, nearly choking on the salty taste in the back of my throat.

Lily laid her head on my shoulder. "I can't believe we lost her," she muttered, fighting back tears of her own.

Annie, too, was unusually sober. Her usual quips of sarcasm were absent as she struggled to maintain control of her own emotions. She cleared her throat and said in almost a whisper, "The Sentinel can fix this…" her voice grew stronger. "Yes! Sosthenes… he can fix this. They have the technology, they can just send us back before she fell. We nab Hesiod and they'll—"

Sean interrupted, "It's not that easy…"

"Stop it," I shouted, "Just stop it! We've lost her and she…"

"No, we didn't," said Sam, matter-of-factly.

Annie slapped at him and began to chastise him for being insensitive, but his eyes were fixed on the pile of hay below and, looking down also, I noticed a hand extending up out of the hay. The whole mass was rustling, as one hand became two. We all were now looking down as a disheveled crown of strawberry blonde hair peeked through. Wiping the mess of hair and straw from her face, Morgan called up to us. "A little help here!"

We stood motionless, each of us with expressions of disbelief etched on our faces.

Morgan called up again, sounding a little impatient as she fought her way around the sea of hay, "Come on you guys, get me out of here!"

I was the first, as we all rushed down the ladder in the old barn and ran out straight into the pile of hay. We laughed and threw handfuls of it at one another.

The nightmare was over, and Morgan was safe.

Never has there been a finer celebration as we romped around that mound of straw and hay. I held so tight to Morgan, who herself seemed to still be in a bit of shock.

"I slipped from the ledge and the next thing I knew I fell into this. What just happened?"

I didn't know what to say. I could only shake my head. The complete and total relief that Morgan was alive washed over me, and tears of sorrow had now given way to tears of great joy.

I hugged Morgan once more. "I don't know, sister… I thought I lost you."

"I heard everything you said up there," Morgan said. Then she smiled and laughed, saying, "You can't get ridda' me *that* easily."

I pulled back, slightly embarrassed. All this while, I avoided talking to Morgan about my feelings and our friendship out of fear of smothering her or pushing her further away.

"It's okay, Hannah," Morgan said. "I've felt the same way at times. You moved away. You couldn't help it. We've both made new friends… but I also know how you feel, and I know how I feel. We've never, ever been *just* friends. We're sisters. Remember? Maybe not by blood, but by heart and no matter where we go or what we do, nothing will *ever* change that."

I was overwhelmed by the warmth of what she said, and my heart felt as though it was going to explode in my chest. A smile slowly stretched across my face. It was not a usual smile but much, much bigger and ever so much brighter as any I had ever had before. I embraced Morgan and Morgan embraced me. We clung tightly to one another as the others continued to play in the scattered straw that was, a moment ago, a neatly piled mound of hay. Then I took Morgan's hand and pulled her out into the grassy clearing.

"Hesiod," shouted Morgan.

"Got away."

"No way," said Morgan. "He opened that portal just in time. I don't think it was a happy accident. He can't be far… what do you say we go get him and then find this guardian."

I corralled the others with a whistle, and we looked at the locator. The field projected on the background of my left arm was lit up. A green symbol, resembling an open square with a dot in the middle, was in motion. A red symbol, that appeared to be a kind of crosshair appeared, chasing it across the gridded field. Distinct yellow cursor arrows connected the symbols to an egg-shaped blue dot that had a line down the middle, which I had determined represented our group. It appeared the alien device was again pointing us in the direction of Hesiod and the Pyxis. There were other characters that, previously, Sean said he believed were *Kalosian* and represented distance and other information.

The red crosshair locked onto the green symbol, which I thought specifically represented the Pyxis. I looked up at the others, who were huddled around me. "What do you all say we catch him and go home," I said, before we all took off walking toward the hayfield.

But before we reached the nearby line of trees, I stopped. The others kept walking, but I felt strangely compelled to turn back and look back at the barn, which stood proudly over the once neatly piled hay in the picturesque clearing. Morgan quickly noticed me standing, unmoved, staring curiously at the old wooden structure. "Hold up, you guys," she said to the others, whose chatter fell silent as they turned back, wondering what had captured my undivided attention.

"I know this place," I said.

"It does look oddly familiar," Morgan remarked.

Annie chirped, "It's a happy barn, and these are happy trees. I've seen a dozen paintings that look like this scene."

"It's nice to see someone's feeling full of herself again," said Lily, as she gave her sister a friendly shove.

"This place… I know it well. And, more importantly, I know exactly where we can go to get help!"

I turned away and walked briskly toward the tree line. The others stood for a moment, confused and uncertain, watching me march away with confidence. Sam fixed his eyes on the old barn and scratched his cheek, as I looked over my shoulder. I think he was trying to put together what I was thinking. I just kept walking and waved back to them, saying "Come on, you guys!"

"Where are we going?" Sean called, as they all ran toward me.

"Home," I exclaimed.

It was a couple of hours before anyone had asked to stop. The six of us all shared the last of the bread and passed around the clay jug of water Annie had grabbed before leaving Isadora's home. Sam offered the final sip to Morgan, who sat rather quietly, still pulling straw and grass from her strawberry blonde locks. She turned the jug over after emptying it of its last remaining contents and then handed it back to Sam, who drew back his arm to throw it into the dry creek bed nearby. I quickly objected and snatched the pottery from his hand, scolding him for even *thinking* of throwing away what I termed "an ancient Greek artifact." Sean looked curiously at Sam, who blushed and turned his head to not be noticed.

Sean asked Sam. "Does it bother you to get berated by her because she's a girl?"

Sean and Sam exchanged a few awkward looks before Sam rolled his eyes and turned his attention to throwing pebbles into the creek bed. I later discovered that Sam's embarrassment was actually because he saw that I noticed him doting on Morgan. After that, Sam must have decided to dial back on any attention he was showing her. While I saw right through him, he most likely wouldn't have wanted anyone else picking up on the fact that he was starting to have feelings for her. He played it cool, for the most part, from here on out.

"So, you still haven't said where we're going, Hannah," Sean said, turning his attention away from Sam.

"I told you… we're going home."

Sam looked around as it all started to become more familiar to him. "This *is* home… well, sort of. I think I know this road," he said with enthusiasm.

"Uh-huh," I said in agreement, knowing he was catching on.

Sam leaped to his feet, pulled me up onto mine and exclaimed. "If I'm right, your place is not more than a mile and a half down this road!"

Everyone else jumped up and followed, as Sam took off in the direction of the Learner Ranch. I reached into my pocket and pulled out a hair tie, pulling my long brown hair back into a pony tail before giving chase to the rest.

We were very happy, and it showed, as we made our way down the old farm road. Not one of us gave much thought to the fact that even though our surroundings were familiar, they weren't entirely as we had known them.

Our happiness turned to pure joy and great relief as we approached the driveway to the ranch. Here, little was different from how I had always known it. In fact, it was always a comfort to me knowing that, no matter what changes occurred around me in my life, I knew that my Nan and Paw-Paw's ranch was a constant. I felt a sense of security here that I didn't know anywhere else in this world... or any other for that matter.

As we approached the house, I saw a woman sweeping the porch. She stopped, holding the broom, and watched us as we neared the house. From her curious expression, we must have been quite a sight. Taken aback by this crazy, marvelous opportunity, I stopped short of the stone walkway that led to the porch. And to the woman with the broom.

My Nan.

Unlike the young lady with the red lipstick and bright plaid pants I had seen just a day or two ago in downtown Dallas, circa 1963, this Elizabeth Learner was as I remembered my great-grandmother before she passed away. A happily plain woman, she had her slightly graying hair pulled back into a bun, accentuating her gentle face which bore the quiet strength and wisdom she was always known for.

I pondered for a moment, contrasting the two versions of this same woman I so admired, and considered the nature of life and how very much one person can change over time. Such thoughts were fleeting though, as Nan gripped her broom tightly, smiled brightly, and called out "Paul... they're here!"

With that, Paul Learner stepped out onto the porch. He, too, looked so very different to me, in comparison to the young man with the rugged, clean-shaven face I had seen in Dealey Plaza. Paw-Paw stood tall and straightened his checkered shirt. He was wearing his signature dirty white Stetson and a broad smile, partially hidden behind a thick, graying mustache. His coffee mug was still in his hand, and he set it down on a nearby wicker table, brushing his hands on his jeans before taking his place at his wife's side.

We stepped up and stood before the couple in an almost ceremonious fashion. I looked up, deep into Paw-Paw's eyes. Those eyes were always the most serious but loving eyes. As always, they reassured me that I was in good hands, and for the first time since we began this quest, I felt totally safe.

"You haven't aged a day," Paw-Paw said, with that familiar throaty voice, as he looked me up and down.

"Well," I said, with a coy smile, "maybe a day or two." I collected myself and tried to remain calm and reserved, before saying, "You're both just as I remember you."

"So, you know who we are?" asked Sam, his voice a little shaky.

"I remember you from the... well, I never forget a face... especially when it hasn't changed in nearly forty years," he said.

"You seemed to be expecting us," I remarked, nodding to acknowledge what Nan had said upon our arrival.

Paw-Paw looked lovingly over to my Nan, who sidled up closer to her husband. He smiled, pointed to the sky and said, "I think we might have a mutual friend. Kalos?"

"Sosthenes," Morgan bellowed.

"He said you'd be along sooner or later."

My great-grandparents ushered us inside. Paw-Paw said very little as Nan poured glasses of lemonade. I felt a little awkward at first, walking into the house, but it wasn't long before it started feeling more like those wonderful visits I had always enjoyed while they were living. She and Paw-Paw made eye contact with one another numerous times, and both were trying far too hard not to be noticeably uncomfortable.

Each time Nan passed by, I had to fight the urge to reach out and hug her. It had been so long since I had seen my Nan, and even longer since I had seen her like this—healthy and vibrant. As Nan walked by once more to refill the near empty pitcher, I could no longer contain myself and finally reached out to grab hold of her hand. Nan looked down at me sitting on the chair. I think we both were rather caught up in the moment.

I broke the strange silence. "I'm… I'm…"

"You're what?" Nan asked, with a smile.

I wanted so much to tell her how proud I was to be her great-granddaughter. I wanted to tell Nan how much I loved and missed her. There were a bunch of things I wanted to say, but couldn't muster the words to form a complete sentence.

Nan could see me straining. She set the pitcher down and put her hand gently to my cheek, as she had done so many times before. Her hand was warm and soft, and her touch filled me with such peace. "You look so much like your mom," Nan said to my great surprise.

"You really do know who I am!"

Nan smiled and winked as Paw-Paw drew close. "Well, more or less," he said jovially, with his gravelly voice. "You really do favor her—well, except for your adorable little crooked smile. I think you must-a-got that from Charlie."

Paw-Paw sat down beside me and joked that my uncanny resemblance to my mother *was* a dead giveaway, but that they had been expecting us. I felt that Paw-Paw had insinuated more than he was willing to say but I was satisfied to leave it at that for now. As I thought on this, I couldn't help but feel the tugging of my more curious nature. I wondered what might be appropriate to ask. So, I threw caution to the wind and spoke up, "So have I even been born?"

Nan replied, "As far as we know, your mom isn't even expecting."

"Oh, this is weird," I said, as Nan refilled my lemonade.

Annie leaped up and said, "Weird is an understatement… truly."

Paw-Paw nodded in agreement and said, "You'll get no argument from me there, young lady. Even with everything *I've* seen and experienced, this is pretty out there."

Elizabeth grabbed an empty chair and pulled it up next to mine, as I tried to explain to them exactly why I was there. Even with the liberty to speak candidly about the bizarre nature of how we arrived more than thirteen years in the past, I struggled to put it into words that didn't sound… well, *crazy.* I started by describing how I had come to find the Pyxis in the field.

Paw-Paw stood to his feet and walked out of the room for a moment, retrieving a small hand-made wooden box. He returned and set the box on the table. Opening it, he revealed the Pyxis that was in his possession.

"I found this shortly after I dropped you kids off at the hospital," Paw-Paw said, as I looked even more confused. "You know… the day of Kennedy's assassination."

"So, you have it," I shouted with excitement.

Paw-Paw held up his hand and stopped me. "I know what you're thinkin', young lady" he said. "We can't use this particular one. Temporal mechanics… it just won't work."

"Temporal mechanics." These were words that sounded foreign, even *alien,* coming from the mouth of this elder ranchman, but they were words Paw-Paw seemed all too familiar, even comfortable, with. He sat the wooden box down and wiped his hand across his mustachioed face trying, as he might, to think of something.

Sam swatted at Sean, "It's just like science fiction, dude," he said. Sean, however, seemed none too impressed, as he listened intently to Paw-Paw.

"This Pyxis was lost in 1963," Paw-Paw continued. "Now I don't know the whole story, but I *do* know it was the strange fellow who slammed into Elizabeth in Dealey Plaza. Broke her camera. I remember the six of you were there, too." Gesturing to the Pyxis, he said, "I found that on the floorboard of the pickup later that evening… must have gotten caught on Elizabeth's sweater, or something, and fallen off during the ride home. Anything could have been possible that day. It wasn't long after that it just opened up and swept me off to Kalos. Never in my wildest imagination… Well, the Sentinels showed me how to use it and asked that I keep it from falling back into that fella's hands. I can use it to go back in time, I can go to other worlds, I can even enter other realities and dimensions—and believe me, Elizabeth and I have had our share of adventures over the years. There are two rules, though, that I remember above all others: One, is to never travel forward in time, and the other is to never move a person from one time, planet, reality or dimension to another."

"Wait," said Lily. "By using the Pyxis to move through time, aren't you kind of breaking the rule," she asked.

Paw-Paw gave her a look.

Lily chirped, "Why the stink eye, Mr. Learner? It's a legitimate question. It may be a silly question, but it's *my* question."

He let out hearty chuckle and then said, "I can help you kids, but I can't use the power of this Pyxis here to do it. It could cause a tear in the fabric of time and space, considering that other fella used the Pyxis from his space-time to bring you here. I know that's not the answer you were hoping for, but it is what it is."

"Don't feel bad, Mr. Learner," Annie quipped. "I'm still trying to figure out how all of space and time fit inside that tiny box. If you can explain *that*, I think we'll be good here."

We all shared a laugh, but it didn't last as we all looked around at one another, no one certain of what to say or do next.

I finally broke the silence. "Regardless, I know I'm where I'm supposed to be. Nan…" I said, as I turned to my beloved great-grandmother, "you made sure I would be here—now, at *this* moment. So, I know that whatever we come up with, it'll be enough. It will be what it's supposed to be."

I told them about the photograph of the barn at Peach Creek, the trips to the ice cream shop and the words Nan always told me: "It's important to know the way things were. It may help you find your way to where you're going someday."

"Well…" I said, "I need to be here right now, but I don't know how long we have before Hesiod decides to open the box again."

Paw-Paw said, "I'd say he can't use it for a while, still. Depending on where, when, and so on, the Pyxis has to have time to regenerate its power."

Sean spoke up, "Which should give us plenty of time to come up with a plan and track him down."

"Well," blurted Annie out of the blue. "Mr. Learner's story does settle a question that's been eating at me since Dealy Plaza."

"And what question is that, young lady?"

"I've wondered if we didn't miss an opportunity to grab smelly Hesiod from the hospital and take *him* back to Kalos."

"You're thinking it might have prevented the future events, which brought us to Kalos in the first place," Sean said. "It's a valid idea but misses a few key points. For one, *that* Hesiod didn't even have the Pyxis when we found him unconscious."

Sam looked at Sean oddly. He must have sensed what I had. Something seemed off. He had mentioned it to some of us already, but we just dismissed it as "Sean being Sean."

Of course, Sam seemed off as well. The thought crossed my mind that it might be a little weird for him to be here with Paw-Paw. I guess I didn't take into account just how much.

Paw-Paw had also noticed Sam seemed increasingly uncomfortable, even awkward. Paw-Paw mentioned it to me in passing as we talked, and said he only hoped it wasn't something amiss that would prove detrimental to me completing this quest and getting home. I thought I should put his mind at ease.

"I think he's okay. Time travelling is taking some getting used to for us all."

"I hope you're right," said Paw-Paw with a grin. "Because I have precious little time to figure him out."

It was about then that Paw-Paw recognized the white band with the thin colorful screen on my arm. "That's *Kalosian* tech, isn't it?"

I tapped the delicate, narrow screen and activated the projection. Pushing up my sleeve, I began to attempt to decipher the lights and symbols. "I'm still trying to figure this thing out," I said, with frustration. "Every time I think I've got it..."

Paw-Paw drew closer to me, sliding on his reading glasses and said, "Well, it's fortunate for you that I've had a little experience with this kind of technology." Then he turned to Nan and said, "Honey, could you get me my county map?"

As Nan stood, the phone on the wall rang loudly. She quickly answered it but turned away and spoke quietly, twisting the coiled cord with her hand. Hanging up the phone, she turned to Paw-Paw and said, "Paul, whatever we're going to do, we need to do it quickly."

Paw-Paw could tell by her voice that the phone call had left her anxious. "What's wrong, sweetheart?"

She looked at me, then to Paw-Paw, and said, "Sarah and Charlie are on their way over here." She mustered a nervous smile and then continued, "And they say they have some wonderful *news* to share."

CHAPTER 14: THE FACE-OFF AT WILLOW GAP

NEARLY A FULL hour passed before Paw-Paw appeared in the barn. The anxiety level was building among us; especially Sean, who seemed plenty irritated and concerned that Hesiod would get another chance to bounce. Worry lingered that Hesiod had a dark agenda, which could do irreparable damage to the fabric of time. Sean was fueling much of the speculation. None of us, however, wanted Hesiod to have the opportunity to elude us once more and drag us off to another time or place.

I had tried to pass the time by brushing one of the two horses stabled in the barn, but when Paw-Paw walked in, I quickly sat the brush down and ran over to him.

Paw-Paw looked around before he walked in, to make sure no one was following and spoke in a hushed voice. "Sorry about that. I was trying to hurry them along without being suspicious."

"Is everything okay?" I asked curiously.

Paw-Paw fondly looked down at me and smiled, "It seems Charlie and Sarah are expecting a baby."

My eyes brightened, and I put my hand up to try to cover my smile. I had gotten a glimpse of my parents as they arrived and noticed my mother hiding a slight baby bump under a baby doll top. So, the news came as no real surprise, but still, this experience was surreal, nonetheless. Morgan reached out her hand and put it on my shoulder. "Wait," Morgan said. "You don't think Hesiod's here to…"

My smile faded as the horror of that possibility entered my mind. I looked at Paw-Paw, who could clearly see the grave concern on my face. "Now, step by step, darlin'. He's not going to hurt your mom and dad," he said sternly. "I'm not going to allow it—*we're* not going to allow it."

"Paw-Paw, I *do* think he's trying to change his history somehow."

Paw-Paw took a good look around at all of us, who were each looking to him for direction. Looking back down at me, he said with sure certainty, "…or maybe yours."

You could have heard a pin drop, until the stirring of the horses alerted everyone that Nan was approaching the barn. I could hear the sound of my parent's old VW Beatle putting away. "Okay, they've gone," Nan said, as she entered through the large, opened barn doors. "Do y'all have any idea how hard it is to look convincingly astonished when you already know what the big surprise is," she asked, laughing. "Still, they've been trying for years to have a child." She put her arm around me. "And I can already see what good parents they're going to be."

I could feel the warmth of my cheeks as I blushed, before saying, "And I can tell you, I have the best Nan and Paw-Paw there is."

Nan put her hand over her heart. She looked deeply touched by what I had said. Choking back a tear, she looked at Paw-Paw, who looked as though he too, was moved. It was something I had always wanted to say to them and now I had been given my chance.

Quickly composing himself, Paw-Paw said in his heavy Texas drawl, "Well, we better get a move on."

I wasted no time saddling one of the horses as Paw-Paw prepared the other. Stepping over to check my tack, he gave a gentle tug at the billet strap and nodded his affirmation of my competence in getting the horse ready to go.

"You seem to know what you're doing, young lady," he said to me, as he gave the horse a pat.

"You taught me well," I responded. "You know—you're going to get me a horse one day and teach me to ride."

Paw-Paw gave a throaty chuckle. "*Now* it seems I'll have to make sure and do that."

I hated to ruin the moment, but I couldn't shake the seriousness of something Paw-Paw had said moments ago. I turned soberly to him. "What did you mean about Hesiod changing my history?"

Paw-Paw stepped away, taking my hand, and walked several feet from where we were standing with the horses. We walked toward the hayfield with its tall blades blowing in the wind. Putting his hands in his pockets, he spoke softly to the me as I stood beside him feeling suddenly as though the weight of the world was about to be put upon my shoulders. "I'm getting too old to be bouncing around the universe, traveling through time, satisfying my curiosities. I found out a few minutes ago that I'm about to embark on one of the greatest adventures I could ever have. Elizabeth and I raised a son, and from the tragedy of his loss we were given the joy of raising his daughter. Now it seems, I'm going to get to spoil a great-granddaughter." He paused as he looked off into the horizon. "I know a lot of good men that never got such a privilege."

I immediately thought of the U.S. Navy chest I had discovered in the attic. It was easy for me to forget that Paw-Paw lost friends in the battles of the South Pacific during World War II. It was clear by what he said that he hadn't. I wanted to speak up and say the right thing but couldn't think of adequate words. I was more than a little relieved as he continued. "Now, it's apparent to me that you're pretty special and I truly believe that, while we have personal agency to make our own choices in life, at the end of the day, not even our free will can stop the universe from unfolding as it's supposed to."

He pulled his right hand from his pocket and in it was the small metallic cube that had started this whole trek through time. Paw-Paw drew his arm back and launched the Pyxis far into the hay field. I gasped but was reassured when Paw-Paw put his hand gently on my cheek and said, "I think, right out there, is where *your* adventure begins. If that fella wants to prevent you from finding Pandora's box, then, by God, he's going to have to search every last inch of every acre I've got to do it!" He added a snappy nod with a wink, and I could see a reassuring sternness in his eyes.

Paw-Paw put his arm around me, and we stood staring at the hayfield as Sam came near. Paw-Paw turned to see him approach but Sam quickly looked away and then lowered his gaze down at the ground, noticeably avoiding any prolonged eye contact. "You okay, son? You keep staring at me like you've seen a ghost."

Sam opened his mouth like he was going to speak up. In fact, I think he seriously considered, for just a second, spilling his guts and telling my Paw-Paw everything. But before he did, he looked at me, and every expression on his face was like a cry for my help.

I started to speak up and say something on Sam's behalf. I wanted Paw-Paw to know that Sam thought so very highly of him, but Paw-Paw silenced me. "Wait up, I don't think I want to know. A man shouldn't know *too* much. I've found in life it's best to be mindful of yesterday and make the wisest choices you can today, because *tomorrow* hasn't yet been written."

I giggled at what to me sounded like something from a Texas fortune cookie and asked rhetorically, "What was all that you were just saying about everything happening like it should."

"I know," said Paw-Paw, smiling. "You'll find out, I suspect. That box has a way of confounding everything. Don't get me wrong. I believe in fate. We're all meant for something. But I also believe that our choices have a lot of power. I've experienced things that are beyond explanation. Heck, I've filled journals with details about my encounters of the natural and supernatural..."

I interjected, "Yeah, I've seen them."

Paw-Paw grinned. I think he pondered his words for a moment, looking as though he was carefully considering what he should and shouldn't say to me. "Well, maybe now's not the best time to discuss philosophy."

Sam had turned his attention to checking the saddle on his horse. Paw-Paw watched him for a moment, quietly studying the young man. Turning back to me, he said with a grin, "Better saddle up while I find out if this kid really knows how to ride."

I retrieved my horse and walked away from the two as my great-grandfather began to rapidly fire horsemanship questions at Sam. I could only chuckle, because I had gotten the same quiz at least a hundred times from Paw-Paw as he was teaching *me* to ride. With the horse's bridle in hand I started out toward the others, who were huddled around the old faded red truck and as I got closer, I mounted the horse.

Nan was walking toward me, and I turned my horse to glance back at Paw-Paw and Sam. I could tell they were having a serious conversation, but I couldn't hear what they were saying. I felt Nan's warm, gentle hand reach up and take mine as I held to the horse's reins. I looked down at my great-grandmother's face, which was aglow with shimmers of sunlight. She looked up so lovingly at me, unaffected by the rays of sunshine beating down into her eyes. She said nothing, and yet at that moment, it felt as though we both spoke volumes. The affection we felt for each other was like a deep ocean.

Nan gave my hand a final pat and began to walk toward the house. I watched as she slowly walked away. Out of the corner of my eye, I caught sight of Paw-Paw reaching out to embrace Sam. However, I didn't want to miss this opportunity I'd been given. How many times I wished for this; another day with my Nan. And so, turning back to her as she slowly glided away, I called out, "Nan."

She turned again to look at me atop my horse. Lifting her hand to wave, Nan shouted back with her smooth southern voice, "Y'all go catch your thief, pumpkin."

As Sam mounted his horse and came up alongside me, Paw-Paw moved quickly toward the truck. "Well, you heard the lady. Let's go get him before he decides to skip!"

With that, Morgan gave me a determined nod as she, Lily and Annie jumped into the truck bed. Sean rode shotgun in the cab with Paw-Paw. Starting the engine and rolling down the window, Paw-Paw said to Sam and me, "Remember the plan. No unnecessary risks, I mean it. We flush him out and corner him. He surrenders the Pyxis, and you take him and the box back to the Sentinels." He paused to make sure we understood the plan and then said, "Alright, good luck." With that, Paw-Paw pulled away.

Sam and I carefully turned our horses in the opposite direction. I gave a glance back to Nan, now standing on the porch of the old house. Turning to Sam, I asked, "What did you say to him over there a minute ago?"

Sam sat stoically in his saddle, took a deep breath and said, "Something I've wanted to tell him for a long time." He gave the reins a pop and a with a whistle, signaled his horse into action. I took off immediately behind him giving chase.

The two of us rode past the pond where we had first met, although it looked better maintained than I had remembered it. Taking what Paw-Paw had called the *Piney Trail*, we made excellent time with the shortcut, and after I stopped to check the locator, we looked to be very close to Hesiod's position.

I had ridden ahead, arriving first at the edge of what was known as Willow Gap, a narrow clearing lined with willow trees and thick ground cover. On the other side of the clearing, a densely overgrown wooded area was known to be hazardous, with a barbed wire fence not far inside the perimeter—a leftover from bygone days.

Sam, finally having caught up with me, quickly dismounted. "The horses can catch their breath while we—"

Sam stopped mid-sentence. We could hear the sound of rustling debris. Then, the sudden snap of a twig echoed through Willow Gap. I carefully climbed down from my horse. My eyes were wide as I scanned the clearing. Just then, a deer emerged and crossed a few feet from where we were standing. The young buck sprang quickly through the clearing as we both let out a deep sigh.

"It's just a deer," Sam said, relieved.

He had barely finished speaking when the horses became unsettled. I crouched down low as the sound of something or someone else could be heard.

"It's probably just more deer," Sam said, as the rustling of leaves and snapping of twigs grew louder.

"No," I replied. "That deer was startled out by something else."

Sam crouched beside me as we watched an obscured figure emerge from the wooded area. It was Hesiod, dressed as he had been when we followed him up the mountain in Greece. His dingy, white robe made him easy to spot, as he slowly came out of the shadows and carefully looked to his right and then to his left.

It was apparent that he had not seen us, nor did he notice the horses, as he stumbled toward our post. I could feel my heart pounding. The sound of it almost overwhelmed me. I wondered if Sam could hear it beating. What I didn't realize is that, even if the hammering of my heart was audible, Sam would not have been able to hear it over the thunder of his own thumping heart. The two of us were virtually frozen as Hesiod continued to move clumsily toward us.

While he was still a respectable distance from us, one of the horses snorted, alerting Hesiod. He stopped cold. Startled, he began surveying his surroundings to identify the source of the sound.

Still petrified, I watched as nervous sweat trickled down between my shoulder blades. The tall, dark, well-manicured man was now dirty and bedraggled. He seemed to shiver as he feverishly tried to find where the noise had come from, and then his eye caught the two horses. Then, he saw the two of us crouched down, trying to hide, just feet from where he stood.

I was nearly flattened by a sudden jolt as our eyes met.

Oh crud! He sees me!

I swallowed hard, as I sprang to my feet and sprinted toward him as fast as I could run. Sam's reaction was delayed, and he was behind me—but not for long.

Hesiod spun around and fled in the opposite direction as Sam yelled back to me, "We got him!"

Hesiod stumbled but regained his footing, darting through the clearing.

"Go back and get the horses, I'm on him!" Sam shouted.

"No," I cried. "I'm right behind you. He's not getting away from me this time."

But he *was* getting away.

I was struggling to keep up. Although Sam was moving fast, Hesiod had nearly doubled his lead on us. Then, without warning, Paw-Paw's old red truck slid into the clearing, directly in front of Hesiod, cutting off his hopes of escape. The truck came to a momentary stop before Paw-Paw hit the accelerator and charged straight for him. Frantically, Hesiod turned to duck into the woods. But just then, Morgan, Annie, and Lily burst out form the cover of the trees and brambles and into the clearing.

Hesiod was completely surrounded.

Nowhere to go.

Struggling to catch his breath, Hesiod laughed between gasps. Bent at the waist, he pulled his long black hair away from his face as he spat on the ground in front of him. Turning to me, he smiled with that same charming smile I had seen in the antique shop when I first made his acquaintance. Now, though, it seemed dark and sinister rather than charming. His forehead furrowed, his dark eyes blazed with contempt as they narrowed. "You don't give up easily, do you, my dear," he panted, still laboring to breathe.

Paw-Paw emerged from the cab of his truck with a polished shotgun in hand. I called out and waved for him to back off. One thing was certain, I didn't want a violent resolution. I knew my Paw-Paw well enough to know he wouldn't have hurt the man, but he also wasn't afraid to give a show of force in case Hesiod decided to try something desperate to get away.

Hesiod began to regain his composure and glanced at my great-grandfather before turning his unsettling gaze once more on me. "Paw-Paw? It was with your grandfather all along. How *interesting*."

I took a cautious step toward Hesiod. "You're going back to Kalos, and me and my friends are going home," I said, with unwavering determination.

"You might be surprised to learn I was actually trying to *take* you home when we ended up... *here*," Hesiod asserted. Then to everyone's shock, he said, looking around at all of us, "One of you fell from the narrow pass on the east side of the mountain. Yes, I heard the ledge give way, and the screams."

One by one, we all looked toward Morgan, as Hesiod caught on and addressed her. "Are you okay, young lady?"

Morgan, somewhat disarmed by his unexpected expression of concern, nodded, as Hesiod turned again to me. "I opened the portal in haste, hoping to prevent her from being *injured*."

"She nearly died," I said. "She almost died trying to catch *you*, so we could all go home."

"I know," replied Hesiod. "Let me go. Allow *me* to return home, and I'll take you back to your time. You have my word, I'll never trouble you again."

I fired back, "You know I can't do that. You need to give up the Pyxis. The Sentinels want you returned to Kalos."

"Ah, yes," Hesiod said, with a grin. "The *Kalosians*… such a noble race, wouldn't you agree?"

"You would know better than me," I said. "You're one of them. You don't belong here; not in this time or any other."

Hesiod immediately broke eye contact with me. I don't know whether he was embarrassed that I knew he was from another world, or if it was something else that triggered him, but he looked almost contrite. The defiant look on his face was fading to reveal something softer— broken—as he spoke again. "No, child. I *was* a *Kalosian*, but I'm just as human as you now."

"We know you can mimic us," said Sam sternly.

"No, my outspoken young friend," Hesiod replied. "You saw my wife, my child. I'm a husband, a father, a friend, a philosopher, a poet. I love, I hate… these aren't the stations or acts of a *Kalosian*. I'm no different now than any of you." Hesiod's voice began to crack a little as he spoke. A tear shimmered in his eye, which all seemed to betray the villainous façade to which we had become accustomed. He quickly collected himself and uttered a plea. "I'm asking… no, *begging* you, to allow me to go back to my wife, Isa, and my daughter," he said. "I've been away from them for well over fifty years, stuck in *your* time. Like you, I just want to return home. Surely you wouldn't wish to leave my child without her father."

I couldn't believe my ears. My eyes also shared in the betrayal as my resolve began to wane. Hesiod's words seemed sincere, and I thought of my own mother and the regrets she had growing up without her Dad. It appeared, to me at least, that Hesiod genuinely meant every word. Or was this just an attempt to manipulate us. I looked over at Paw-Paw. He slowly lowered his gun. Hesiod seemed to have struck a chord with us all.

Sean, however, broke the silence as he stepped out and spoke up, "I think we've all heard enough. You need to be returned to Kalos. Surrender the Pyxis!"

Hesiod opened his hand, which had to this point been tightly closed. In it was the box. He looked down at it, sitting snugly in the palm of his hand, as a solitary tear fell from his face and landed on the alien surface of the Pyxis.

"The child will adapt," Sean said flatly.

Hesiod spun toward Sean and looked up from his opened hand, catching Sean firmly in his gaze. Sean's face flushed as Hesiod stared him down.

Tension built as Hesiod, his feet dirty and bleeding, widened his stance. I had no idea what just happened between them, but clearly, the situation had suddenly become volatile, Hesiod's rage unmistakable. I took a step back, as though retreating cautiously from an unpredictable wild animal.

"Hesiod… Sean, let's all take a breath," I said.

He held up his opened hand and shouted, "HER NAME IS… PANDORA!!"

The Pyxis lifted itself from the palm of his hand and came to life. The box opened, and with brilliant light of every color exploding from it in expanding bands, the vortex started to appear, stirring everything around us. The blinding illumination made it impossible for anyone to see clearly what was going on. The fissure had formed, and Hesiod moved quickly into the portal. I cried out. "NO! We can't let him get away!"

Paw-Paw, thrown backward against his truck, called back to me. But just as suddenly as Hesiod had opened Pandora's box, the portal had closed and we were whisked away from Willow Gap almost without warning, with no power to stop it.

CHAPTER 15: INTO THE DARKNESS

I WAS COLD.

Chilled to the bone.

Something didn't seem quite right.

I fumbled through darkness as I called out for the others. One by one, they answered back, giving me at least some reassurance. For the moment, that would have to do.

Lily called out to Annie, asking where she was. "I can't see a thing… I'm scared," she cried.

Annie consoled her younger sister. I could see almost nothing but could tell, by the way the sound of her voice moved as she spoke, that Annie was trying to draw closer to Lily. I slowly reached out my hand and gingerly stepped forward. I took another cautious step and then another. Trying to focus on the muffled sound of voices and the noise of shuffling feet around me, I looked down to see if I could discern the terrain but saw nothing in the thick darkness. I held my hand out once more and realized the density of the darkness made it impossible to see anything more than twelve or fourteen inches away.

Fear began to grip me. I could barely breathe. I was not at all afraid of the dark, but this place had an unsettling vibe. It was more than an absence of light.

I closed my eyes and slowly began to inhale through my nose and exhale through my mouth. I took three long breaths and then said, "Everyone, freeze! Don't move. We have no way to know where we're going. We need to stay together."

My voice, however sounded strange. It seemed deeper and strangely distorted. I took another deep breath, breathing the stale air deeply into my lungs.

Morgan began to call out. Her voice also sounded different, but seemed close as I heard her say, "Look up. I see some kind of tiny lights."

I looked upward and saw what appeared, from a distance, to be small specks of white and rose-colored lights in motion above us, but how far, no one could tell.

"I see them," said Sam with a deep bass tone. "Looks like fireflies."

"Guys, what's going on here?" I asked, noticing my intonation dipping even deeper to a noticeable baritone.

An eerie silence swept over us for a few moments as everyone watched the curious swirl of light above our heads. An almost trance-like state seemed to wash over me as I watched the specks drift through the air. I was so disconnected I didn't even notice that the pattern of the lights changed as they seemed to grow larger.

What I wasn't immediately able to recognize was the feeling of *emptiness* building in me, growing in my heart and mind. It seems strange to think of emptiness growing as though it were a living thing.

But it was.

As it grew, it pushed out fond memories and positive thoughts. It forced out joy and happiness… everything that drives the human spirit to exhibit the best virtues, leaving only a vacuum of apathy and destitution. I was slowly becoming numb inside, without the slightest awareness that it was happening.

Just then, a hand caught hold of my arm, snapping me out of my trance. I let out a scream and jerked away.

"It's me, Hannah… Sean," a deep voice blurted.

My heart raced, my breathing becoming heavy and labored. I clutched my chest and turned toward Sean, who I could now *almost* see. "You scared the heck outta me," I exclaimed. "Dude! Don't *ever* grab me like that again."

"Sorry," said Sean. "I wasn't trying to scare you. You were just off in your own little world. I don't know if you noticed, but I think those lights are moving down toward us."

I looked up and, at last, noticed that they were rapidly closing in and, as they drew near, the area around us was becoming increasingly more visible. I also realized that the longer I stared at the lights, the more captivated I became.

In fact, when Sean again tried to get my attention, I didn't acknowledge him.

I was entranced.

Again.

Finally, he snapped his fingers in front of my eyes. I spun toward him as he asked, "Did you hear anything I just said?"

Clearly, looking at those firefly things was not awesome. They seemed to arrest both my mind and body, leaving me in a daze. And worse, the trance state seemed to leave me feeling vulnerable. Susceptible. But exactly to what, I wasn't altogether sure.

"Guys we need to huddle up. Don't look up at the light," I said.

No response.

"Guys," I called out.

Nothing.

"Annie… Lil?"

Suddenly, I heard Annie yell out, "Marco!"

Sean grumbled, "Marco? I don't understand. This is not a time for one of your games."

"No," I said. "I get it… Polo!"

Again, Annie called, "Marco!"

Lily, Morgan, Sam and I all shouted back, "Polo!"

Within a few seconds, we had all found one another, and with the strange pattern of lights getting closer, we were close enough to see one another. Our surroundings, however, were still a mystery.

"We need to avoid looking at the lights," I said. "They seem to induce some sort of weird hypnotic state."

"Yeah," Lily agreed. "And what's the deal with our voices. I sound like Mr. Learner."

Annie sidled close to her sister, "Lily… *I* am your father," she said in a hushed voice directly into Lily's ear, her vocal tone dipping ever deeper.

Lily gave Annie a playful push as Morgan chimed in. "Inhaling sulfur hexafluoride will make your voice lower, kind of how helium will make it higher."

Sean seemed genuinely surprised. "I'm impressed. How is it you know about sulfur hexafluoride?"

"You know me," Morgan said proudly. "Math is my jam, but science is my bread."

"Beauty *and* brains," Annie sneered.

"So, are you're saying the air is unbreathable?" I asked.

"I don't know about unbreathable, but it sure does stink," said Lily holding her nose. "What is that horrible smell?"

"Yeah. It smells like rotten eggs," Sam added.

"Sulfur," replied Sean. "If the atmosphere was not breathable, we wouldn't be standing here talking about it. Sulfur hexafluoride is odorless though, so that doesn't explain the odor."

"If it is SF6," Morgan said. "We have a problem. It's six times heavier and will displace oxygen, so we couldn't breathe this very long."

"Whatever it is, it's dense, judging by the way the sound of our voices is traveling through it," I said. "I *am* feeling a little lightheaded, so either way, we need to get out of here."

"So, where is *here*?" asked Sam. "Where did Hesiod bring us this time?"

"Something's very different about this," Morgan said.

"A fine deduction, Sherlock," snarled Annie.

"Hey," Lily snapped. "No need to troll on everyone."

"No, seriusly," Morgan continued. "It was like we were being pulled in one direction and then all of the sudden, something got hold of us and pulled us in a whole other direction. I know that sounds weird but…"

"No," said Sean. "I felt it too. It was definitely different than the other times."

All of us agreed that we each felt the same sensation as well, but none of us could agree on what it could possibly mean. We wondered whether something had gone wrong or whether the *Kalosians* had interfered somehow.

I pulled up my sleeve and looked intently at the device on my wrist. I had a difficult time getting it to switch on, and when it finally did, the projection seemed to cut in and out. One second it appeared to suggest that Hesiod was nearby, and then the icon would completely disappear, leaving a blank field. "I've got nothing," I said with frustration. "I can't tell if it's the environment or what."

Sean quickly glanced up at the approaching lights, then turned his face away and said, "It might be whatever those things are above us. They could be interfering with the device in some way."

Sam spoke up, "Try not to look right at them, they're getting really close."

"Are they alive?" Lily asked.

"They sure seem like it," replied Morgan. "They're moving like schools of fish."

"Or flocks of birds," said Annie. "Beautiful."

Sean cleared his throat, indicating that we should all divert our eyes, but it was getting harder to ignore them as they drew ever nearer.

"Any ideas?" I asked, noticing that we could now see the ground below us. "We could try to move away from here but the further we get from them, the darker it will be."

"What *are* they?" asked Lily.

The strange lights were completely alien to us. They seemed to possess bioluminescence and moved through the air with the grace and ease of jellyfish in the ocean. Sam turned to take another look and noticed that they had different shapes and sizes. While some appeared as bubbles, floating delicately through the air, others had the appearance of swirling ribbons, spinning in pairs.

"They look like a double helix—like DNA," Sam said.

Sam was the first to feel it. "The air current around us… it's moving. They're disrupting the air flow around us. I think they're right on top of us."

We all looked up, almost simultaneously. Panic set in, seeing the curious creatures just above our heads, continuing to move in an almost fluid unity. The light they emitted seemed to change color, from brilliant white light to a soft rose, and then purple… It was both beautiful and horrifying.

Because the lights were now so close, the landscape all around us was quite visible, appearing onyx-like, with an almost smooth surface in places but with jagged formations of the same hard stone protruding upward all around us. I couldn't see anywhere we could take shelter. No one else offered up options, either.

A low rumble billowed through, causing the alien flock above us to move with more haste. Sam looked up as one of the bubble shaped creatures wafted slowly toward him, taking a stationary pose in front of his face. I was mesmerized by what I saw.

"It's like it's checking me out," Sam said.

The curious bulb hovered, almost motionless, with nothing but the faintest flutter of its near transparent form. The luminescent glow slowly transitioned through a rainbow of colors, moving along a track of strand-like fibers inside the thin membrane-like outer skin. Sam seemed to believe it was alive and curious about him. "Look," he said excitedly to us. "It's trying to figure out what I am."

Sam slowly lifted his hand and moved toward it. His fingers carefully extended and just as he was about to touch it, Sean shouted, "No, Sam! Don't!"

Sam quickly pulled away, his hand dropping to his side. The jellyfish-firefly began to pulsate. The once gentle flutter became faster, and the color patterns changed at an incredible speed, until it appeared to be something like magma. Truly, it looked like a swirling ball of volcanic lava. The object darted forward and brushed Sam's shoulder, sending Sam to his knees, crying out in pain.

As I rushed to Sam, the creature pulled back and retreated, rejoining the rest of its kind and floated away within the swirl.

"Sam, are you okay?" I cried.

Sam grasped at his shoulder, which appeared to be seriously burned. It was as though he had encountered something super hot or some corrosive chemical.

He writhed in pain.

A sharp clap of thunder sent the glowing orbs darting quickly in swirls, just above us. In something that resembled Van Gough's *Starry Night*, the chaotic swirls flowed endlessly, lighting the dark and barren terrain, where Sam now lay gravely injured.

"It attacked him," Morgan cried, as we all tried to help Sam back to his feet. "Why did it do that?"

"I don't know," I answered, looking at Sam's arm. "It doesn't matter, we need to find a safe place where we can figure out what he needs. He looks badly burned."

"Where's a first aid kit when you really need one?" Annie asked.

"It hurts," Sam cried out.

Sean was busy surveying the area around us. "It looks like there's a place over there where he can at least sit comfortably," he said, pointing the way.

Sean and I helped Sam as we all slowly made our way toward a formation of black stone. As we dragged ourselves across the barren landscape, we tried to keep a close eye on the sea of light above us. I began to fear not only the physical effects of the atmosphere here, but also the strange psychological impact of the glowing orbs—or something else in this wasteland.

Sitting down, Sam was dripping wet, and his skin was pale. "Something's wrong," he said with a weak voice. "I'm so sleepy."

"Stay awake, Sam," I said.

"I just need to close my eyes for a few minutes," Sam said, nodding off.

Sean gently slapped Sam's cheek. "She's right, Sam. You have to stay awake."

We were feeling helpless to do anything, but afraid Sam's condition might be critical or even fatal.

Far from home—far from anything familiar, or even civilized—I held little hope of finding anyone who could help us… who could help us save Sam.

Another massive clap of thunder shot across the sky. Morgan jumped and looked up to notice the alien swarm was swirling around directly overhead. "They're circling, guys," she said fearfully.

"Like vultures," Lily added.

I sprang to my feet. "We have to find a cave, or something. Like, now!"

"We have a serious problem, people," Annie said, motioning upward. "They're coming closer again."

Sean looked down to see that Sam's eyes were closed once again. Tapping Sam's face, he said with a raised voice, "Wake up, Sam."

Sam was not responsive. Sean called to him again, and when Sam didn't respond, Sean grabbed Sam's burned shoulder and jammed his thumb right into the center of the injury. Sam bolted up, screaming out in pain.

"What did you do?" I shouted as Sam's screams echoed all around us.

"Sorry, Sam," Sean said. "You need to get on your feet. We have to move out of here."

Helping Sam to his feet again, Sean asked him if he could walk, but before Sam could respond, my ears popped. Everyone grabbed at their ears as the air pressure changed. It was like we'd been sucked into a vacuum.

Then, I felt weightless and began floating head over heels through space. Like something from a weird dream, I swear that we were drifting across a vast abyss of nothingness. *Are we dead? Have we succumbed to the toxic atmosphere?* I felt sick to my stomach, though, and a painful ringing reverberated in my ears, both suggesting I was still alive. At the moment, I wasn't sure if that was a good thing.

Seconds seemed like hours, but I soon felt baking heat bearing down on me, as I opened my eyes to the blinding light of a sun in the sky above me. I wondered for a moment if it was our sun or some other. The smell of salty air wafted on the breeze, and I quickly realized I was lying on the ground, with my friends scattered around me.

Sam!

Springing to my feet, I made my way to him as the others began to sit up and get their bearings. Sam lay flat on his back next to a patch of tall grass, which danced in the gentle breeze. He was motionless as I drew near, with Sean and Morgan following close behind.

"Sam," I called out, standing over him.

Annie helped Lily to her feet, and the two ran over to where we were gathered. Annie fell to her knees next to Sam. "There's no burn! His hoodie isn't charred or anything!" Sure enough, his shoulder bore no evidence of the severe burn he'd sustained just minutes earlier.

"Then why isn't he responding?" cried Lily.

Morgan clung to me as Sean paced back and forth. Then reaching out to Sam, Annie gave him a violent shake. "Time to wake up, buttercup. Rise and shine, sleepyhead."

Sam opened his eyes and, with a hint of ire, looked up at Annie, who smiled with relief and leaped up, before reaching down to pull Sam to his feet. Sam's face was expressionless as Annie threw her arms around him and hugged him tightly for just a moment before catching herself and pushing him away, covering her embarrassment with classic Annie sass. "Don't get any ideas. I'm just glad we didn't have to carry you."

We all broke into laughter. Even Sean, who was being uncharacteristically pensive, let out a hearty howl. I almost felt bad for Annie. To her chagrin, Lily now had something to hold over her big sister's head for a very long time, and I could tell she knew it.

We were glad—relieved—to be away from that desolate place and still in one piece.

Sam seemed awkwardly reserved when Morgan reached out to tenderly touch his shoulder. He looked nervous but managed to muster a smile. Morgan looked into his eyes, and I could see from his expression that Sam was trying to read her actions. "I'm okay," he blurted.

Morgan snatched him into a hug. He returned the embrace while rolling his eyes at the absurdity of what he'd just said. I was quietly entertained that Sam couldn't manage the courage to say anything meaningful or to express his feelings, but knowing Morgan, she didn't care. At that moment, what he said was enough, and, I'm sure, it was just what she needed to hear. She let go, stepped back and said tenderly, "I'm so relieved."

A smile emerged on Sam's face, and he stepped closer to her with a little swagger. Just then, Morgan punched him in the arm that had just been wounded and said, "Don't scare us all like that again."

Sure enough, the severe burn that had reduced Sam's shoulder to something akin to charred hamburger appeared to be gone. He was in no pain, and other than a traumatic memory, Sam seemed to be perfectly fine, urging us to spring into action and get back to the business of tracking down Hesiod.

However, at that moment, I feared for Sam. He later told me that he felt bad that his curiosity and adventurous nature could have endangered us—and cost *him* his life. It was an inner conflict that I believe would haunt him for a long time to come.

And while I was relieved to have escaped that dark place, deep down, I knew the darkness had not escaped me. Two close calls had nearly claimed the lives of my friends. I began to wonder if this was a fool's errand, doomed to fail. I started to question whether we would ever make it home. Catching a time-traveling thief was one thing, but finding this *Guardian* was going to be another problem entirely. If he *did* exist, I feared, it would be like trying to find a needle in a haystack. It was all becoming overwhelming to me, and a growing feeling of hopelessness was tightening its grip.

CHAPTER 16: THE FAMILIAR ROAD

HESIOD HAD INDEED managed to increase the distance from our weary group, but to my relief, the locator at least seemed to be working correctly now and assured us he had not gotten too far. The muted hues of green and tan seemed familiar as we surveyed our surroundings. More familiar still was the rolling mountain that crowned the valley trail we walked.

"I'd give just about anything for a field of bluebonnets and a bottle of Cherry Dr Pepper right about now," Annie said, as we trekked along the stony way.

"Well, at least we know where we're at this time," Lily replied.

"Still, the Dr Pepper *does* sound good," added Sam.

Taking in the sight of the quarry stone buildings with baked-clay roofs surrounding the *acropolis*, we were sure that we had returned to Hesiod's village in ancient Greece. I was quick to remind the others that Hesiod would have the advantage, because he knew the lay of the land and could easily blend in. We found a secluded area in the market where I could carefully study my locator with hopes of pinpointing his position and tracking him, knowing he had to be somewhere nearby.

As I worked to locate Hesiod, Lily spotted a familiar face in the crowd. It was Isadora, Hesiod's wife, just as we had seen her before. She held her child, Dora, in one arm and her basket in the other, working her way through the crowded *agora*. Lily pointed her out right away and leaped up to go catcher her. "She might help us."

Sean caught her by the hand. "No, don't, Lily," he said, pulling her back. "That wouldn't be smart. We could have traveled back to a time before she met us. If not, she knows we're trying to apprehend Hesiod and may not be willing to help—or worse, might help him evade us."

Lily tried to pull away, but Sean had a tight grip on her hand. She winced as Sam stepped in and took Sean by the arm. "Let her go, amigo!"

Sean shrugged away and cast a sharp indignant look toward Sam, who was growing increasingly irritated with Sean and his arrogant attitude. "What's with you, Sean?"

Lily rubbed her hand and said, "Yeah, you've been acting weirder than usual."

Annie blasted, "He's not the center of attention, so he's going to boss everyone around." Then turning to Sean, she said, "If you hadn't blown off at the mouth to Hesiod back there at the gap, we might have talked him down and made it home by now."

"Stop it," I shouted, drawing their attention. "You guys are arguing while Hesiod is getting further away."

Morgan came near to console me, leaning in and whispering, "You have to admit, he did seem to get under Hesiod's skin back there at Willow Gap."

I didn't immediately acknowledge Morgan's observation. While Lily kept an eye on Isadora, I continued to consult the locator. Glancing up, I finally said to Morgan, "It wasn't what he said so much as how he said it. It seemed so... cold—even for Sean." I took another gander at the projection coming from the device and continued. "It struck a nerve, but what I can't figure out, is why. It seemed personal." I gave Morgan another look. "Still, it doesn't give any of us a license to point fingers and bicker about who's fault any of this is."

"Yeah," said Morgan. "I get that. Although, I'd like to pop him, for dragging all of us into this mess."

Something about hearing her suggest Sean had dragged us into this stung. Sure, he didn't exactly help matters much back at Willow Gap. At the moment, I felt like there was only one person to point the finger at for getting us into this up to our necks. "I'm the one who dragged us into this crazy situation."

"It's not your fault. We all agreed to go after him together."

I looked at Morgan's reassuring expression and said, "I couldn't have gotten this far without you."

Checking the locator once more, I pointed east. "OK, guys... this is it. I think he's heading in that direction. He's heading home."

We moved quickly into the throng, carefully scanning the faces of every man in the bustling square.

"We should split up and flush him out," Sean said.

I sighed and turned around to Sean, directly behind me. "Why does everyone keep saying split up... split up," I growled with frustration as the others circled around.

"That's what they always do in the movies," Sam answered.

"That may be... but this isn't a movie. If we split up, he could still give us the slip. One of us could easily get lost—or worse. Besides that, if one of us did catch him, he would have no problem overpowering any one of us," I warned. "We're stronger if we stick together. *Together*, he doesn't stand a chance against us."

"Together it is," Morgan declared, as we tightened up our ranks.

"Eyes in every direction," I said. "He's close. I can feel it."

We worked our way through the horde, each of us looking in a different direction, hoping to catch sight of the cunning thief.

Suddenly, I caught him in my sights. I locked my eyes on him as he meandered around, presumably looking for Isadora. I tapped Lily and Morgan, to my sides. They turned to see Hesiod less than a hundred feet away, talking to one of the merchants. All six of us had eyes on him now, and we moved quickly to corner him. As we drew closer, a tall, muscular man collided with Sean, who fell to the ground. The man stood over him and shouted, telling him to watch where he was going. Sean got up quickly, but it was too late.

The commotion caught everyone's attention, and Hesiod looked up from his conversation to see what was happening and saw me, now running straight for him with Morgan, Annie, Lily, Sam, and Sean right behind me.

Hesiod shot out into the crowd, at first toward us, but then he darted left, overturning a cart of vegetables to slow us down.

I cut to the right, followed by the others. Sam leaped over the mess, as Sean cut to the left. "Stay on him," I shouted.

Hesiod ducked in between two merchant canopies and lowered his head, hoping to give me the slip. He quickly realized, however, that his attempt was futile and burst out into the crowded *agora* once more, trying to elude our pursuit. A livestock merchant was moving some goats, and Hesiod got ahead of him, putting the nervous flock between us. As I gave chase, the goats scattered, causing an even greater disturbance in the square. In the confusion, Hesiod gave us the slip.

Gone. Again.

I. Was. Furious.

I threw my hands on top of my head. I couldn't believe he had led us on a wild goose chase through the crowded market and managed to dodge us yet again. I pulled the others aside to a secluded nook and once more consulted the locator, hoping to pick up the chase.

Everyone was panting, hot, sweaty, and thirsty. Sean was preoccupied, however, trying to get a good look at the projection the *Kalosian* device had cast on my arm. With labored breath, he asked, "Well, did he flee the market?"

"Yes... yes, he did," I answered between gasps. "But I know *exactly* where he'll end up—eventually."

"Then that's where we need to go," Sam growled.

Once we had all sufficiently rested, we turned back toward the square. As we pushed our way through the turmoil left in the wake of the chase, a hand reached out and grabbed me.

I spun around to see the grave face of the woman I had befriended during our last visit to the Greek *agora*. "Isadora…" I said, alarmed.

The basket Isadora once held was now being trampled under the feet of passers-by, who had returned to whatever business had brought them to the square. She held tightly to my arm, her baby cradled snugly against her chest. "What is your business with Hesiod?" Isadora asked, suspiciously.

I could tell from her tone that Isadora's trust in me had all but eroded. But my priority was catching up with Hesiod before he could use the Pyxis and make another break for who knows where. "Isadora, I can explain, but I need you to take me back to your home."

"He did not come back last night. I don't know where he has gone or why he is running from you." Isadora gave her baby a gentle rock, then shot me a wary look. "Perhaps you and your friends are trouble… Come down from Helicon bringing evil and mischief with you."

She looked deep into my eyes, and her suspicious glare softened. It was as though she was looking for something. Something deep. Strangely, it started to feel as though we had known and trusted one another our entire lives. I couldn't explain it, but the feeling was profound. Isadora's tone changed, as she let loose of me and said, "I'm sorry, Hannah. That wasn't fair of me to say."

"It's okay," I said. "You're worried about your husband. I kind of understand."

"Like most of us, he has his secrets, but this one… this one is driving him from me, and I fear I will lose him forever."

The baby opened her eyes and began to cry. Isadora gave the baby a gentle bounce to comfort her. "There now, Pandora," she said, as the child whimpered.

"This must be a piece to the puzzle," I thought. In my continuously spinning mind, I was beginning to bring some order to all the random events and coincidences surrounding Hesiod and the Pyxis.

You see, Pandora's box, as Hesiod had written the story in ancient literature, was a story about a container forged by the gods and filled with evil, before it was given to a girl who opened it and released all its evil into the world. "Could it be," I murmured, "that the story is a metaphor for a truth, and it was Hesiod's intent to pass the box on to the child one day. Could she be the Guardian?" I couldn't quite put all the pieces together for this idea, and while I felt I was getting close, I doubted my own intuitions. Still, I was determined to put it all together. "So, Dora… her name is Pandora?"

"Yes, it was my husband's idea… a character in one of his stories."

Morgan had begun to console the crying baby and had offered to hold her. Isadora was reluctant, but I assured her that we meant no harm and were as interested in finding Hesiod as she was. Despite her misgivings, I sensed Isadora wanted to trust us. And so, after a minute or two with Morgan, Annie, and Lily doting on her, the baby's cries subsided, while I set about to try to convince Isadora to help us.

"He's in trouble, Isadora, and we have to find him," I told her. "We've come a very long way, and we can't return home until we do. Please, believe me. I only want to locate him, so we can get back home to our own land and return a small box he's taken. It's priceless and very dangerous." I took her by the hand, trying to reassure her. "I can't help him unless you help me."

"You mean the small silver rune he keeps in the jar at home," Isadora said. "I've seen it. He takes it with him whenever he goes to the mountain. I think it must conjure the power of the gods or ward off the evil that is up there."

Morgan was busy bouncing the baby but stopped cold. "Did she say mountain? Please, let's not hike back up there again."

"After the scene here a minute ago, I think he might go and try to lay low at home," I said. "How about it, Isadora? Will you help me?"

Isadora said nothing at first but then quietly set off in the direction of her house as we followed. While we walked, Morgan carried Pandora, staying close to Isadora, with Annie close by. Sean had fallen back a short way, clearly distancing himself from the rest of us. I sidled up to Lily and Sam, who kept looking back to make sure Sean was still following.

The three of us talked quietly about what had taken place at Willow Gap. While I was still oddly convinced of Hesiod's sincerity during our encounter, Sam and Lily were both unsure. One thing we all seemed to agree on was that Sean had somehow set Hesiod off, but none of us was certain what it was that triggered his sudden change in demeanor. Sam said he thought Sean made it personal when he mentioned Hesiod's daughter and Lily agreed, pointing out the way Hesiod was staring Sean down, before he opened the box and activated the portal.

"I realize I don't know Sean that well," Sam said. "But he seems more uptight than he was when we first met. Then again, I suppose we're all a little on edge, given this whole situation."

Lily added, "Yeah, our whole world's been turned upside down for sure. But still, I've known Sean Evans my entire life, and I've never seen him act so weird… and that's truly saying something for Sean."

I couldn't help but snicker. "Are you saying Sean is just naturally weird?" I joked.

Lily didn't miss a beat and said with a straight face, "Yes, yes I did."

Lily and I shared a refreshing giggle; something our circumstances had given precious little time for, and the feeling was like a misting of cool water on a hot day. But I, all too quickly, returned to the moment and the task at hand. "We just have to get our hands on the Pyxis, so *everything* can get back to normal… if that's even possible."

"So, what's the plan when we get to the house?" Sam asked.

"I think you guys know what we have to do," I said. "Any ideas?"

Lily turned her attention solely on Isadora, who was walking briskly, several feet in front of us. She lowered her voice, to ensure she could not be overheard. "I know

I was the one who wanted to go to her in the market, but are we sure we can trust her? I mean, how do we know she isn't going to help him escape again?"

I thoughtfully considered her concern. Lily wasn't usually the suspicious type, and I knew it was a fair question, but I was growing more uncertain of my own pre-conceived ideas regarding Hesiod and his motives. I had assumed he was simply a fraud and a thief, who would stop at nothing to have the power of the Pyxis for himself. I was sure he had some dark agenda to change events in time. To what end, I wasn't sure.

Still, I couldn't shake what he had said to me when we cornered him at Willow Gap. I wondered if he was sincere about taking us back home, and there was also the question of Morgan and the timing of the bounce that, for all intents and purposes, had saved her life. All these thoughts swirled around in my mind, along with the many questions I still had.

Finally, I drew in a deep breath as I continued walking while Lily awaited an answer. "I don't know, Lil. I don't know. I am starting to think there's more going on here than what we're aware of."

The road narrowed, and everyone knew we were close to the house. Isadora stopped. She took Pandora from Morgan and turned to me. A noticeable tension knifed through our ranks. Isadora was choking back tears as she held tightly to her child. "Hesiodos…" she began. She paused thoughtfully, before continuing. "Hesiod is a good man. He is a good father. I told you he has secrets… He's tormented by something. Spirits from the mountain… the magic in that box. Something I do not know. I will help you because I believe *you* can help *him*. If you cannot, or will not, please go. Leave here now. I will not betray my husband if your intent is not to help us, as you say."

I put my hand reassuringly on Isadora's arm, but said nothing.

"Then what I do now, I do to save him, or I will not do it all," Isadora said.

I was moved by the sincerity of her words. It was evident to me that Isadora loved Hesiod deeply. I nodded intently to Isadora, who nodded back, then turned and walked into the courtyard of the home. Whatever suspicions that may have existed between us were gone, and that single non-verbal gesture forged a profound understanding and agreement between us I was determined not to betray.

Isadora walked straight ahead, past the well, as we all fanned out slightly. Sean had moved in much closer to the rest of us and approached me. Grabbing my shoulder, he spun me around to face him. I felt like I was looking into the face of a stranger.

My friend—my cocky, theater-loving co-op buddy— had seemed increasingly irritable and distant since we were first pulled into the time portal, and the Sean I was face-to-face with seemed little more than a shadow of the boy I knew.

He loosened his grip on my shoulder and noticeably relaxed, rolling his eyes as he spoke. "I know I've not been myself," he said. "This is all a little much... even for me. I'm sorry. I just want Hesiod and the Pyxis back where they belong. That's the mission we were given by the Sentinels."

"Listen, Sean…" I quietly interjected.

"No, Hannah," Sean said, cutting me off. "You need to think this through. Our mission is to return Hesiod, and the Pyxis, to Kalos."

"You're so wrong, Sean," I argued. "Sosthenes didn't say anything about what to do with Hesiod. He wants the Pyxis and this Guardian… and *I* want to get *us* home. That's all that matters."

Sean stood for a moment, sulking, tugging nervously at his ear. I turned, frustrated and walked toward Isadora. Sean growled, muttering something under his breath, and then caught up with the rest of us as we took positions near each entry to the house.

Isadora paused as she approached the main entry, with me directly behind her. She looked back as I placed my hand on her shoulder, reassuring her, and then she entered the home alone.

"Isa," yelled Hesiod. "Isa, my bride. We need to talk about what has happened. I want to explain…"

I stepped through the door. Hesiod fixed his dark eyes on me. They widened, then closed, as he covered his face before running his hands back across his head. I could see the consternation as he tried to consider his options. The settling reality that he had come to the end of it, with his bride and child present to witness the shame of his capture, was written on his expression. It was difficult to watch, as his shoulders sunk, accepting his defeat.

Isadora, still holding Dora in her arms, stared at her husband for a moment and then said only, "Hesiod, please…"

I moved closer to the man but stopped when Hesiod instinctively took a step backward and assumed a defensive posture. I wrung my hands, which were soaking wet with sweat. Heart racing, I found the courage to reach my hand to him and say, "I just want the Pyxis, Hesiod. Give it to me, so I can return it to the *Kalosians* and go home."

Hesiod stood motionless. Only his eyes moved, as the sound of the others converging on the room gained his attention; first Morgan, Annie, and Lily, followed by Sean and Sam. Hesiod was cornered, and with a relatively short amount of time passing since he last opened the portal, he was literally left with nowhere to run. He knew to try and flee again would be futile. Holding his hands up to indicate his surrender, he gazed at me and, smiling, said, "You are nothing if not persistent, Miss Goodheart."

I took a deep breath before responding. "One of my better qualities."

"Yes," said Hesiod. "You *are* more than meets the eye—much like some of your friends here, I suspect." Looking down, he noticed the band on my left wrist and quickly took hold of my hand. "Clever," he said. "Very clever. I see now how it is you have been so hard to evade."

I reached out with my other hand and grabbed his wrist, fearing he would try to take the tethering device from me. He noticed the fading bruise on my wrist and looked embarrassed.

"I'm sorry," he said sheepishly. "You have no reason to believe me, but I never meant you or your friends any harm."

Isadora handed the child to Lily, who was standing close by. "Hesiod," she said. "What is this about? You've taken something. The little box from your story. Give it back and let them be on their way."

"You don't understand, Isa," Hesiod said, reaching for his wife. "I've missed you so much. It was all to get back here to you. It's been so long, and all those years all I could think about was coming home to you and our daughter. This you must believe."

Isadora embraced her husband and said, "But my love, you've only been gone for two days."

Dora stirred and began to cry. Isa instinctively took the child into her arms. "She's getting hungry."

I smiled reassuringly and said, "If you want to feed her, I think everything here is under control."

Isadora looked over at Hesiod, who nodded tenderly, telling her that he would explain everything when she returned. She took the child and left the room, leaving Hesiod alone with the six of us.

"I will return you to your home, but I cannot permit you to take me away from *mine*," Hesiod said in a hushed voice.

Sean spoke up, "This is not your home. You're *Kalosian*."

Not wanting a repeat of what had happened at Willow Gap, I quickly shut Sean down, as Sam shot him a look. A clear warning to keep quiet.

"So, let me see if I have this right," I said to Hesiod. "You came here with the Pyxis, as an envoy of the Sentinels, to find the Guardian. You fell in love with Isadora, married and had a child. You continued to bounce through time, using the portal, until you got stuck in Dallas, circa 1963, lost the Pyxis and spent the next fifty or so years trying to find it, so you could return here to ancient Greece. Did I miss anything?"

Hesiod smiled wildly and clapped his hands, "Not bad, Miss Goodheart. Not bad, indeed. Somewhat over simplified, but reasonably accurate. Now you understand why I can't allow you to take me away from here."

"Why go from here, where you wished to stay, and bounce to somewhere like Dallas," asked Sean. "Why November 22, 1963? What was your purpose?"

Hesiod started to seem agitated as he side-eyed Sean. "Wherever there are light bearers, the Darkness will be near, waiting for an opportunity to strike back against those who threatens its dominion."

Sean's shoulders fell as a fearful look washed over him.

"You... you didn't have anything to do with the Kennedy assassination, did you?" asked Sam, as he tried to reason what Hesiod meant by his answer.

"Of course not," replied Hesiod emphatically. "I was in pursuit of something dark and destructive, something your young *Terran* minds could not begin to comprehend; A threat to this world and every other. I was determined to stop it, but I failed, and the punishment for my failure was more than 50 years of exile, searching. The 60s were difficult enough, but I had to endure the horror of bell bottoms and mullets, and don't get me started on the millennium. Your world would do well to learn from its mistakes."

"What about the other envoy? What about Theseus?" I asked.

Hesiod took a step back and rested his back against the wall, "Theseus..." he said, as he slid down the wall and sat. He put his face in his hands as his expression fell. Looking up at me he said, with great regret, "Theseus sits in the Bowel of Hades. I put him there."

CHAPTER 17: THE BOWEL OF HADES

MY HEART SANK. I had just grown accustomed to the idea that Hesiod was not necessarily what he seemed to be, at least on the surface. I was beginning to see glimpses of a more *human* side to the time-traveling thief. Now, I shuddered at the thought that he could be guilty of murdering his fellow envoy, Theseus. "Could he actually be the villain that everyone was painting him to be; what my preconceptions pegged him to be? Worse?" I questioned quietly.

It just didn't seem to add up. According to what he had said at Willow Gap, Hesiod acted to prevent Morgan's death when she fell from the narrow pass on Mount Helicon. He seemed genuinely sorry for bruising my wrist. He had finally convinced me that he was a committed husband and father; even Isadora contended that he was "a good man." Little by little I was getting a very different picture of him than what I saw in my first black-and-white assessment. In fact, I'm discovering how difficult it can be to judge someone once you peel away what's on the surface and take a deeper look. So, the moment he uttered the words, "Theseus sits in the Bowel of Hades" and admitted to putting him there, I started to question every intuition I had about the man now sitting on the floor before me.

Sean drew near to Hesiod as the man sat chewing on his regret. "So, Theseus is dead?"

Hesiod looked up at the freckled face of Sean, who stood over him. "No," he replied. "You should know… *Kalosians* do not *easily* perish. Ours is a resilient race. No, I'm reasonably certain he's very much alive."

Annie threw Lily a look, a raised eyebrow signaling her confusion. In fact, I think all of us were thoroughly confused at this point, until Isadora stepped back into the room. "The Bowel of Hades… it's a cave on the mountain," she said abruptly, pointing off in the direction of Mount Helicon. "Strangers passed through the *agora* a few years ago, saying they heard voices—tormented voices, coming from inside the mountain."

Hesiod added, "A cave was discovered there many, many years ago." He perked up a little as he continued. The flair and excitement of the master storyteller peeked through the surface of the broken man as he added a bit of dramatic motion to his tale. "But now, no one will go near that place for fear that *Hades himself* will drag them down to the belly of Hell."

"That is, no one, but you," Sam said, glaring at Hesiod.

"Is that right, Hesiod?" I asked. "You created a lore around the mountain to keep anyone from finding the other envoy. You hid the whole truth, so you could stay here with your wife."

"Please do not involve her in this," Hesiod said, pleading with me. "She... she doesn't know..."

"Hesiod," said Isadora "I know... I *know*. Somehow, I've always known. You came here with Theseus and told me you were from a distant village. The things you know, the stories you tell; and then you said Theseus wanted to return to your country."

"Yes, yes," said Hesiod. "It's true, all of it. He insisted we leave and continue our journey, but I couldn't bring myself to leave you." Emotions ran high as he spoke and I, once more, held no question of the sincerity behind his words. It seemed he was drawing most of us in as he continued. "We traveled up the mountain together, to ensure we would not be seen as we were leaving. Theseus fell into the cave. It was a straight drop, and at first, I did fear him dead. When I realized he was alive, I thought to try and rescue him, or perhaps even use the Pyxis. I could prevent him from ever falling into the cave. Then..." Hesiod began to scribble with his finger on the dusty ground as he continued. "Then I knew. This was my opportunity."

"Your pilgrimages to Helicon... the box. It's a magic box, just as in your story, and not of this world." said Isadora suddenly, as her understanding began to unfold.

"I would go every few days. I take Theseus food. I've been able to provide him everything he has need of. I drop it down the entrance and usually leave."

No one knew quite what to say, nor did any of us try. It was evident as he sat drawing swirls on the floor that

Hesiod felt the absurdity of what he had done, and the guilt seemed overwhelming. He put his hands in his lap and stared at the dirt floor as tears began falling from his face to the ground, creating a small, muddy pool.

Hesiod rose to his feet, turning away to cover his shame. Isadora reached for her husband and, taking his head into her hands, said, "Hesiod, my love, I don't care from where you have come or what magic you possess. I know the man you are. We have to make this right. We have to fix this."

Retrieving a stone jar from the corner, Hesiod took Isadora's hand, palm up, and placed the small pot there. She removed the lid and turned the vessel over into Hesiod's open hand. The Pyxis fell from the container, and Hesiod held the small box once more. "With this," he said to her, "I can travel to places beyond your imagination. It brought me to you, Isa. And though I could go anywhere in the universe, I have always come back here to you."

Isadora stared at the metallic object for a moment and then turned, walking gracefully across the room to face me. "Help my husband return Theseus from the cave, and you have my word the box is yours," she said with sincerity. Then she furrowed her brow and asked, "Will you then leave here and allow my husband to stay?"

I looked up into her soft brown eyes and then turned to Hesiod, who was returning the jar to its spot in the corner of the room. "Do you have any rope?" I asked.

Morgan immediately sprang forward. "You're not thinking of going back up on that mountain?" she asked, in horror.

I turned to the others, none showing any enthusiasm for the plan they all knew I was about to propose. Sean stepped in front of me. "Take the Pyxis, Hannah," he said pointing to the stone jar nestled in the corner. "Let's take *it* and Hesiod back to the Sentinels and let *them* decide how to resolve this."

Frustrated and ready to blow, I side-stepped him and nudged him away, "Sean, we've been friends a long time, and this may mean the end of that friendship… but I've had just about enough of your attitude. Before we do *anything*, we're going up there and get Theseus out of that cave. If you have a problem with that, you can stay here." Then turning to Hesiod, I said, "I need enough rope to get down into the cave, and *your* help to lower me down. It's going to take all of us working together."

With a resigned nod, Hesiod pledged his help, giving Sean a peculiar smile as he led us out of his home.

It had taken a few hours to walk back to the market, buy the rope and then trek to the base of the mountain. Hesiod had complained that an extra few hours' walk to the nearby sea ports would have saved him a few drachmas on the purchase, but his groanings fell on deaf ears. Nearly everyone agreed that the sooner we could get to Theseus, the sooner we could get home.

Everyone, that is except Sean, who continued asking me to reconsider the plan and return Hesiod and the Pyxis to Kalos. When that didn't go over well, he tried to stir dissent among the others. Even Morgan, though petrified at the thought of going back up the mountain, defended my idea to rescue Theseus from the cave. It wouldn't be right to leave Theseus sitting there another moment, in peril, all alone.

Isadora had stayed behind with her child, secure in my promise that Hesiod would be home to eat his evening meal.

As we walked, Hesiod talked at length about the Pyxis and told us of the many time periods and interesting places he'd visited. His stories were colorful, even entertaining, but I felt he was holding something back. I had nothing to base my hunch on, but it just seemed he was careful about what he shared with us.

We stopped at the base of the mountain to rest briefly. Hesiod poured some water on his feet, washing away dirt and blood. Tearing a piece of cloth from his garment, he wiped them clean. Annie watched, but knowing her, she felt little pity after he'd dragged us across time and space. I've often noticed she can be a little salty that way. Sure enough, scoffing, she said, "Looks painful, dude."

Hesiod humbly nodded. "What I wouldn't give for a pair of quarter brogue oxfords. I'll have to get used to traipsing around in sandals once more."

Annie was a little disarmed by his candor, and they chuckled. Hesiod stood and announced that we were going to ascend the mountain from the *western* side rather than take the eastern trail. "The cave is not far and it's a much easier path."

"So, no death drops?" Morgan asked anxiously.

Hesiod reassured us, to Morgan's relief, that this was not only a much safer route to the cave, but much shorter as well. As promised, it was not long after beginning our ascent until we arrived at our destination.

The mouth of the cave was little more than an opening in the rocky ground below our feet. Brushy growth obscured the orifice, and it was easy for me to see how someone could stumble and fall in.

Sam lay down on his belly, at the opening, and holding tightly to a protruding rock, he lowered his head inside. "It's too dark to see," he said, his voice echoing off the cave walls below. I was thinking "flashlight" and trying to figure out how we could get a better look inside. Morgan perked up, suddenly remembering that her cell phone was tucked securely in her pocket. Pulling it out and checking, she announced, "Hey, I'm at forty percent! No signal, but my flashlight app might still work."

"Mine's dead."

"Mine, too."

"Yep, so's mine—and why didn't you think of that when we were blindly poking around that *dark* place with the psycho light balls?" asked Lily.

"I don't have one," Sam said, looking a little embarrassed.

"Sean?" I asked, knowing his parents got him a new one for his birthday.

"I do not," he said, to my surprise.

Hesiod's head had snapped at Lily's comment. "*Dark* place?"

"Yeah," I asked. "What *was* that place anyway?"

"Oooh, was it some kind of galactic hideaway?" Lily asked through a playful squint.

Hesiod didn't look amused as trepidation bolted across his face, leaving us all feeling uneasy. But he quickly collected himself and turned back to the opening of the cave. "I'm uncertain. It's most likely no place of concern," he said, trying to dismiss the question. "Quickly… let us not waste daylight."

Snagging Morgan's phone, Lily hit the icon on the screen, activating the bright light. "Yep, it works," she said, as she handed it down to Sam.

Moving the light around, Sam grunted as he strained to survey the cave. Jumping up, he said, "So cool! It's almost a straight drop though… about twenty feet, or so." Then looking at me, he asked, "You sure you want to do this?"

I reasoned that Lily, or even Morgan, were probably the lightest of the group. I'm not always comfortable in my own skin and, at times like these, I'm painfully reminded that while I'm a little tall for my age, I also think I'm a bit overweight. While Morgan has a solid athletic build, Lily is fairly average and lean. Annie is the oldest by a few months over Morgan and was physically the most mature of the four of us. It's hard for me sometimes, not to compare myself to my friends or even models on magazine covers and television. But this wasn't the time or place, I thought, to beat myself up about how I'm built or what I see in the mirror.

Whatever angst I had about my body, I accepted this task as being *my* responsibility. I knew that *I* needed to be the one to go down into the cave. It was, after all, my idea. Sean argued that this was Hesiod's mess to fix, but Sam reminded Sean that it was going to take Hesiod's strength, along with everyone else on the surface, to anchor the rope and pull Theseus up and out of the cave.

While they were debating the plan, Hesiod stood over the cave opening, cupping his hands around his mouth and shouting down into the cave, "Theseus!"

He paused and listened for a response.

"Theseus, my friend."

Still, no reply.

Hesiod looked anxious.

"Answer my old friend," he whispered, with uncertainty.

Annie wiped the sweat from her forehead and asked, "You don't think … you know …"

"Dead?" asked Hesiod. "Doubtful, but there's no way to be certain. I was hoping he would answer, and we could just throw the rope to him, and then *no one* need go down into the cave."

I didn't waste another minute. I grabbed the rope, and with Sam's help, began to tie it about my waist. Lily, Annie, and I had plenty of camping experience and were comparing notes on the best knots. We debated for a couple minutes about the best one to use and decided on a simple clove hitch.

"I think our troop leader would approve," Lily said as she cinched the knot tighter.

"Yeah," said Annie. "Maybe we can get community service hours credit after all this is over."

I couldn't help but smile at Lily and Annie's banter. Those two could always find something to laugh about, no matter the situation. "That would be fine by me," I said, checking the knot one last time. "Do you think they offer a time traveling alien rescue badge?"

Laughter erupted from our huddle. The others looked over curiously at us as bit by bit, they began to distribute the long line. Hesiod secured the other end to a lonely tree that stood, resolute, nearby. As Sam handed Morgan's cell phone to me, Hesiod told me, based on old legends, he was certain the cave had only one passage that would lead back into a large cathedral room, on the other side of a natural spring. Once more, I could see a sincere concern in Hesiod's eyes.

Standing on the precipice, I took a moment to look into the faces of my friends, who all had expressions of fear and dread. Mustering every ounce of courage in me, I took a deep breath and carefully stepped into nothingness.

Hesiod slowly lowered the rope as Sam, Sean, Morgan, Annie and Lily anchored it. I held tightly as I dropped in short bursts down into the chasm. My descent came to a brief pause as I activated the flashlight on Morgan's phone and tried to look around. "That's way more than a twenty-foot drop," I yelled up, before muttering under my breath, "How could Theseus have survived that fall?"

Another short burst down, and then another, brought me within fifteen feet or so of touchdown. "I'm almost there," I shouted up.

Just then, I could hear a muffled roar of voices above. Lily yelled, "I'm losing my grip!"

A swell of commotion from the surface echoed off the cave walls.

Suddenly, the rope jerked as I plunged downward several feet.

I let go of the phone and grasped the rope with both hands. Hesiod cried out as the tension on the line gave way, sending me plummeting the final few feet to the cave floor.

I hit hard!

Lying flat on my back, disoriented, I barely noticed the dirt and debris raining down on me. The impact knocked the wind out of me and I hurt from head to toe.

Once, a horse threw me and this pretty much felt the same. Reliving the experience all over again in my mind, I fought to remain calm and catch my breath.

The ghostly echoes of voices from above were muffled in my ringing ears. I saw flashes of light and couldn't tell if they were real or imagined. At that moment, just as I had the day I was thrown from my saddle, I could hear my Paw-Paw's gravelly voice asking me if I was alright. Strangely, however, the voice seemed near and not at all a memory from my past.

My hands swept the ground around me as I began to push up into a sitting position. The voices above were chaotic and becoming clearer as I started to get my bearings. Sam shouted down from the surface, "Hannah!"

"Miss Goodheart, say something," Hesiod called.

"I'm okay," I shouted back. "I think," I muttered.

Still sitting on the cave floor, aching and dripping with sweat, I started to stand up when I noticed the unthinkable. The broken pieces of my locator, on the cave floor, caused my heart to sink. The impact had shattered the face, and only the band remained on my wrist, along with a cut where a small piece of the device was now lodged. I slowly wiped the blood from my hand, wincing from the piercing sting of the fresh cut.

My only link to the Pyxis was now destroyed.

Before I could even process the gravity of the situation, Sam called out to me again, with relief. "Thank God you're alright!"

"Yeah, I'm okay, but my locator's broken."

As I said this, I heard a shuffling sound coming from a dark corner, near the passage leading to the cathedral room. I turned to see what it might be. My first thought was that it was an animal and I began looking around for Morgan's phone, praying that it had not suffered the same fate as the *Kalosian* tracking device. I was so focused on my present situation that I didn't even notice the swelling ruckus on the surface; that is until a burst of cold wind blew into the cave from the opening above, sending a chill all over me.

Keeping one eye on the darkened corner as I scanned the cave floor for Morgan's phone, I hollered, "Guys, what's going on up there?"

Silence.

Sean's voice finally sliced through the quiet. "He's gone… Hesiod is gone."

"What do you mean, 'gone'?" I shouted to him, looking upward toward the cave's opening.

Once again, an uneasy silence fell, until Sean again called down, "He opened a portal, Hannah. He's gone."

I staggered backward toward the entrance to the passageway. My hands shook as I began to untie the rope about my waist. "This can't be happening," I thought. I started breathing heavily, panic setting in. The dreadful reality that we were now trapped here was overwhelming, as I pried at the tight knot until I was freed from the rope. I tossed it aside, stumbling further back until I bumped into what, at first, I thought was the cave wall.

Two hands reached for my shoulders as I spun around. I stepped away, first one step, and then two more. A shadowy figure emerged from the dark corner. I swallowed hard and then spoke. "Theseus?" I asked, hoping with every last ounce of hope… praying that it was the lost *Kalosian* emissary and not someone, or something, else.

Then, a voice echoed through the pit. "Welcome to the belly of Hell, child."

CHAPTER 18: ENTER THESEUS

A TALL MAN stepped into the light of the cave opening. His surprisingly clean-shaven face was weathered, but handsome. He put his hand up to block the natural sunlight, which poured into the cave. His soft eyes squinted in response to the stark brightness. His mouth opened slowly as he moistened his lips with his tongue. I waited for him to say something.

Anything.

Then he gently spoke. "Don't be frightened. I'm Theseus and you are… *injured*."

I was genuinely struck that his concern was not for the gravity of *his* situation, but for *mine*.

He took my bleeding hand into his and carefully removed a protruding shard of glass.

"Ouch! That hurts!"

"I'm terribly sorry. I didn't mean to cause you pain, but we must first hurt before we heal," he said looking up from my bleeding hand with a warm grin.

Tearing a piece of cloth from his tunic, he gently removed the band and tied it around my wrist. "We need to wash that out, so it doesn't get infected," he added, checking to make sure the wound was adequately wrapped.

The arguing and blame game that ensued above had subsided. It was a blow to my already fragile self-image hearing my friends arguing about pulling me up out of the cave. Theseus, on the other hand, didn't seem at all concerned about getting out. He called up to the surface to make sure the rope was anchored to something, and then said he needed to gather a few things before he climbed out.

I had decided to follow him through the cramped passage, into the cathedral room of the cave, which had served as his home for nearly three years.

It was easy to forget that Theseus was *Kalosian*. Like Hesiod, he had that same dark olive skin tone, and was otherwise like a lot of the men we had seen around here. His curly, dark locks were long but groomed, and crowned a hardened, yet gentle appearance. I was sort of taken off guard from the get-go, considering I figured on him being a bit more… well, beastly. Everything about him seemed to inspire trust and confidence.

He said nothing as we made our way through the passage until we came to a natural spring, just where Hesiod said it would be. It was a welcomed sight!

The water seemed to come from nowhere and ran down the rough wall, rich with mineral deposits, and into a pool. Two torches were lit on either side, illuminating the cool, fresh pool of water, and Theseus did not have to ask me twice if I wanted a drink. I cupped my hands and raised the cold water to my mouth, drinking it in before going in for more.

A half gourd, hollowed out and clearly well-used, sat on the dusty ground in front of the pool. As Theseus filled it with water, I removed the cloth wrap from my wrist.

"Looks like the bleeding stopped."

"This might sting a little," he said, pouring water from the bowl.

"Ack. Yes, just a little." I said as the water washed away the blood and cleansed a few other small cuts on my wrist and hand.

"A civilization here only a few hundred years ago believed this spring was magical."

"Magical?" I replied, wanting to know more.

"They believed it had once flowed out of Eden itself, untouched by the corruption of man's fall," he said. "Of course, that is only the stuff of legend. I found no magic in it, save that I never discovered it dry."

I filled my cupped hands one last time with clean, cold water and splashed it on my face, wiping away the dust, dirt, and sweat before continuing on with Theseus.

"Strange," I said as we walked, thinking about the legend. "A spring flowing from the Garden of Eden into a place called the Bowel of Hades."

Theseus looked back and grinned. "I find nothing strange at all about it. A reminder that grace can always find us… even in the darkest of places."

We continued through the maze of passages, some of them quite cramped, and at last made it to the cathedral room within the cave. The vast chamber was lined with exquisite stalactites and mineral deposits. Various torches placed throughout the chamber caught deposits of quartz, which caused the walls to sparkle with wonder. The ceiling was at least thirty feet above us, and the entire room reverberated with the faint echo of the nearby spring flowing into the pool.

Theseus picked up a large basket made of twigs and reeds and began to riffle through it. Gesturing toward a large natural stone structure, resembling a bench, near the center of the room, he told me to have a seat while he looked for a salve he had made with roots to treat his own occasional cuts and scrapes. I took a seat and marveled at the incredible beauty of this place.

"I have a blanket if you're cold," Theseus said. "The temperature never changes in here. A little cool, but I've gotten used to it."

He rambled under his breath as he rummaged through the basket. As he did, I realized for the first time since our meeting, moments earlier, that I could understand him without the aid of the now broken locator device. "I just realized you're speaking…" I began.

Theseus turned, with a small crudely fabricated clay vessel in his hand. "English?" he asked, finishing my sentence. "Sure. I'm fluent in over two hundred twenty-seven forms of communication. It's one of my more useful talents; especially when translation devices are broken after falling into a cave."

Theseus smiled, sat next to me and began to apply a small dab of the pungent salve, which resembled a very oily, brown mustard. It burned at first, and I pulled away, but with little more than a look, Theseus reassured me. "It looks like we did get all the crystal removed. That's good."

His voice was crisp and pleasant—like the perfect narrator. Unlike Hesiod, who had a thick Greek accent, I couldn't get a read on a pattern in his speech. His voice wasn't as deep, but much like Sosthenes, sounded mildly *English*. He talked a bit about the geology of the cave as I tried to take my mind off the sting of the cut and our situation. "What is this thing you needed to come back here for?" I asked. "You said we needed to get a *pirithous?*"

"Pirithous is not a thing, young one," Theseus said matter-of-factly. "Pirithous is my friend. He should be lurking about, I would imagine."

I began to entertain the thought that Theseus may have lost his sanity while all alone in this cave. It certainly would have come as no surprise. I said nothing but could hardly control the expression of uncertainty on my face, as he continued.

"All the while I've been here in this place, I had no one to talk with save Hesiod on the rare occasion he would stay and chat after bringing food. The bats certainly aren't very good company. They hide further back in the cave and sleep all day, spending their nights out there," he said, gesturing upward. "Pirithous wandered in here one day and never left. I like to think he enjoys my company as much as I enjoy his."

Just then, a brown lizard, about eight inches long, scurried across my leg and into Theseus' lap.

"Right on cue, old friend. I knew you were close by," a beaming Theseus said, as he carefully took the curious creature into his hands.

"*That's* Pirithous?" I asked, with surprise.

"Of course," laughed Theseus. "What were you expecting?"

I managed an awkward smile and shook my head. "So, what else do we need to grab before we try to climb out of here?" I asked, trying to remain on task.

"Well, let me collect a couple things, and we can be going," Theseus replied, springing to his feet.

Handing Pirithous off to my reluctant care, Theseus pulled a wool bag, with a long woolen strap, from the basket where he had previously located the balm. Throwing it over his shoulder, he began to gather various items—notes scribbled on crude parchment, a tattered cloak, even the small vessel of salve was tossed into his bag. While he packed, he started to tell me about the many hours he sat, feeling almost chained to the rock on which I now sat. He described the great loneliness he felt and how he had all but forgotten the life he once knew on Kalos.

I listened, as Theseus explained his plight of living in the cave these past few years. His words echoed in my soul and seemed to magnify a feeling that was slowly eating away at my spirit. But I couldn't help but notice his optimism. I was sure it was simply a reaction to having someone else besides Pirithous to talk to.

Whether in this cave, or in ancient Greece, I could feel the hopelessness of my current circumstances. My bout of self-pity, however, quickly began to give way to something even darker. "I'm sure you're probably as eager as I am to get your hands on Hesiod," I said, biting the inside of my cheek in anger.

"Oh, no," Theseus said, to my surprise. "I hold no ill will toward Hesiod. He's misguided but—"

"But he left you trapped, alone in this cave," I blurted, cutting him off mid-sentence. I wasn't buying for a minute he wasn't ready to get back at Hesiod for what he had done. "He betrayed and abandoned you. How can you not hate him for what he's done?"

"Hatred is a murdering savage, Miss Goodheart," he said, with such gentle conviction. "Even *if* you never act on it, when you harbor such dark emotions, you die inside—little by little, piece by piece. And to what end?"

Theseus called to Pirithous. "You better hop aboard, my friend… unless of course, you prefer to stay here," he said to the unusually affectionate reptile, who quickly scurried over and climbed into the bag.

As we made our way back to the cave entrance, Theseus shared with me how the Sentinels had chosen *him* to remain on Earth with the Pyxis, but that Hesiod met a woman and had fallen in love. To my surprise, Theseus went on to say that Hesiod had made a deal with the woman's father and they married secretly. Convinced they both needed to stay, Hesiod had pleaded with Theseus to allow him to remain.

"I told him we needed to leave here and return to Kalos together for further guidance," he said. "Then I fell into this cave, and Hesiod took advantage."

"Wait," I said. "Did you just say, Hesiod, made a deal with Isadora's father to marry her?"

"Certainly," replied Theseus. "It is common for families to arrange marriages in this culture. It is their way. I'm not for certain, but I believe Hesiod bought out another suitor before negotiating with the woman's father. He always was a skilled negotiator."

Approaching the cave entrance, Theseus took hold of the rope as I shouted to my friends, quietly waiting above.

"I'll climb up first and then help pull you up," he said, handing his bag off to me, before ascending quickly up the long rope to the surface.

Watching him climb with ease, I wondered to myself why I even took the risk to descend into the cave, to begin with. I felt regret, and it further fueled my suspicion that Hesiod had somehow planned the whole thing. Hesiod, no doubt, knew Theseus would be able to climb up without help. I didn't think anything of it at the time, but he gave up calling to him awful fast. Surely, based on his previous visits, he knew it would take Theseus several minutes to travel through the passage. I considered that the entire show of concern and fear that Theseus might have perished, was nothing but an act. I was deeply conflicted, angry that I had possibly fallen for Hesiod's scheme.

Within minutes, however, I felt a little relief as I was reunited with my friends. Night was falling, however, and the chill of the air sent us quickly down the mountain and into the village. I had little assurance when or how we were ever going to make it back to our own time or place. A growing dread squeezed my chest as it coiled itself around me, tightening its oppressive grip on me with each passing minute.

As we made our way down the mountain trail, talking away, none of us *really* knew for sure if Hesiod had planned the whole thing or just capitalized on the news that my locator was broken. It was a clever deception for him to pretend to put the Pyxis back into the jar, which lends itself to conspiracy. But so far, he had shown himself to be more opportunistic than malicious. Theseus certainly seemed to believe so. One thing alone was certain.

Hesiod was gone.

The rest of the journey had been a quiet one. Lily apologized to me repeatedly, taking responsibility for my fall, despite my continued reassurance that it wasn't her fault. While despair settled in, taking deep root in my heart and, from all observations, my friends' as well, Theseus seemed more upbeat. He appeared thoughtful, but he had such a presence of joy and peace.

My first impression of Theseus was leaving me confused. He had spent the better part of three years in a pit, trapped, alone and destitute. His only friend, a lizard named Pirithous, provided little in the way of company. In fact, as I took note of Pirithous, now happily riding upon the broad but gaunt shoulder of Theseus, it seemed clear that Pirithous benefited most from the odd relationship. The thought drew a smile, but only for a moment.

Then there was the issue of the ease with which Theseus exited the cave. It seems he could've probably managed an escape anytime he wanted. Perhaps he did and failed. It just didn't seem to add up.

I drew near to Theseus as we continued walking. "You're quite a climber."

Theseus turned to me, briefly, as if to assess my intention. "Yes, I am."

"Another one of your more useful talents?"

We continued walking, as I tried to figure him out. He would side-eye me much the same way I was doing to him as we strolled along. I think he was as engaged in trying to size me up as I was him. Finally, I broke the momentary silence. "Why did you live so long, alone in that pit?" I asked. "I'm guessing you probably could have found some way out a long time ago."

"Had I done that, *you* would have been …"

I pondered just a second what he could have meant, then asked, "Been what?"

Theseus stopped dead in his tracks, turned to me and answered, "Alone."

His response fell like heavy drops of rain on the arid Texas plain and raised a host of questions all too fantastic to be pondered. I was speechless at the thought that he was not there in the cave by an act of ill will, or even by some freak accident. I wrestled with the notion that perhaps he didn't suffer by chance, but rather by choice.

Theseus lead us through the dimly lit square that earlier had been a bustling village market. The *agora* was now crawling with raucous, disorderly types. It was an unsettling sight, for sure.

Theseus quietly told us to remain alert and to avoid making eye contact with anyone.

Suddenly, a dirty, sweaty giant of a man emerged and grabbed Lily's arm.

Lily shrieked, as he began to drag her away. He was howling and snorting like an animal.

Annie took off running. "Oh, no you don't," she said, leaping onto his back and smacking at his fat, hairless head.

The rest of us jumped to help, but Theseus wasted no time snagging the burly man firmly by the wrist. Twisting the brute's arm backwards, Theseus tightened his grasp, eliciting a howl of searing pain, forcing him to let go of Lily. Annie had been thrown off the brute when Theseus first caught the lug. She immediately sprang back to her feet and gave him a swift kick, doubling him over. I helped Lily up as Annie spun around to check on her little sister.

Seeing Lily was safe with us, Theseus rebuked the man. Though none of us could understand his language, we were sure, by his tone and intensity, it wasn't small talk. The lug's face was like a catcher's mitt, and it was evident he was in excruciating pain as Theseus continued his tight hold.

Theseus swiftly released the man, pushing him away and started toward us. We watched as the man snorted then spat on the ground as he straightened to stand upright. He tilted his head, sneering as Theseus turned his back and walked away.

Suddenly, the brute lunged toward Theseus, both fists like sledge hammers, raised, ready to strike.

"Theseus! Look out," Sam cried, rushing toward them. Theseus ducked to the right, barely evading the blow. Spinning around, Theseus struck the man with an open hand in the center of his chest, sending the beast flying backward several feet into a pile of crates.

The brief fracas had drawn a crowd. Theseus stepped back cautiously while, one-by-one, bystanders scattered. Theseus offered a reassuring nod and then suggested we get out of the square as quickly as possible.

Lily stuck like glue to Theseus as we turned back toward the *agora*. "What did you say to him?" she asked, brushing her long blonde hair out of her eyes.

"I told him to go home and work on his manners."

Lily raised her eyebrow and shot us a look that said she wasn't buying his answer. Annie shrugged her shoulders and quipped, "It's all Greek to me."

Theseus stopped briefly and spoke. "There is a woman, Phaedra. She sells olives here in the market with her sister. She might give us a place to rest tonight, and then tomorrow we can figure out how to get the six of you home."

Moving swiftly through the square, we came to a row of clay brick buildings. Theseus approached one of the rough timber doors on the far end and knocked. "Phaedra, it's Theseus," he said, in a quieted voice. "Phaedra, I have returned."

Not so much as a stir.

Theseus knocked again and called out once more, but still, no answer. He turned to us and began to say something when the door behind him flew open.

A statuesque woman with dark flowing hair, and eyes as dark as the night sky, stood in the doorway. She spoke, but only Theseus knew what she was saying. Theseus responded to her, and the two embraced. She quickly waved us all in. and as we entered, Theseus asked, "How's your English, Phaedra?"

"It's a little not so good since you're not here to teach me."

Sean spoke up. "You taught her to speak English? Why would *you do* that?"

Theseus shot Sam a curious look, who shrugged and shook his head. Then he made brief eye contact with Sean before looking back at Phaedra. "Can my friends and I stay here tonight?"

"First, you tell me where you go for all this time," she barked. "Then if the answer is pretty okay, I'll think about it," she said with a smile.

"All in good time. I promise."

Phaedra hugged Theseus tightly. Then she stepped back, adjusted her long, faded garment and said, "We eat and talk, okay?"

Within minutes, Phaedra brought fluffy pita bread and the very best olives we had ever tasted. Moments later she was back with salted tomatoes and bite-size bits of roasted meat on a stick. "It's Souvlaki," Phaedra said with a smile, as she handed one off to Sam, who received it enthusiastically.

Everyone got a laugh watching Sam gobble down the savory treat. I have to admit, despite feeling pretty down about our predicament, it was pretty funny watching him go after the food. Lily, Annie and Morgan teased him about his "meat obsession." He paid no attention as he reached for another.

As we ate, Theseus talked openly about the cave, Hesiod, and the Pyxis. It was apparent to us that Phaedra was aware of who Theseus actually was and seemed most curious about the six young travelers that were sitting in her home. "So, you were tied to Hesiod by some device," Phaedra asked.

"Yes, until it was smashed in the cave, we went *where* and *when* he went, but we somehow keep ending up empty handed," I responded, feeling broken by what felt like total failure.

Theseus popped an olive into his mouth as I was talking and then stroked his chin thoughtfully. "Have you noticed any pattern to where he has traveled… any specific time periods or places?"

"Not really," I replied. "At first, we thought he was trying to change certain points in history; a majorly terrible tragedy in *my* country's history, then here in Greece." I paused and thought for a moment, then said, "Oh, that horrible, dark place."

"Don't go there," Sam said, rubbing his arm. "I thought that evil little ball of light was going to be the death of me."

"Or the super heavy gas atmosphere," Morgan added.

Theseus' expression changed immediately. "The Darkness!"

"It was dark, alright," Annie chided. "We couldn't see past the end of our noses."

Theseus spit an olive pit into a jar, exhaled and scratched his furrowed brow. I could see his concern as he stared aimlessly at the bowl of olives. His wheels were turning.

"You know something about that place?"

"I know *Hesiod* was not responsible for taking you there, and if they have become aware of you, it is more critical than ever to get the Pyxis away from Hesiod and into the hands of the Guardian."

Now my interest was piqued! I wanted to know more about this *Guardian,* but Theseus looked away, staring off with such intensity. I feared prying any further might provoke him in some way, so I decided to let it go for the time being.

While Sean sat quietly picking at his food, Sam listened as Phaedra had struck up a conversation with Morgan, Annie, and Lily. I leaned over to Theseus. "Hesiod *will* come back here. I'm sure of it. He's not going to leave Isadora and their child."

"Hesiod has a child?" Theseus asked as his eyes widened.

"Pandora... she's just a baby," I replied. "I actually believed he would keep his word and give up the Pyxis after we got you out of the cave. Was I ever wrong."

Theseus relaxed, patted my leg and said, "This is one of the reasons we chose you, you know... I mean humanity... you, here on this world. You have an incredible capacity for *optimism*. You choose to see the very best of what is possible. It is a remarkable attribute."

"Yes, well," I started as Theseus popped another olive into his mouth. "You can clearly see where that got *me*. I mean, how could you pick humanity to safeguard such an important and powerful thing? After what my eyes have just been opened to, we have such a totally long way to go."

"You are quite right," Theseus said. "Humanity *is* flawed. In your time, your world has nearly torn itself apart in two great world wars. In this time, they fight over something as trivial as a tract of land or natural resources, and nothing will change—not in a hundred years, not in a thousand. You allow yourselves to be divided over the natural pigments in your skin and ignore the common things that make all of you uniquely *human.* Your appearance, religion, philosophy, politics… these things should never drive people down the path of hatred. You have yet to figure it out, but your diversity is one of the pillars of your world that makes your species strong. Tragically, however, humanity has a long history of trying to wipe out anyone, or anything, that is different—including one another."

Theseus continued. "In contradiction to this narrow mindset, your world sends radio signals deep into the heavens, searching for intelligent life, naively thinking that out there somewhere are *benevolent* beings, eager for contact. Oh, Hannah Goodheart, if your world could only see what you are able to become and what you could accomplish; if you only knew the potential laying just below the surface, underneath these destructive human flaws."

I was floored! His passion for what he could see in us blew me away, and I wanted to hear more.

He sat back, paused thoughtfully as he studied me, then said, "Your species puzzles me. Humanity is a mystery, a riddle I am unable to solve. To the rest of the universe, yes, yours is a primitive, backward world… too self-absorbed to matter. But they do not know you as we do, which makes you a perfect choice. I know you are ready to take this leap. Even now, you transcend your shortcomings with your capability to show compassion *and* strength, to embrace logic *and* emotion, and to push the boundaries of what is possible by pursuing the impossible. That is what I see before me. And soon, with the help of the Pyxis, so shall you."

These were not the ramblings of a man secluded for years in a cave. I could hardly believe what he was saying and how deeply he seemed to understand human beings. I was able to see through his eyes humanity's incredible potential. And in that brief moment, I, too, believed that my world was capable of building a brighter future.

As the night grew ever darker, Lily was first to nod off to sleep. I sat quietly watching the fire burn down, trying to concentrate long enough to think out a decent plan to corner Hesiod before we ended up stuck here forever. Then, beating myself up for worrying so much about my situation, I wrestled with the weight of what this could mean for the world if we didn't catch him. *Close your eyes, Hannah. Breathe. It's only the fate of the entire universe. No biggie.*

Theseus and Phaedra talked quietly in one corner of the room, while Sean sat brooding in the other. Sam lay on his back staring off at the ceiling as Lily was joined in her slumber, first by Morgan and then by her sister, Annie.

My mind wandered from the possibility of universal oblivion to something a bit more positive. Theseus's words. He had described humanity as "optimistic," and yet it was *his* optimism that fanned the fading flame of hope in my own heart.

I was tired—no, *exhausted*—and had endured setback after setback. I had no sense of how long it had really been since any of us had slept. The unrelenting peril we faced was taking its toll. I recalled how hopeless I felt in the cave. Though I should have felt grateful to be out of there, bitterness swelled instead. The anticipation of ending this quest successfully and returning to my family was gone—Hesiod was gone, and I was trapped. *We were trapped.*

How quickly things change.

Feeling hopeless, I had all but surrendered to despair. But then, Theseus had somehow managed to keep my fading hope alive. But as Phaedra's fire started to die down and the air cooled, I feared that I was also growing colder and weaker in my spirit. Could I even endure another setback if we're unsuccessful in getting the drop on Hesiod, come morning? Regardless, I knew morning would come, and for now, that was as far as I chose to look. I could hear my Paw-Paw's voice in my mind, saying something I had heard him say a thousand times: "Step by step." Now, for the first time, I truly understood what he meant when he said it.

Phaedra arose and left for her bed chamber, bidding both me and Theseus "peaceful rest" as we were the only two still awake. Theseus stood and walked toward me. "You should get some sleep," he said. "I'm guessing it's been days since you have rested."

"I look *that* good?" I asked, in jest.

Theseus gave me a reassuring smile and said, "Sometimes the gulf between despair and hope can be bridged with a little rest."

I continued to watch the glowing coals as Theseus stood over me. "He'll come back for Isadora and the baby. I'm sure of it," I said. "That's where we need to be as soon as the sun comes up."

"Then, that is where we will be," Theseus said. "When the sun comes up."

I sat for a few minutes longer, but my busy mind was no match for heavy eyes. Lying down with a wadded-up wool blanket for a pillow, I drifted off to sleep, hoping against hope that the new day would lead us to Hesiod and, ultimately…

Home.

CHAPTER 19: THE RETURN OF HOPE

THE AIR WAS cold and crisp. Morgan was shivering, her teeth chattering, as she waited by the well with Lily, Annie, and me. Theseus had taken Sam and Sean ahead, to the now familiar tawny house where Hesiod lived with Isadora and their child, Pandora. The three of them had quietly surveyed the area and I could see them very carefully making their way back.

The sound of crickets chirping and other strange noises filled the early dawn, nearly drowning out the sound of the approaching team bringing news to the rest of us.

"You were right, Hannah. He's definitely here," said Sean, with tempered enthusiasm, as they arrived.

"Then what are we waiting for?" exclaimed Annie. "Let's go in there with guns blazing!"

Lily was quick to reply, "We don't have guns, bonehead."

Annie punched Lily's arm as I held up a hand. "Stop it, you guys."

Now, I usually enjoy their sibling banter, but I was too anxious and much too tired. "We can't risk going in there without a plan."

"No," said Sean. "I agree. We shouldn't wait. We have the element of surprise. I say we storm in and seize him before he has a chance to flee."

I turned to Theseus with hands up and shoulders shrugging. He didn't immediately catch on, but then said, "I am actually inclined to agree with the boy. We do have the element of surprise. Everyone is still asleep, but not likely for long. As soon as the sun rises from behind the hill, this place will surely come alive with activity."

I couldn't believe my ears. I shook my head with a growl, letting everyone know what I thought of *that* plan. "No one wants Hesiod as much as I do," I said. "But there are other people in that house we have to think about."

We huddled quietly behind the well.

"What are you suggesting?" asked Sam.

Taking a moment to think about my best ideas from the night before, I paused, then said, "We close in and wait." I drew a crude diagram of the area around the house in the dust on the ground. "We cover points here, and here," I said, pointing at the simple map. "Sam takes the front door with Theseus since that's his best way out. The first sign of activity, we move. The key is to make sure we have every possible escape route covered, then we draw in the net."

"Risky," Theseus said, as he studied my dirt doodle, scratching his chin. "It gives him an opportunity to react.

If he opens a portal and takes the woman and child with him, you will again be trapped here—possibly for good."

"If that's his play, why hasn't he done it already?" I asked. "I totally understand what's at stake, but Isadora trusts us—she trusts *me*. I'm not going to break that trust by going all pre-dawn raid of her home while she's in bed sleeping."

Morgan cupped her hands together and held them to her face, blowing her warm breath into them. "I'm with Hannah, we can't bust in there and traumatize these people."

I was relieved to know at least one person agreed with me. I spoke up again to try and strengthen my case. "I don't think we lose surprise, and if we can isolate him from the rest of his family, I'm willing to bet he'll not be going anywhere for long."

Sean clenched his jaw and huffed, showing his displeasure, drawing everyone's attention for a second.

"We should at least spread out a little more to ensure we have both entries *and* the windows adequately covered," Theseus said.

"Not a bad idea," I conceded. "There's still a risk that he could overpower one of us and make a break for it."

"How is it the saying goes?" asked Theseus. "The greater the risk…"

"The greater the reward," replied Sam with a grin and confident nod.

Annie reached over and slapped Theseus on the back, signaling the coming wisecrack. "You're well versed for a cave man."

Theseus smiled awkwardly and scurried away toward the house, followed by the rest of us. We each took positions near doors and windows, agreeing to stay within sight of at least one other person. Remaining silent, we listened carefully for any sign of activity. I signaled that the sun was starting to become visible. Sam, who had taken a position with Theseus near the main entry, moved to a nearby window, where Sean sat alert but motionless, directly beneath it. Sam quickly popped up to look inside and ducking back down, motioned back to me, indicating no movement inside.

Suddenly, a rustling could be heard, followed by the cries of the child. Sam, looking panicked, ducked down. He pointed up and then moved his fingers to sign "walking" as Isadora sprang past the window where he and Sean were crouched. Her voice carried, but only Theseus could understand what she said.

Theseus held up his hand to ensure no one moved too soon. Sam, resting his head against the clay brick wall, eyes closed, sucked in a deep breath. Theseus raised his finger to his lips, signaling silence and stealth were necessary.

Sean, ignoring Theseus' commands, sprang to his feet, turned and leaped through the open window. Theseus looked unhappy and shook his head, grimacing with disappointment, but quickly signaled everyone to move in.

Within seconds, everyone was inside. Isadora emerged with the crying baby in her arms. Her eyes were low and her expression fearful as she protectively cradled her child. "Hannah," she cried. "Den Ide-eye edo," she said, repeatedly.

"What is she saying?" Sam yelled.

"He's not here," Sean said.

"How do *you* know what she's saying?" I asked, suspiciously.

"I *don't*, but Hesiod's clearly not here."

"That *is* what she is saying," remarked Theseus. "I fail to understand. He was here, in bed asleep, just a moment ago."

I charged the door and threw it open, hoping to catch a glimpse of Hesiod making tracks for the market. I ran into the courtyard, toward the well, where we had hidden only a short while ago, but found no sign of him anywhere—not even a dust cloud.

As I ran back into the home, Theseus was calming Isadora and talking to her, while Sean stood curiously, as though eavesdropping nearby. I stepped closer, as Isadora took my hands into her own. The only word I could understand was my own name, as the kind woman said it over and over. It seemed very much like she was pleading with me. She finally let go and gestured toward her child, who found momentary solace with Morgan and Lily.

"I don't understand," I said to her, as Isadora continued talking. "I'm sorry." Turning to Sean, I asked, "Do you understand her?"

Sean blinked awkwardly with a scowl as he tugged at his ear and barked. "I don't know what she's rambling on about!"

Theseus spoke up. "She said he came home late last night from the mountain. When she woke up, he was gone. She is afraid you intend to take him to a distant country, away from her and the child. She is asking you about what happened on the mountain."

I mustered a smile, but Isadora's fears and frustrations burbled up and over as a single tear fell down her cheek. Theseus turned to her, speaking softly.

I listened, though I couldn't understand. My own emotions were a bit all over the place. I felt broken. Once more, I had been so close to getting Hesiod and the Pyxis, and once more I had come up empty. But my growing frustration and despair turned to anger as I spied Sean once more in the corner of my eye. I marched toward him, boiling over. "This is your fault, Sean!"

"If you had listened to *me*, you would have the Pyxis back now," he spat back. "Your plan gave him an opportunity… you have only yourself to blame."

"So here we go. I suppose it's time for the Sean Show," I snapped, backing him against the wall.

Sean stood with little expression and said nothing in response as I stood over him.

I was defused by his lack of reply. *No 'best lines' comeback?*

Studying Sean carefully for a moment, I felt as though I no longer recognized him. It was like he was an entirely different person; cold and calculating—nothing like the Sean Evans I knew. Maybe this whole ordeal had changed him.

Maybe it's changed me.

Annie stepped between us. "This isn't the time or place to second guess things. He can't be far."

"He couldn't have opened the Pyxis and bounced. We would have known," Lily added.

Theseus drew near, putting his hand on my shoulder. "I agree." Speaking up, so the others could hear, he said, "I think it best we leave here and search the square near the *agora*. Hesiod often goes there to tell his stories and debate philosophy. Our best chance of finding him is there."

With that, he took the baby from Lily's arms, gave the child a gentle kiss and handed her to her mother, before politely bowing his head and saying, *"Erroso."*

Theseus quietly exited the home as we each bid Isadora goodbye and followed.

We had not gotten as far as the well before Sean sped up and began throwing his opinion around, saying Hesiod would likely stay near the home.

"For the first time since we've left home," I said, "I actually agree with Sean."

Theseus, however, kept walking, as we followed close behind. Once out of sight, he turned quickly to me. "He *is* still there. He could not have exited his residence without us knowing, and Miss Little is correct that he could not have escaped using the Pyxis without drawing attention."

"Logically," I added, "He would have stirred the dust up tearing out of here. I think he *has* to be there."

"Yes," said Theseus kneeling down. "Our unsubtle intrusion, however, has cost us the element of surprise."

I figured out that he must have heard the commotion and managed to find a place to hide. "He'll lay low now to throw us off balance until he can pull off another bounce."

"What we need to do now is throw *him* off balance," said Sam.

Theseus nodded enthusiastically. "Point well made."

Sam raised his fist to offer Theseus a bump but was left hanging. Lily giggled and demonstrated for Theseus, who quickly gave Sam his bump, as Sean rolled his eyes.

Theseus grinned. "We need to move quickly, and we do not chance taking our eyes off the house. If he tries to leave, we need to know where he goes. If he opens a portal, the six of you must be ready to move in quickly and, whatever it takes, enter the event horizon before it collapses. It may well be your one and only opportunity."

"What about you, Theseus?" I asked.

A conniving smile appeared across his craggy face as he sprang to his feet. "I'm going to go buy some olives."

As he walked toward the *agora*, he admonished us again to make a run for it if Hesiod used the Pyxis. So, we laid low. We watched, and we waited.

The wait was utterly brutal.

Although it seemed much, *much* longer, not more than half an hour had passed before Sean signaled us that he could hear someone approaching. We all scattered and watched with the expectation of Theseus returning. I, on the other hand, paid little mind to the southern pathway, where the sound of footsteps approaching was easily heard. My attention was focused solely on the house in the distance, which I watched diligently for some clear sign that Hesiod was still there.

As the rustling sound grew louder, I heard a soft, assured female voice.

"*Elpis*," said Phaedra, greeting us as she emerged from the cover of the twisted trees that lined the winding path.

One by one, everyone stepped out from their hiding places onto the stony walkway, while I remained vigilant at my post.

"I thought you spoke English," asked Sean.

"I do," replied Phaedra in her now-familiar mellow tone, as she moved a large basket of olives from under her left arm.

"*Elpis* is Greek," said Theseus, emerging from the shadows nearby, startling everyone. "It means, 'hope.'"

Forlorn and exhausted both physically and mentally, the last few days had drained me. Beyond drained.

But at this moment, Phaedra's greeting registered in my spirit, and I felt a fresh wind blow over me.

That word.

Hope.

Hearing it spoken aloud brought light into darkness. Doubt and fear cowered as hope rang once more through my spirit. A warmth seeped in as desperation began giving way to courage. Whatever wave had washed my hopeful expectations out to sea, like a returning tide, they were swiftly rushing back in.

Mind you, it wasn't what Phaedra *said*, so much as how her unexpected arrival reminded me of something I've always known.

I could suddenly see things much more clearly. It was like waking to the morning after a bad dream. The monsters that haunted my sleep were nothing more than shadows behind a distant veil. For all the fear and struggle, I now understood, that with every difficulty and every uncertainty, something—someone—was there to turn to. Nan and Paw-Paw. Theseus. Phaedra. My friends—loyal to the last. I also realized I carry the lessons my mom and dad taught me, assuring they are forever as close as my own heart and mind. Theseus reminded me after escaping the pit, I was not alone. I realized… I've never been alone.

I also remembered something Daddy once told me: "Hope is the fuel of the present, propelling us ever forward toward a brighter future."

All this truth had suddenly rushed in and put down the lies that tormented me because right now, at this moment, Phaedra had come and had brought with her a powerful ally: hope. In my darkest moment, she reminded me that hope could sustain me and carry me through. Suddenly, I knew this was it!

Hope said to me success was sure.

"I take it that all is still quiet with our friend. Nothing to report," Theseus asked Sam with a pat on the shoulder.

"Nada, amigo."

"Ahhh. Muy bien!"

"Yes. Not a peep," I added.

Theseus squinted at me and tilted his head, as if he could see a change in me as well. "You are looking quite confident, young lady."

"I'm suddenly feeling very optimistic."

"Then I think the time has come to surprise my old friend with a gift."

Phaedra flashed a flirtatious smile before sashaying toward Hesiod's home like a model on the runway.

"No one moves until she is inside," ordered Theseus.

"Sean," I said, "that goes double for you!"

Lily gave me a solid non-verbal that Sean was rolling his eyes after I looked away. It didn't matter, though, because he *did* patiently stand by with the rest of us as Phaedra approached the door. We watched with surprise as Hesiod opened the door and looked cautiously around, before welcoming the familiar olive merchant into the house to complete her delivery.

"She's in," I said, just a little surprised at the ease with which she managed to enter.

"Yep, I see that," responded Lily.

"Let's move," Sam said, spurred by a determined nod from Theseus.

First to the well and then to the door, the seven of us skulked forward before bursting into the home. Everyone inside was astonished, except for Phaedra, who grabbed Hesiod's arm to prevent a quick getaway attempt. "Let's not do anything unwise."

Sean reached into his pocket and pulled out a tiny pod of neon green powder and broke it, blowing it into Hesiod's face. Hesiod gasped and collapsed suddenly, pulling Phaedra down with him.

"What was *that*," cried Phaedra struggling to get back up.

"A little souvenir from Kalos. Mizcus pollen."

"Well great," I said, frustrated. "How long is he going to be out?"

Theseus snatched the pod from Sean's hand. "There could not be enough here to put him out for very long. He should be waking up…"

A garbled sound emerged from the heap that was Hesiod, laying on the floor. "Theseus," a groggy Hesiod uttered.

"Ah… Right about now," Annie said, finishing Theseus' statement.

Hesiod sat up immediately, stunned, looking around. Seeing Theseus for the first time, from his perspective, in over fifty years he reached out with a broad smile. Then his hands dropped into his lap as his face fell. "I'm so ashamed… I'm so ashamed."

Stepping forward, Theseus crouched down and put his hand on Hesiod's shoulder. "All is forgiven, friend," Theseus said. "This is the way of our people, is it not?"

Hesiod slowly stood to his feet with the help of Theseus, who embraced his friend and colleague. Hesiod nodded and humbly hung his head.

"Please," he said. "I intend to offer no resistance."

Isadora quickly retrieved a clay jar. She said nothing but put the pot in my hand. She smiled cautiously and stood by her husband, who watched intently as I tumped it over, the silvery box tumbling into my hand.

Once again, I held the incredible object that had brought me and my friends through time and space, to this moment. I had been stripped of every pre-conceived notion of the universe and had my entire life turned upside down. The emptiness of despair had nearly consumed me. but now, surrounded by my friends, I felt the fullness of hope, and I knew I would soon be able to return home.

Hesiod drew near to me, taking my hand. Closing my fingers around the Pyxis, he said, "A wise friend *recently* told me that 'time is truth.' We cannot hide from either of them forever."

"A wise friend? Theseus?"

"Actually, it was you, my dear—in another time and another place. But perhaps I shouldn't say any more. One should not know too much about the future."

"So I keep hearing."

I looked into Hesiod's eyes, and was amazed at the kindness I saw in them. I wanted to know more, but I wondered whether he was right. Maybe one shouldn't know too much. The thought frightened me a little, knowing that sometime in my future I would encounter this man again; as friend or foe, I wasn't at all certain. I pondered those potential circumstances as Hesiod continued.

"I will say, *this* moment," Hesiod added, "it is real. It is true. I have learned that when you leave it, it is not gone—it still exists. The moment is fixed for eternity and it ripples through to the future in the most unexpected ways." His intensity and passion was captivating. "Please hear what I am about to tell you, Miss Goodheart. You must redeem the time. Make *every* moment count. Beware of the idleness of busyness; the barren pursuits which can lead one to be prey to the Darkness. It is easy to lose sight of this, especially when one possesses such a power as this thing you hold in your hand. It is when you least expect it that what you fear will find you, unless you are both patient and most vigilant."

I literally stepped back, struggling to understand what he was trying to say. A fervent urgency in his words excited and frightened me all at the same time. Isadora tried to brighten the mood as she invited everyone to sit and to be refreshed. But Hesiod was preoccupied and zealous to talk to us.

"I am a fool. I gave in to my fears and betrayed everything I held sacred." Hesiod turned to Theseus, who was also listening intently. "I don't deserve your forgiveness, my friend. Mine was the worst betrayal. I knew the Pyxis belonged to you and to your descendant. I just don't know what frightened me most, leaving Isa and my daughter, or becoming a pawn in the temporal conflict."

He paused and clinched his fist in the air, showing his resolve. "I swear to you, I intended to put an end to it and make everything right once again."

I barely heard the latter statement about this temporal conflict. My mind raced as I was sure Hesiod had just confirmed what I was beginning to suspect since the cave. I was now certain *Theseus* was the Guardian I was instructed by Sosthenes to find. What other reason could Hesiod have to imprison him in the pit? I considered what Hesiod said about the Pyxis belonging to Theseus and his descendant. I was certain now I had all I needed and could return to Sosthenes and the Sentinels on Kalos.

Isadora had come back into the room with bread and oil. "I know you still have much to discuss," she said, shifting the platter nervously before setting it down. I was relieved to once again understand what this sweet woman was saying. With the Pyxis in hand, all of us could understand.

As she sat down, Isadora turned to me. "I know you will be true and allow my husband to remain."

Theseus diverted her request and turning to Hesiod, asked, "You seem most concerned, Hesiod. What of the Darkness and the conflict? Surely, they cannot have gathered power enough to mount an offensive."

I listened carefully, consumed with both curiosity and dread at the mention once again of the Darkness. Something about it all sent a chill down my spine.

Hesiod looked confused. "I was completely caught off guard when the child made mention of it on the mountain."

He turned to me. "I had every intention of honoring our agreement and helping you pull Theseus from the cave. I would have never allowed you to remain trapped there. Please, believe this," he pleaded.

I nodded in agreement, though I was confused. I wasn't sure what he referred to or what was said on the mountain that caused him to panic—if anything. Hesiod had given little indication that he was at all trustworthy, and yet, I saw in him perhaps what Isa saw. Maybe it was in Theseus' gesture of forgiveness. Maybe it was the explicit trust between the two men that existed in spite of their complicated history. Whatever it was, I did believe him and trusted what he was about to say was sincere and true, whether I understood it or not.

"At first, I was content to remain here, but he found me, Theseus. I don't know how, but he did."

Dismay colored Theseus's face. He tried to hide his expression, but I could see his immediate distress.

Hesiod continued. "I had gone to Dallas, in 1963, chasing him through time." He turned to me and continued. "The blow to the head when I fell. I completely forgot. But I was there to stop him. I think when I saw my future self, I became frightened. All that nonsense about temporal mechanics and seeing another version of yourself is simply superstition and hyperbole. I know— I've proven it. Stranded in that time for over fifty years, I realized that my selfishness had endangered everything and everyone. To think, in my arrogance, I actually *caused* the event that marooned me in Dallas. I thwarted my own plan." Hesiod's shoulders drooped, and then he straightened, turning to face me. "I had to try and correct my error. So, I took advantage of the opportunity your misfortune at the cave afforded me. I retraced my steps and did everything I could to erase or minimize my footprint through time. If the Darkness could not track *me*, perhaps it would never find the Guardian and never seize control of the Pyxis. My last stop was to be here, to retrieve you all and return to Kalos to face the Sentinels. But even this was a foolish strategy. I fear I've only hastened the coming conflict."

"Then why did you try to hide from us just now?" asked Theseus. "Surely you knew you could have turned yourself over, if that were your intent."

"Indeed," said Hesiod, as his eyes began to moisten. "I had but one final footprint to erase," he said, as his soft baritone voice was breaking. He turned and looked at his beloved Isa. "I wanted one last chance to tell her and Dora goodbye, before I erased all of this from time."

Isa took his hand, and they drew strength from each other to hold themselves with dignity in the moment, knowing that this could be their last together.

"I made a promise. Hesiod stays," I blurted, leaping to my feet.

"I don't think that's a good idea," Sean replied.

"I don't think carrying alien pollen around in your pocket is such a good idea either, but let's not debate questionable choices," Annie quipped.

"Seriously? Mizcus?" I asked. "How did you even get hold of that?"

"An entire patch of it was near where they found me," Sean said. "Don't you think we should stay on topic?"

Theseus agreed. "As a Kalosian emissary, he *must* be returned to Kalos to face the council and answer to the Sentinels, who commissioned him."

"No," I said, turning to Theseus. "In my time, Hesiod is a renowned poet, a philosopher, and writer who helped shape the course of civilization. Economics, government, religion; remove *him*, and the tapestry of *my* history unravels."

"The Sentinels may not agree," warned Theseus.

"Which is exactly why *you're* going to come along and help me convince them," I said, handing the Pyxis off to Theseus. "After which, my friends and I will return home, and you can go off wherever and fulfill *your* destiny."

Theseus gave me that same curious squint as he scratched his jaw. I could see he was weighing the merits of my argument, but I couldn't begin to read what he was thinking.

Leading me and my friends to the well in the courtyard, he bid Phaedra "*Elpis,*" and asked her to look after Pirithus. She agreed with a flirty grin and asked Theseus for his promise to return, joking that she would not care for the creature forever.

As Hesiod stood resolutely beside his bride, Theseus gave him a nod, before uttering the word that sent the Pyxis into motion, opening the portal.

"*Elpis,* Hesiodos," Theseus said. "She spoke well, old friend," he added. "You remain with your family," he finally said, as we were swept away. As I saw Hesiod, Isa, and Pandora fade in time, the expression on Hesiod's face was burned into my memory. It held kindness and warmth, such as I had not seen in him before. He looked admiringly at me and I'm almost certain he winked lovingly before I was caught away. It was as though he knew some grand secret, like he knew what I was getting for Christmas. For me, I had a lingering feeling that this was somehow only the end of one chapter, in a much larger story.

CHAPTER 20: WHAT DO WE WRITE NEXT

I WAS GROWING more and more impatient. Feeling quite anxious, I sat once again in the hall of the Sentinels, inside the grand Praetorium, my mind racing. Weary from our travels as we arrived, we were led through a chamber that, in many ways, reminded me a little of the body scanners at the airport. Entering in, we were instructed to raise our arms above our heads. The massive machine had three large rings that passed over us, crossing over one another as it worked in one direction and then the other. As it slowly moved over each of us, the dirt and filth of the past several days lifted from us and was dissolved instantly. Cuts and scrapes were healed, torn clothing mended, all in a complete cycle.

My hand, where the *Kalosian* tracking device had cut me during the fall into the pit, was as though it had never occurred. Even the remnant of the bruise Hesiod left on my wrist was gone. It was remarkable. However, impressed as I was about how clean I felt, I wanted nothing more than the satisfaction of being home and taking a long quiet bath in my own tub.

I longed for the safety and comfort of having my parents close once more. I genuinely missed them and though I was unsure how I was going to explain all of this to them, I couldn't wait to tell them everything I had seen and experienced.

Everyone was feeling lighthearted, anticipating our imminent return to our proper time and place.

Sean, however, sat across from me nearly expressionless, as the others were enjoying Annie's jokes and wisecracks. The *Kalosians* were attending to us as though we were visiting royalty, treating all of us as honored guests. A couple of our *Kalosian* hosts, including Thekla, who we met previously, even took a moment to talk with us about some of the "more interesting" things about Sophia, the capital city, inviting us to stay and explore. I think they found us as fascinating as we did them.

All the while, Theseus and Sosthenes were off somewhere having a private confab. *What could be taking them so long?* Being doted on was nice, but I was ready to get down to business and finally be reunited with my mom and dad.

To me, the whole thing—everything since we arrived—was rather unsettling. Sosthenes said next to nothing, nearly ignoring me altogether once Theseus entered the hall after our arrival. *Of course, he is their long-lost Guardian.* It seemed to make sense, but still, I wondered if, by not returning Hesiod to Kalos, I had made a horrible mistake or failed in some way. Surely the success of our quest was cause for happiness.

I guess I had expected celebration—joy, even—at the return of both the Pyxis *and* the Guardian. Other than the warmth of our hosts, though, the atmosphere felt quite formal. Distinctly not a party vibe. I was starting to feel uncomfortable.

"I'm overthinking all this as usual," I mumbled, as I continued to wait impatiently.

Theseus returned the Pyxis to me almost immediately after we arrived on Kalos, insisting that it was *my* duty to present it to the Sentinels when they convened.

"This is your moment," he said to me, before being ushered away by Sosthenes.

I now held it in my hand and marveled at the immensity of power contained in such a small box. The mythos of Pandora's box was little more than a story—an ancient fable. Yet, in my hand was a truth that proved much more incredible than the myth, as I'm discovering is often the case. I wondered what other powerful truths were out there in the universe, shrouded in myth, waiting to be discovered. But I quickly cast down such thoughts, considering all that the six of us had just been through.

As the massive chamber doors suddenly opened, I rose to my feet, holding the Pyxis tightly in my grip. Sosthenes entered, walking ahead of another *Kalosian,* who was dressed in a long, starkly white robe trimmed with a golden braided cord tied around his waist. The two strode ceremoniously across the chamber. They curved to the right of the room's central attraction, the time pool that the 24 Sentinels used to keep their vigilant watch.

The regal Sosthenes took his place among the others, who had stood to acknowledge their entry and were then seated. As it was during my previous visit, I could see one of the twenty-four majestic thrones on the platform still sat empty. I considered that perhaps it belonged to the robed one that followed Sosthenes into the chamber. However, he only walked to the base of the platform and gracefully bowed to the twenty-three, who stood once more and greeted him in kind. From our places, we watched all of this in awe—though we didn't altogether understand what was going on.

I was the first to notice that the appearance of this new *Kalosian* had begun to change as he turned to face us. Right before our eyes, the being was transformed into someone much more recognizable. As his stature and likeness became fixed, Theseus gave me a nod, indicating that I should join him at the base of the platform, near the pool. He adjusted the golden cord around his waist as two *Kalosian* stewards quickly escorted our entire group to his side. The hall was beginning to fill as more *Kalosians* poured in from the various entrances around the great room.

Sosthenes stood and prepared to address the entire assembly. He had an inscrutable look as he scanned the *Kalosian* Sentinels, first to his right, then to his left. I remembered that *Kalosians* had the capability to speak telepathically and wondered if he was communicating non-verbally before saying anything aloud. Or had he simply forgotten that humans from Earth did not possess this ability?

Sosthenes paused before turning his piercing gaze to me, saying, "Theseus has made known to us the decision to allow Hesiodos to remain on Earth, in what you would consider antiquity."

His booming voice seemed more imposing than I remembered. Of course, the whole atmosphere here was different than before; much more ceremonious and rigid—if that were even possible.

Already on edge, my nerves ramped up at this point, feeling that I was being called out. My stomach flip-flopped, but I knew I had to give a defense for my decision. So, I collected myself, cleared my throat, squared my shoulders, took a deep breath and spoke.

"In my time, Hesiod is a well-known historical figure. His influence is, well… immense. You can't remove him from our timeline without the potential for negative consequences."

The Sentinels traded glances among themselves. Sosthenes' eyes lowered, and his head remained still. He appeared to be listening actively to what I had said but was uncomfortably silent for a moment. I swallowed hard as I waited for his response.

"You speak the truth," replied Sosthenes, finally. "The circumstances notwithstanding, I agree with our most *honorable* Theseus that you demonstrated uncommon wisdom. According to our calculations, permanently removing him and returning him to Kalos would have set your world's cultural evolution back five hundred years, perhaps more."

I let out the breath I had held for what seemed like an eternity and allowed my stiff posture to relax—just a little.

I was relieved to know that, at least in the *Kalosians* eyes, I had done the right thing. I glanced over for just a moment at Sean, who had opposed and challenged my decisions almost entirely from the beginning. He only looked straight ahead at the platform, seemingly unaffected by the verdict. I was mildly irritated that even now, it felt as though he were second guessing me; still disapproving of my choices.

As Sosthenes and Theseus locked their gazes upon one another, I had no doubt that something was being shared telepathically between the two. They were communicating, but about what I did not know. Sosthenes suddenly stood and bowed to Theseus, who then turned to me and said, "It is time for me to return to Greece and fulfill my purpose."

My heart sunk. I knew I would be saying goodbye to Theseus soon enough but had not realized that it would be like this—so abruptly. Confused, I looked up at him. I had questions but couldn't manage to utter even one word, as Theseus continued.

"It has been pure joy for me to know you, Hannah. As long as I live, I shall never forget you."

He reached forward and touched my cheek and then, looking around, bid the others farewell before walking toward the glassy pool.

"Wait," I said, with alarm. "You're forgetting something."

I opened my hand and held up the Pyxis.

Immediately the twenty-two Sentinels on the platform rose to their feet, joining Sosthenes and standing reverently with semi-bowed heads. Every *Kalosian* in the hall, in fact, came to an immediate halt. All of us, even Sean, were taken aback by the sudden change in the room. Looking around the great room, we saw that everything and everyone was completely frozen in place, and every eye was now trained on me and the box snugly nestled in my hand.

The atmosphere was electric. Every *Kalosian* face held an expression of wonder and pure joy. It was as though a long-missed friend had suddenly returned home to celebrate a holiday. I couldn't read the *Kalosians'* unfamiliar facial expressions like I could my friends' faces, but I knew somehow—these faces showed clearly expressed anticipation now satisfied and waiting expectantly to see what would happen next.

With that, I turned again to Theseus. "I think this belongs to you."

"No," replied Theseus. "It belongs to you. I told you, this is *your* time."

I paused, astonished by his statement, then fired back, "But… but you're the Guardian."

Theseus took a long stride toward me. "I am not," he said confidently, as his gentle face lit up. He reached for my hand.

"*You* are the Guardian, Hannah Goodheart."

I stumbled backward.

I recalled Hesiod's words, saying the box belonged to Theseus. I was so sure he was the Guardian I was sent to bring back. Theseus took hold of my shoulder with his other hand and held tightly. "It is *you*."

I turned to the twenty-three Sentinels, standing before the twenty-four seats of authority. It seemed too magnificent to me. Like a dream that I would soon awaken from. As I tried to grasp what was taking place, the unimaginable suddenly happened.

"I must concur," a voice said, boldly.

It was Sean!

Stepping away from our group and ascending the steps to join the Sentinels, he strode to the empty throne.

Sosthenes paid no visible notice to his actions, but said directly, "And what say you of her, Sentinel?"

Sean sat in the previously empty chair, followed by the other Sentinels who also took their seats. As he sat, Sean was transformed before us, revealing the truth.

He was a *Kalosian* Sentinel impersonating Sean this entire time.

His appearance was that of the other *Kalosians,* with his chiseled features and deep, dark eyes that reflected the light. He looked at me with the faintest hint of a smile. Something I'd rarely seen.

The newly revealed Sentinel sat back in his chair and said to the entire assembly, "She is *far* too impulsive, sometimes irrational, emotional, and headstrong." He briefly paused and looked once more at me, standing at the base of the steps leading up to the platform he sat upon, before continuing. "However, she is also wise beyond her years, compassionate, devoted, ever loyal and steadfast. It would seem Paul Learner has prepared her adequately. She *is* the Guardian, and of her companions, I can say that they are also of impeccable character. A testament to her own."

I was utterly speechless.

To be told that *I* was this Guardian I had been searching for! And now to discover that a *Kalosian* had been impersonating my friend was almost too much to process. Still, it was all suddenly beginning to make sense. Sean—or rather, his doppelganger—had acted quite oddly for much of our journey. His behavior had grown less and less like Sean, to the point that *everyone* had completely lost patience with him.

I suddenly found myself worried, as it all began to come into focus. Had the real Sean somehow gotten left behind, when Hesiod first opened the Pyxis or did something else happen?

Sosthenes must have sensed my concern for Sean and spoke. "Your friend is well. He is being attended to and will join you soon."

The *Kalosian* that had impersonated Sean interjected. "It *is* true what you were told... the boy was found unconscious near the outskirts of Sophia. Sosthenes dispatched me to bring him here. It seems he must have been too close to the fissure. The temporal wake, when the cycle is complete, can be explosive. The energy discharge would have thrown him away from the rest of you after reentry. I found him near the *mizcus* patch sound asleep, and carried him back here. He was exhausted, hungry and frightened, but unharmed. It was an *opportunity* to have an observer join you."

Relieved to hear Sean was well, but feeling some contempt for their methods, I said, "*Opportunity*... hmm. So you could see if I measured up."

Sosthenes didn't look fazed in the least by my salty jab. He only gestured in the affirmative. Then, turning to the newly revealed Sentinel, he bowed his head and said, "Our gratitude, Neanias. I look forward to a full reporting of your mission."

And so, the identity of Sean's doppelganger was the young, eager *Kalosian* Sentinel, who I was not surprised to learn had vigorously argued against entrusting humanity with the Pyxis, saying it was "too much power for a world still unable to find its way in the universe."

Neanias bowed his head to Sosthenes, and then to me. Though slightly put out by the whole ruse, I returned his gesture of respect, unsure whether or not it was even proper for me to do so. I didn't agree with the means, but I would eventually come to understand it was not only necessary, but it was their way.

Feeling a bit overwhelmed by the complexity of what was happening to, and around me, my confidence waned. "I'm just a teenage girl from Texas," I blurted. "I'm not sure…"

I turned again to Theseus. I was trying to find the words, but for a moment I could see my reflection in his eyes. He stopped me mid-sentence and interjected. "Do you not see it? It was you all along." He smiled widely as he continued.

"You are more than the sum of your years. Never allow anyone to tell you that you are *just* a girl. Do not let them marginalize you because you are young. Do not let them dismiss you because you are human. You are a brilliant light. You embody the most noble virtue. When the best laid plan failed, fate still brought you to the

Pyxis. You are the chosen… the Guardian, and now even time itself has testified of this."

"It is true," said Sosthenes, as though he were addressing his remarks to the entire hall. "Time would have unfolded somewhat differently before Hesiod interfered, but now it has all been set right again."

Theseus looked once more at me and said, "Hesiod and I were sent to affirm your lineage and reconcile it against the prophecy of the Guardian, and then to find you. You were to be prepared for the responsibility you are being given. Hesiod was actually chosen to be your teacher, and I discovered *my* destiny was to return to Greece—to Phaedra. This is what I must now do, just as you also will go with your friends and find yours."

He took my hand and gently kissed it, before stepping into the pool. Everyone watched in awe as Theseus slowly began to descend, slice by slice, into time. Annie opened her mouth to speak but hesitated; a rare occurrence for her. Then, as he continued to descend, she said, "See you around, cave man."

Theseus turned one last time and smiled fondly. I was full of emotion and questions. I could barely contain myself.

"Theseus," I said, as though I were about to bust. "You said fate brought me to the Pyxis. How will I know when I find my destiny?"

Theseus looked down into the pool for a moment and then said kindly as he looked back at me. "We write it with each passing day, Hannah."

Though his answer stirred more questions within me, it had somehow lifted my spirit and gave me courage, as

I was about to take up a mantle that transcended my imagination.

Theseus turned around, raised his right hand and placed it over his heart. Bowing his head, he said to me, *"Elpis."*

"Elpis," I replied, as Theseus turned away, stepping into time.

The silence seemed deafening as the rippling pool began to still.

"It will soon be time to reunite you with your friend and return to *your* own time, as well," Sosthenes said, while I watched the final ripple of the pool subside.

I felt a sadness at having to say goodbye to a friend.

I turned to the wise Sosthenes. "So, what destiny awaits him in Greece?"

"Yeah, and if Hesiod is exiled to ancient Greece, who's going to be Hannah's teacher now?" Lily asked, boldly.

Annie gave a hearty "yeah" as the others rallied around me. "Don't forget the rest of us here, too. Hannah may be the Guardian, but we're a package deal. You're getting a whole time *troop* here.

"Your friends are fiercely loyal," said Sosthenes. "I admire that quality."

"Then honor us with an answer," said Sam, with respect.

"Indeed, I shall," replied Sosthenes. "Hannah, you were chosen by the one who forged the Pyxis from pure gold and used it to set time, as we know it, into motion," he said, to nods of agreement from the other Sentinels, who sat regally upon their thrones. The crowd in the hall seemed to press in as he spoke.

"Your lineage is nothing of chance. Your parents, your grandparents, Paul and Elizabeth Learner... and those before; they were men and women, common and uncommon. Scholars, artisans, kings..." he paused, then said, "heroes, philosophers and poets."

"Theseus!"

"He *is* your ancestor," Sosthenes said, solemnly. "It was long ago decided that one chosen from among us would sacrifice his heritage to become fully human and go make a life on your world, at a specific moment in time, when mankind was beginning an age of discovery. Theseus and Phaedra will be blessed with nine children. The first born, a son, will take a wife. Until you returned here today, we were unable to see into time and know *who* his wife would be."

"It's the child," said Morgan. "Isa's baby, Dora, isn't it?"

Sosthenes offered his affirmation. "As to your training, Paul Learner recorded his experiences and thoughts in journals to make sure you would be ready. When Hesiod took the Pyxis and ran, we could not have foreseen it falling to Paul and Elizabeth. But then again, time somehow has a way of unfolding as it should. Still, the temporal conflict brings uncertainty to the future."

That mention of the "temporal conflict" sent a shockwave through me, nearly taking my breath. I remembered Hesiod's brief reference. "What about this conflict?"

"All in time, Hannah," Sosthenes said, as the crowd parted allowing for the real Sean Evans to walk into the hall, much the same way his doppelganger had during our first visit.

As Sean exchanged hugs and fist bumps with Sam and the others, I found the courage to climb the steps to the platform and stand before the Sentinels. "It seems you already know what the future holds. I guess I'll just have to trust you," I said to Sosthenes, who rose to greet me.

"I am privileged to receive occasional fragments of the hidden knowledge, but we only know for certain what is past," said the giant man, softly. "There is only *one* who knows for sure what is ahead, and you should know that it is forbidden for you to use the Pyxis to travel forward in time. The future is shrouded for a reason and must remain concealed until the fullness of time."

"The Darkness..." I said inquisitively. "I think we were there. Sam nearly died in that place. All of us could have died. It has something to do with this conflict you mentioned, doesn't it? How did we end up there? Who's doing was that?"

Sosthenes' sculpted face showed concern and uncertainty, as he lowered his voice and replied, "It is, I'm afraid, still a mystery. Although I have my suspicions. Someone, yet unknown to us, tried to pull you and the others out of time, it would seem."

"The tracking device."

Sosthenes nodded. "Fortunately, it connected you to the Pyxis and prevented you from remaining there."

"We were tethered—like a rubber band. It was stretched when we were pulled into the Darkness, and then it snapped back," I said, before asking. "What about Sam's injury?"

"The Darkness is a realm of shadows… a dimension outside of time."

"So, it wasn't real?"

Sosthenes peered over at Sam and then back to me. "It was all too real, but only so much as a shadow is real, and then is gone. Be vigilant. Sam has been marked, I fear. He would be wise to guard his thoughts. For as he thinks, so will he be."

My heart sunk at what this could mean for Sam, and for me. "Those strange luminescent beings, they seemed so beautiful and tranquil."

Sosthenes smiled, reassuring me. "Beauty is irrelevant *and* subjective," he said. "Evil often assumes the most pleasing form to achieve its dark objective. There is much for us to discuss, but we should talk of this in depth at another time."

I had to smile when Sosthenes said, "… another time." Time had taken on an entirely new meaning for me, and I realized, at this moment, that I had taken my first steps into a much larger universe.

So "another time" it would have to be. But for now, my thoughts were once more of home on the Leaner ranch, in North Texas, and my parents. The journey had taken me far from home, and far from the Dallas skyline I was always so fond of seeing. I wondered if it would even look the same. Would any of it ever feel the same? The journey had been incredible, but long. None of my friends were certain just how long we had been away, but one thing was sure, it felt like the right time for us to return.

Morgan came up to me from behind and embraced me. Annie, Lily, Sam, and Sean—the *real* Sean—ascended the steps and joined us. I looked around at the five of them, thinking how fortunate I was. I considered the uncertainty of the future and the rule Sosthenes had just thrown down against using the Pyxis to see what it held for us. Still, I knew there were bound to be risks.

Honestly, my biggest worry right now was once again how to break all this to my parents. *Or do they already know?* A whirlwind of thoughts spun tumultuously through my head.

Lily whispered, "Can we go home now?"

"I think we've had enough excitement for the time being," I said, with a giggle. "Is there anyone here who hasn't nearly died at least once on this little expedition of ours?"

We thought for a moment and took a quick count. Sean had been knocked unconscious, abducted by aliens—friendly as they may be—and replaced with a doppelganger. Morgan had nearly fallen to her death in a gulch while crossing a narrow pass on Mount Helicon. Sam had been burned and almost died in another dimension. I fell into a pit, narrowly escaping serious injury. Lily was nearly kidnapped by a brute in an ancient *agora*. Then all eyes turned to Annie. Even Sosthenes peered at her with surprise.

"Hey! What are y'all looking at me for?" she asked. "I suffered… I've endured peril… Does anyone even *know* how long it's been since I've had a green M&M?"

We all shared a laugh, although going forward, it would often be mentioned in jest that Annie was either lucky or covered in non-stick coating because nothing bad stuck to her.

As the others enjoyed their laugh, I opened my hand again and peered at the Pyxis that, strangely, looked a bit brighter and more polished than I had ever seen it—almost transparent. The bright silvery-golden markings appeared vibrant and renewed, against the sheen of the cube. The gears on each side were ready to go into motion and open the doorway home.

Standing there, I remembered once again, the story of Pandora's box. I recalled that, in the story, when Pandora had released all the evil within the box into the world, Pandora found all that was left in the mythological container was hope. The thought warmed my heart, and once again, I felt courage rise up in me. Hesiod had wrapped the truth within his story so well.

"Time," I said to Sosthenes. "Hesiod's myth tells a truth. All the dark things people do. Being wasteful with the time we've been given. Maybe *that's* the evil that escaped Pandora's box." I paused for a moment to gather my words, then continued. "The hope that's left inside is the potential for all the good that can be done with each minute we live out with purpose; when we pursue our best destiny."

"You speak well, Guardian."

Then, pondering the words Theseus had said to me earlier about my own destiny, I said aloud, "Yeah, I think Theseus is onto something... we write it with each passing day."

Morgan cracked a determined smile and put out her hand. Then Sam put his hand on hers, followed by Sean, then Annie, then Lily. They looked at one another and then to me. I could see hope in *their* eyes and a mutual resolve that filled me with confidence, knowing that whatever happened, I would have the companionship of my friends. They held their hands centered in a pile as Morgan asked me, "So, Guardian… what do we write next?"

I put my hand on top and contemplated the potential of those words. Before I could say anything, I heard Neanias behind me. "There are endless possibilities, you know," he said to us. "So, may I challenge you to write it together? For, I recently heard a very wise person say, 'we're stronger if we stick together.'"

I took the large gangly paw of Neanias and placed it on our pile. His dark bronze hand nearly covered all our hands put together and shimmered with color as it caught the light. He looked down at the assembly of hands, stacked atop one another with a curious gaze. I nodded to him and he managed a conservative smile. I could tell he was puzzled and unsure about the meaning of this gesture but seemed happy to be included.

Finally, he cautiously removed his hand and stepped back, looking at our faces as we looked back acceptingly into his. I brushed my bangs away from my face and said with a smile, "I suppose you're right… um …" I wanted so much to call him by his name but was unable to do so. The surprise about his identity left me feeling uncertain I would pronounce it right if I even remembered it correctly.

"Neanias," he said, completing my sentence. "I suppose I do owe you an apology."

"For impersonating my friend or for being a pain in the neck?" I asked him as I snickered lightheartedly.

Neanias didn't seem to catch my playful poke, and I could see what I thought was a long look sweep across his face. His heart was truly heavy. His posture even seemed to carry the burden of his contrite spirit as he muttered, "For doubting you, Guardian."

I could feel the depth of his sincerity. I took his large hand. "You know—it's weird, but in a way, you'll always be Sean Evans to me. A friend. And real friends don't hold grudges."

Neanias brightened and squeezed my hand gently. "It would be rather odd for you to have two friends named Sean Evans, would it not?"

I giggled at how he took what I had said so literally, and yet he seemed somehow enthusiastic about the prospect. Suddenly, I got an idea. "Then perhaps I should just call you ... Evan—yes, Evan," I said, with a bright smile. "At least I can remember that one."

The young Sentinel bowed his head and raised his right hand to his chest. Sosthenes, overhearing the conversation, came near. "Assume your post, Neanias. We must be ever vigilant, my young friend."

Neanias gave me a final bow and turned to bow to Sosthenes. "Evan, if you will, Principal. The Guardian has given me the name Evan," he said happily, as he turned and hustled to his place on the platform.

Sosthenes summoned an uncharacteristic grin as "Evan" hastened gracefully away. "I suppose you will want to change my name as well, Guardian?"

"No," I replied, smiling. "I don't believe I will. Sosthenes suits you perfectly."

"Good," exclaimed the noble giant. "I am not altogether fond of *terran* names. Far too simple for my taste... they lack *character*," he said, with a deep chuckle.

Annie could hear the lighthearted banter and darted closer to join the conversation. "You know what's lacking in character?" she asked, jokingly. "You guys need to lighten up around here. It's way too serious. The hospitality is amazing but…"

Lily quickly butted in. "Annie, give it a rest," she said, to which Sosthenes offered her a wink.

And so, Sosthenes led me, Morgan, Annie, Lily, Sam and Sean to the center of the chamber. He told me that the Pyxis would decipher the code hidden in my great-grandfather's journals, adding they would prove most helpful as I mastered the use of the Pyxis. "I will summon you back here, in time," he said reassuringly, pledging to help guide me as well. "But for now, I am sure you are eager to get home to your family."

That certainly sounded like an excellent idea. Sosthenes, using a holographic simulation he conjured from his seemingly bare hand, demonstrated the essential controls within the matrix of the Pyxis. I paid careful attention, as he showed me how to select a location and time, telling me to avoid the dimensional controls for now.

I looked thoughtfully at the object that had been known in myth as Pandora's box, then turning again to Sosthenes, I asked, "How do I change the word that opens the portal?"

Sosthenes looked at me. His eyes narrowed and he looked puzzled. "The key, you mean?"

I held the Pyxis up toward his furrowed brow and said, "I think I would be wise to change the locks on this box."

Sosthenes offered no discernible reaction at first, but then his sculpted face brightened as the corners of his mouth turned upward, and a great sound of laughter erupted. The deep bass of his voice reverberated throughout the vast hall. Me and my friends joined him as the sound of both joy, and to some degree, relief, soared to the outer square of the capital city, where *Kalosians* paused in wonder to hear the grand chorus.

Sosthenes looked at the other Sentinels, who continued to preside over the moment. "It did not unfold as we expected, my brothers, but it *is* being worked out for the good of all within the realm." Then directing his statement to the entire assembly, he said, "It was foretold that the Guardian would rise, and an age of hope would drive back the Darkness." He paused, putting his massive hand on my shoulder. Taking in a deep breath, he boldly announced, "Today I say to you all, the Guardian *has* ascended and stands here among us, and so begins the promised age."

Cheers erupted throughout the hall, spilling out into the city, and soon all of Kalos would celebrate the rise of the promised Guardian.

As the cheers and laughter subsided, I moved the Pyxis from the grasp of my thumb and forefinger to the security of the palm of my hand. My fingers closed around it, and I felt, for the first time really, the weight of it. It wasn't a weight which I could ever measure on a scale or quantify in any physical sense.

On what would be my thirteenth birthday, the veil was torn away, and I discovered incredible purpose within myself, beyond anything I could have imagined. I found out I was more than I believed myself to be. But I had also discovered the truth, that there were terrifying dangers all around that I could not see before. With that discovery, came a responsibility that I could not refuse.

This was the weight I now felt, and although it seemed overwhelming, I looked around once more at my friends. I thought of my parents, and even my beloved Nan and Paw-Paw. I also considered Sosthenes, Theseus, Phaedra, Isadora, the child Pandora… even Hesiod and Evan.

I discovered something about myself I had not realized up until this time. Surrounded by my friends, I was absent of fear, and my hopes were lifted. I've always believed myself to be grounded and independent but, whether in this time or any other, I discovered the best way to face the unknown is to face it with friends.

Sosthenes, it seemed, could sense my thoughts and leaned into me, saying, "It is said on your world as similarly it is said on mine, 'A great person does not seek power, for they have power thrust upon them.'" I looked deeply into his dark eyes and, for a moment, felt as though I could see into the depths of the universe itself, as Sosthenes continued, "You do not, however, bear the weight of such power alone, for you already possess the strength of friendship."

EPILOGUE

THREE DAYS HAD passed since the six of us returned to the Learner Ranch. Although to me, it seemed like much longer since my birthday party was interrupted by the uninvited guest. My parents, however, had barely noticed that we had been swallowed up by the portal. Thanks to Sosthenes, our return and the original portal's collapse were nearly simultaneous.

Sam and Sean went home after they gave my parents the abridged version of events. I have to say, they took the news rather well, all things considered. It took using the Pyxis to open the mysteries of one of Paw-Paw's journals before they fully realized the scope of what had occurred. All, however, agreed to keep it under wraps—at least for now. Even Sean, who was quite disappointed to have missed all the time bouncing—especially the trek to ancient Greece, decided that he would remain mum about the whole thing. He said his parents wouldn't believe him anyway and would probably think he was babbling on about one of his roll play games.

Things were much quieter for the moment. Momma and Daddy were still uneasy about the idea of me possessing something as incredible as the Pyxis, but after reading some of the journal entries Paw-Paw left behind about the box, the Guardian, and what was at stake... at least for the now, they posed no objections. Life had quickly returned to some semblance of normal.

Whatever that is anymore.

And so, this particular Tuesday morning came with little fanfare. Daddy sat reading the newspaper. Buried on page six was a story about the closure of *D. Hoise Antique Emporium of Dallas* and, more importantly, the donation of a rare presidential pen, made by the former proprietor, to the JFK Museum.

I joined my parents at the table and began to eat breakfast when I noticed the story, while glancing over as Daddy read. I was quick to point it out, and the three of us speculated about what became of the rest of the treasures in his shop. I shared with them how Hesiod had tried to "cover his tracks through time." I joked that the entire time, not one of us gave a thought to taking a picture or grabbing a selfie. "It was a good thing, though," I told them. "Besides the fact that Morgan's phone was the only one to have a charge, one of the rules, I guess, is that there can be no documentation of historical events—just observation."

Our conversation was cut short, however, when a delivery truck pulled into our driveway. Daddy dropped the paper and raced to the door, thinking it was something for his magazine. I was putting my dishes in the sink when he stepped back in and announced that the package had *my* name on it.

I sat down and began to open the box. Daddy helped with the packing tape, and I pulled at the flaps, while Momma stood over my shoulder and watched. Opening the package and removing the corrugated packing material, I found a bulbous heap, wrapped tightly in several layers of bubble wrap. I set it aside when I saw, at the bottom of the box, a book.

Pulling it out, I announced to my parents that I immediately recognized the old cover from Hesiod's antique store. It was, as I suspected, the very copy of *Works and Days* that Hesiod had on the counter in his shop. Sticking out of the cover was a two-page, hand-written letter.

In the letter, Hesiod explained everything pretty much as he had before, while sitting in his home. He expressed deep regret regarding his behavior and went on to say that he retrieved a few "choice items," which he said were needed to make restitution for his actions. Then, with a single phone call, he liquidated the store and donated most of the proceeds to various charities.

The letter contained account information, where the remaining funds from the liquidation could be retrieved—a gift to be used toward my education. Hesiod also noted that he'd made a couple additional, but "necessary," stops in history before his planned return to Greece, and closed the letter by writing, "The Countess also sends her regards."

Gently, I opened the fragile cover of the book and turned to the title page. Looking to the left side, I saw this hand-written inscription:

> There are flashes of light which streak across the sky and then are gone. A star, however, is sure and steadfast, holding its place in the heavens, showing all who look up, the way home. Such are you, my dear. The conflict is coming, and the world needs your light. Shine brightly! – H

I ran my fingers over the inscription. It moved me to the very depths of my heart, but I could not entirely escape the intended warning that was inked onto the page of the aged book.

Carefully, I flipped through the pages, and as I did this, a tin-type photograph fell to the table. It measured just over three inches long and appeared very timeworn. I delicately picked up the old photo with its worn corners. The aged paper mat was stained and deteriorated, and while the picture itself suffered the same fate, the image was unmistakable.

I could barely believe my own eyes.

In the photograph were two teens, dressed in poufy Victorian dresses and holding parasols. They stood on what looked to be the lawn of a stately manor, visible in the background of the photo. Standing behind was a gentleman in a fine-looking suit and bowler hat.

I studied the faded and discolored photograph quietly, until Momma noticed that I seemed positively baffled by the picture. "What is it, Hannah? Are you okay?"

I turned the image around, so my parents could see what had me so perplexed. One of the two girls in the photograph was clearly *me*, dressed in full Victorian regalia. Momma covered her open mouth and tried to hide her astonishment. "That's *you*?"

Daddy pointed at the dapper looking gentleman standing proudly behind us. "It's Mr. Hoise... Hesiod."

Looking at it once more in wonder, I couldn't even begin to make any sense of where or when the photo could have been taken, nor did I recognize the other girl whose image had been captured. It was easily over a hundred years old, and yet I had no memory of it. "The past is the future, and the future is the past," I said to my bewildered parents. "It's something I read in Paw-Paw's journal."

Setting the photo aside, I could wait no longer and picked up the bubble-wrapped item I had set aside. Inside, in mint condition, was a snow globe. The twin to the one Hesiod had given to me a little over a week ago, that had been destroyed during the break-in. The only noticeable difference was that this one had a brilliant blue jewel set in gold, which embellished the ornate silver base. I turned it over to shake up the contents and to retrieve the key, so I could once again hear the beautiful melody. When I did, I saw an engraved inscription, which read, "With gratitude - N."

Elated by the gift, I recalled the story Hesiod had told me of the snow globe. Two were made for a countess, who gave one as a gift.

Perhaps this countess was the mystery girl in the photograph.
And then again, maybe not.

Hesiod had said he found the previous one in England and that the other had disappeared. As I listened to the melody of Chopin's lullaby, and watched the carousel horses dance inside the glass amidst the falling snow, I reflected on Hesiod's letter and about who the countess was and what her story might be. But that, as Hesiod said to me during my visit to the antique shop, "perhaps *is* a tale to be told another time."

ACKNOWLEDGMENTS

To EVERYONE who encouraged me and cheered me on along the way, I salute you.

Deep gratitude and the warmest expressions of appreciation go to Jodi Thompson, TwylaBeth Lambert and the Fawkes Press team. I couldn't have put Hannah Goodheart in better hands. Thank you all so much for caring about her story as much I do, and for welcoming me into your family with open arms.

To my Collin Creek and CV Church family—I can't say thank you enough. It's my privilege to be counted as one of you.

To Christopher Jones. You graciously convinced me that I had the chops to tell a good story.

I also want to thank my Meta Treks co-host, Zachary Fruhling. It's such fun podcasting with you, and you've taught me so much. There's a bit of you in these pages. (Meta Treks is a Star Trek and Philosophy podcast on the Trek.fm network, available on iTunes and other podcasting platforms.)

To the Trek.fm community, it's a treat to be part of such a talented and creative group of trekkies and trekkers. Thank you for your support!

Thank you so very much, Jude Pilkington of Toronto-based Pilkington Proof. You provided so much more than editing services on my earliest drafts of Hannah Goodheart. You're the best!

I also wish to thank the following, who in one way or another, helped to make this possible—whether you realize it or not. You've inspired me and won't be forgotten. Lily Holbert, Molly Holbert, Shawn Holbert, Jaylyne Morgan, Samuel Christian Thompson, Paul Chambers, (the late) Don McVey, Ron and Hilda Singleton, (the late) James "Bud" Spaur, (the late) Maxine Spaur. This is a Texas story with West Virginia roots.

I owe a huge thanks to my many beta-readers for their time and feedback. You all helped make this story what it is.

To my sophomore year high school English teacher, who once said to me, "John, (yes, he often called me John—it's a long story) you're going to be a brilliant writer someday." Mr. Ludford, you, sir, were the spark.

And finally, thanks to all the great authors, past and present, who have fired my imagination and welcomed me into their worlds through the written word. *This* world is a brighter place when pages turn, and people dream.

WWW.CMICHAELMORRISON.COM

Did you find an error in this book?

Fawkes Press strives to present a perfect product, but being staffed by mere humans, mistakes happen. If you find something we missed, please visit www.FawkesPress.com and click on "bounty program" to submit your find and enter to win our twice-yearly bounty.